Hugh Johnston

A merchant prince:

Life of Hon. Senator John Macdonald

Hugh Johnston

A merchant prince:
Life of Hon. Senator John Macdonald

ISBN/EAN: 9783337173678

Printed in Europe, USA, Canada, Australia, Japan

Cover: Foto ©Raphael Reischuk / pixelio.de

More available books at **www.hansebooks.com**

Jno Macdonald
Oaklands
Toronto

LIFE OF

HON. SENATOR JOHN MACDONALD.

BY

REV. HUGH JOHNSTON, D.D.

TORONTO:

WILLIAM BRIGGS,

WESLEY BUILDINGS.

C. W. COATES, Montreal, Que. | S. F. HUESTIS, Halifax, N.S.

1893.

INTRODUCTORY.

THIS Biography has been undertaken at the solicitation of
friends, outside the family of Mr. Macdonald, who felt that
some record should be preserved of a life which shed so
much light and love and quickening influence upon our
young nation. It was a life not only worth living, but worth
being studied—a life replete with the highest activities,
brim-full of the noblest deeds, and so furnishing an example
as rare as it was beautiful.

Biography is the literature of life, of the individual, personal life, which must always have a distinctness and an
interest which cannot belong to any other kind of history.

The late Bishop Brooks has said : "The intrinsic life of
any human being is so interesting that, if it can be sym-
pathetically and simply put before the world's attention, it
will be legitimately interesting to others." I have sought to
conceive of Senator Macdonald's life as a whole, standing
out distinct and complete by itself ; and trust that his large
circle of acquaintances and friends will find here a true and
living portrait of the man. I have not sought to follow a
strictly chronological order, but simply to give a clear and
connected outline of the chief events in his remarkable
career.

The task has been a delightful one, but it has been
performed under the constant pressure of duties of other
kinds, and each interval during which the work has been
laid aside has involved fresh labour upon its resumption.

In the material available for biographical purposes, there
has been an *embarras des richesses*. Rev. William Arthur,
in his Preface to the life of Gideon Ouseley, says that he
could easily have made two portly volumes, but he did not
wish to bury Gideon in a big book. With a like desire I
have found it no small effort to bring this volume within

its present compass. Amongst the many friends of this Merchant Prince are those who knew him longer and saw him more frequently than did I. But it was my good fortune to have been brought very close to him during some of the most impressive phases of his life; and this gave me a clear knowledge of his inner life and a rare insight into his character. I have been in close touch with many of the events recorded here, and while the work has been done with a loving heart, I have sought carefully to guard against inaccuracy or misrepresentation of facts.

I desire here to express my great obligations to Mrs. Macdonald, who has placed at my disposal diaries, letters, and other documents necessary for the work, and greatly assisted me by her counsel. His eldest son, Mr. John K., and the daughters, Miss Winnifred and Miss Ethel, have rendered invaluable aid in various ways. Indeed, all the members of the family have been most helpful. My thanks also are due to the Editors of the *Christian Guardian* and the *Methodist Magazine*, who have given me unrestricted access to these connexional publications; and to many friends who, by conversations and by letters, have helped to recall important details of his personal history. What has been attempted is the plain record of a busy and eventful life.

I trust that these memorial pages will give stimulus and inspiration to other lives. Because this beneficent life is so worthy of imitation, the narrative of it is worthy of being given to the public. Whilst many who once occupied prominent places in the land will soon be forgotten, the name of John Macdonald will be an abiding monument; and in the annals of Canadian history he will ever rank among the men of "light and leading" of his time.

HUGH JOHNSTON.

Toronto, August, 1893.

CONTENTS.

I.

CHILDHOOD AND PARENTAGE.

Life, like a dome of many-colored glass,
  Stains the white radiance of eternity.
                    —*P. B. Shelley.*

A new sweet blossom of humanity,
Fresh fallen from God's own home,
    To flower on earth.
                    —*Gerald Massey.*

" The childhood shows the man,
    As morning shows the day."

A MERCHANT PRINCE.

JOHN MACDONALD, son of John and Elizabeth Macdonald, was born in the city of Perth, Scotland, on the 27th December, 1824. His father was a Highlander, a native of Inverness-shire, and was born in the parish of Boleston, near the town of Inverness. This maritime county of the Highlands, on account of its numerous lakes and rivers, combines something of the softness of the Lowlands—gentle hill-slopes and river valleys, pasture lands dotted with herds of cattle, gardens and orchards, farm land and woodland—with the bold, picturesque and rugged scenery of mountainous districts—retired glens, green patches and purple heather, with thatched cottages and shepherd huts scattered here and there over the landscape. Those who have traversed the Caledonian Canal know something of the grand and varied scenery of this portion of " Auld Scotia."

Nowhere within the bounds of the Empire of Great Britain can a more strongly marked type of character be found than in the Scottish Highlands. The territory of a community is not only the indispensable condition of national life, but also a determining factor in its development. The effect of natural scenery upon the character of a people is well known. A rich landscape like that of Italy enervates; an inferior and flat landscape like that of Holland dulls the temperament, while a bold and varied landscape excites the poetic and inventive faculties, and awakens energy and activity. What wonder then that a country so stern and wild as "Caledonia," and presenting so many obstacles to be overcome, should force its sons to habits of frugality and thrift, sagacity and industry, and develop those characteristic traits which have made the Scots foremost in the empire of mind and enterprise, the world over.

Sir Walter Scott says that "every Scotchman has a pedigree," and the Macdonald family maintained this national prerogative. The clan was an ancient and noble one. The Macdonalds were a typical household. The father not only possessed those deeper and sterner qualities which are usually considered to belong to the Highlander, but was also strongly imbued with the national spirit, a passionate love of country and devotion to arms. At an early period Inverness-shire was included in the kingdom of the northern Picts, and Inverness was the capital of the Pictish kingdom. Pict, in the old Celtic, means a fighting man. Breathing this air, and inhaling the aroma of the olden time, John Macdonald, senior, at the age of fourteen, enlisted as a drummer boy in Company No. 1 of the 93rd Regiment—the Sutherland Highlanders. The muster-roll contains this entry concerning him : "Light complexion, eyes grey, fair hair, height five feet four." From this it will be seen that the son inherited not a few of the physical characteristics of the father.

The mother's name was Elizabeth Nielson, an Aberdeen lassie, of fine personal attractions, cheerful in disposition, simple, frugal, and like her husband, God-fearing. We can only get glimpses of her appearance and character; through the mists of recollection her lovely lineaments can with difficulty be traced, but she is remembered as being above the medium height, with large expressive eyes, of gentle and sedate manner, having a sweet voice and a superior mind.

An event so common as the birth of a child makes little stir in this busy world; but it was while the 93rd was stationed in Perth that the subject of our memoir was born. He thus became "a citizen of no mean city"; for that staid old town, charmingly situated on the west bank of the Tay, is an ancient and royal city. It early became the seat of Parliament, succeeding Scone as the capital, and was the favorite residence of the Scottish kings until in the reign of James II, the Parliament and Court were transferred to Edinburgh. We know not just how long the child lived in his native place, but long enough perchance to allow its historic associations to mould and impress his lively imagination. The city itself does not retain many relics of antiquity, but in its neighborhood are Culross Abbey, founded by the Cistersians in 1217; Blair Castle, Huntly and other old castles of the chiefs, with the ruins of Castle Dhu, once a stronghold of the Campbell family. Among the adjacent hill-forts is Dunsinane, and near to this the witch-stone where Macbeth is said to have met the witches.

Mr. Macdonald never lost interest in his native city, and desiring in some way to be identified with its young life, he appropriated a sum of money, the interest of which was to be given annually in books for religious knowledge, as a prize to be submitted for competition in the Public Schools of Perth.

Nor do we know much of the home-life of young Macdonald. The father was not cast in a tender mould; he was a man of iron will, and believed in the use of the stick. Though the current of family life ran smoothly on, yet the standard of living was not high, and there could have been no luxuries and but few comforts in that soldier home. Army life, at best, is a hard and weather-beaten one, and young Macdonald's home was a migratory one. Indeed, to follow it, we must trace the wanderings of the famous regiment, and in doing this we are indebted to Captain Roderick Hamilton Burgoyne's historical records of the 93rd. This regiment was organized in 1759, when the Earl of Sutherland received proposals from Pitt to raise a regiment of Fencibles on his estate. Soon 1,100 men were assembled before Dunrobin Castle, and the regiment served the country until the peace of 1763, when it was reduced. In 1779, another regiment was raised, which, in 1793, was recruited to the strength of 1,084 men, and served in Ireland during the rebellion of 1798.

In 1805, this regiment formed part of an armament for the reduction of the Cape of Good Hope, and when the town and garrison capitulated in 1806, the 93rd remained there in garrison until it embarked for England in 1814. In 1813, a second battalion was added, and it was at this time that John Macdonald's father joined the regiment. This battalion also maintained the exemplary bearing which had always characterized the high-principled, self-respecting men of Scotland. The soldiers of this most Highland of the Highland regiments, were always remarkable for their subordination, their respect for military authority, and bravery, as well as for their intelligence and stable religious character. Whenever they were in quarters, the usual precautions necessary with soldiers were entirely inapplicable to them. Many of the non-commissioned officers and privates were farmers' sons, and almost all of them of highly respectable parentage, and of good moral and religious training. The regiment seemed as one large family, bound together by the ties of neighborhood and acquaintance, nay, the stronger ties of relationship; and this inspired the reciprocal feelings of confidence and attachment between the commanders and the commanded. The officers were well-known gentlemen connected with Ross and Sutherland; the regiment was regarded as one great household, and there was the exercise of the clan influence on a large scale. No regiment ever stood in greater estimation for its discipline and soldier-like conduct, and no wonder that its deeds of daring will live forever on the beadroll of fame. The regiment was intensely national, and as blood is thicker than water, the family and social life prevailed wherever they went. One of the most marked proofs of the intensity and genuineness of this family and religious feeling, was the support given to the Kirk and the School.

The Regimental School was kept in a thorough state of efficiency, and this means of culture and discipline was diligently improved by young Macdonald. In the Regimental School and the Soldier Home, though there was not the stimulus of college life, and the daily breathing of a literary atmosphere, yet there was the development of character and disposition, the formation of sound principles and good habits, strict integrity, high devotion to duty, and deep, though undemonstrative affection. He was a precocious scholar, fond of his books, but not less fond of fun and sport.

The regimental teacher was Sergeant Nimmo, now an aged and highly-respected Congregational minister, living in London, England, who still remembers the boy and many of his early traits of character. His teacher took a sincere interest not only in his advancement in learning, but in all that concerned his happiness, and that could affect his future prospects in life. A friendship was formed between master and scholar which time could not dissolve, and in Mr. Macdonald's frequent visits to England he never forgot to call upon his loved and venerated teacher. Mr. Macdonald's diary of August 8, 1868, contains this record : " Received a letter from my early friend and school-master, then Sergeant Nimmo, now Rev. David Nimmo, Independent Church, Melbourne, Australia, to whom I am deeply indebted for leading me, as a boy of twelve, to the knowledge of Christ."

The teacher thus writes concerning his pupil:

LONDON, *Aug.* 15, 1892.

REV. DR. HUGH JOHNSTON.

DEAR SIR,—In reply to your request, made at the suggestion of the family of the late Senator Macdonald, for some account of his school life in the 93rd Highlanders, I have to say that my acquaintance with him began in the spring of 1835, in Daventry Barracks, Northamtonshire, when he was a lad about twelve years of age. He was the son of the hospital sergeant of the 93rd Highlanders—a man respected by the whole regiment for his faithful discharge of the important duties entrusted to him.

The boy was a scholar in the school of that regiment, to the mastership of which I had just been appointed by the late Sir Duncan McGregor, then lieutenant-colonel in command of the regiment.

Almost immediately on entering upon my work my attention was arrested by the appearance of John Macdonald. He was slender of frame and short of stature, for his age. He had a sickly cast of face, and appeared to have lived for some time in a tropical climate. His countenance was earnestly serious. The frivolity of boyhood was not in him. Had he possessed more of boyish sportiveness, his subsequent health would have been better and his life longer. His gravity was that of manhood rather than of boyhood. Such was the impression made on me at my first interview —an impression which deepened in my after-intercourse with him.

In teaching him I found mental powers that placed him abreast of the foremost boy in the school. In soundness of judgment he was older than his years. I had ample opportunities of testing this, as he was frequently in my company. He was a daily visitor in my room and very often accompanied me in my walks. He attached himself to me, and was spoken of by the people as my shadow.

We discussed politics, theology, the different religious sects, the past history of our race and its future prospects, and I dare say often "rushed in where angels fear to tread." His favorite theme, however, was his religious experience. He had an intense desire to live a Christian life, and sometimes would have us pray together in my room. We were more like companions than teacher and pupil. In years, there was not a great difference between us, and in disposition still less. I had scarcely entered my manhood, and he was just emerging from boyhood and had the bearing of a man. If he was still at school, I had not long left it, for on the completion of my training as a teacher I was immediately appointed to my work. The remembrance of my school-days was still upon me. I had not lost sympathy with my stripling speculations. The difference in our years raised no barrier to our very confidential intercourse. It was this intercourse that enabled me to gauge the soundness and penetration of his judgment, and the thorough grip that Christian truth had taken of his soul.

His influence in the school and regiment was a great help to me in my work. The 93rd was distinguished for its religious character. It contained a goodly number of men of all ranks, well known for their consistent Christian lives. The Colonel himself was a pronounced servant of Christ and an effective preacher. Sometimes he gave the soldiers the benefit of his gifts. Led by such a commander, who was supported by many in the regiment, especially of the non-commissioned officers, the corps became as noted for its piety as for its bravery. Stimulated by this state of things, the aim of the school-master was to infuse a religious spirit into the thinkings and feelings of the school life. For this purpose the scholars met every Sabbath, and occasionally on the week-day evening, for Bible instruction and devotional exercises.

Not satisfied with these meetings, John Macdonald sought privately to influence his school companions and awaken in them the same interest in the claims of Chist that he himself felt. He succeeded in persuading some of the boys to follow his example. They organized a weekly prayer-meeting and conducted the singing, praying and talking themselves. John Macdonald was the leader of the praying band; indeed, the suggestion of such a meeting came from him. All this became known among the soldiers, and doubtless helped to raise and strengthen the religious tone of the corps. It was already known in the towns where it was quartered as the praying regiment.

This effort among his school-mates did not exhaust his zeal. He was ever ready to help in any attempt to enlist the soldiers in the army of Jesus Christ, and threw himself with zeal into a series of services held weekly by the school-master in the school-room of Richmond Barracks, Dublin, for the spiritual welfare of the men. At these meetings a course of lectures on the " Pilgrim's Progress " was delivered, The room was crowded with an audience that maintained its attendance to the close. Our protegé threw his whole soul into the enterprise and spared neither time nor toil to make it a success. He went round the barrack-rooms and compelled the men to come in. His prayers for a blessing were as fervent as his labours were incessant. I recall that time with a great deal of pleasure. This Christian activity was not a fitful impulse, but a fixed habit. It was his life —a life received from, and devoted to, Christ. It continued with ever-increasing fervour all the time I served in the regiment. That time, however, was short. Eighteen months from its commencement I was called to enter upon a course of preparation for

2

the Christian ministry, and had to leave my young
friend and the work of the regiment. For some time
after we corresponded, and continued to do so until
the 93rd was ordered for foreign service. We then lost
sight of each other for nearly twenty-five years. After
this long time I received a letter from him. In consequence of feeble health he had gone to winter in the
West Indies. There he became acquainted with one
of the missionaries who, in conversation with him
happened to mention my name. From him he learned
my address, and wrote to inquire if I was the same
Mr. Nimmo who taught the school of the 93rd Highlanders; and requested me to favour him with a letter.
I satisfied him on this point, and asked for an account
of himself since we last heard from each other. I
received a reply attributing to me the commencement
of his spiritual life, and giving a full account of his
doings during our long silence. This renewed correspondence continued until shortly before his death.

In returning from Melbourne, where I had been for
five years, and coming by the American route in 1872,
I was his guest for a fortnight in Toronto. During
that time, "we fought our battles o'er again, and
thrice we slew the slain."

We contrasted his school-boy life in the 93rd with
his then political, commercial and religious life in the
Dominion of Canada. The contrast much affected us
both. After this he had to pay frequent business
visits to the old country. I met him from time to
time in my own home in London. As these visits and
our correspondence are now at an end, my hope is that
I shall go to him as he cannot come to me.

This meagre account would have been much fuller
had it been written when I left the regiment, fifty-six
years ago, or had I kept memoranda or even our correspondence. In the absence of all these I have had
to rely solely on my memory. Little did I forebode

that I should survive him to perform this slight service to his memory. Could I have presaged it, how carefully I would have preserved every laurel I could find to plant it on his honoured grave. "Silver and gold have I none, but such as I have give I unto thee."

Yours in sympathy,
D. NIMMO.

We thus notice in his boyhood the dawning of those mental and moral qualities which afterwards characterised him. His beaming face, bright eye, Celtic impulse and perpetual activity show the wide-awake, genuine boy; while his clear head, ready sympathy, and considerate regard for others, make his presence as sunshine among the soldiers. His father, who was a corporal at the time of his birth, was made sergeant in 1827, and promoted to be color-sergeant in 1831. The regiment was then in the West Indies. After three years spent at St. Lucia, Dominico, and Barbadoes, the company was quartered in Canterbury, England, under Col. McGregor, and here on the seventh of October, 1834, new colors were presented the regiment by His Grace the Duke of Wellington, the great commander of the age. His father being color-sergeant, one can imagine the interest which young John took in this great military display. The Highlanders in their brilliant costume, the rich ostrich plumes waving in the breeze, their tartan plaids gracefully falling from their shoulders, the ancient garb of kilt, hose and sporran, giving a warlike appearance, and displaying to the best advantage their symmetrical and manly forms, march forward to the sound of mar-

tial music, and stand in battle array ready to give the
salute when the veteran " victor of a hundred fights "
delivers an impressive address, and then presents the
new colors, which he charges them to defend and protect with all the gallantr yand devotion that have distinguished Highland soldiers. This memorable event
must have made a lasting impression upon the plastic
mind of the ten-year-old lad. Shortly after this the
father was permitted to resign the colors to be hospital
sergeant, which is a staff appointment.

In 1836 the regiment proceeded to Dublin, where
it formed part of the garrison until removed to Newry,
then to Belfast, from which city, in December, 1837,
it was ordered to Cork to be in readiness for foreign
service. Serious trouble was occurring in Canada,
and the commander of the regiment received directions
to be ready to proceed to Halifax, Nova Scotia.

It was during this stay at Cork, that the first great,
overwhelming sorrow fell upon his young life. The
cholera, that sanitary inspector of the world, scourged
the regiment, and his mother was suddenly attacked
and snatched away. The loss was irreparable, and
the affectionate, impulsive boy of thirteen mourned
like one heart-broken over his mother's death. The
father was made of sterling metal, but the mother
was tender and lovable, and with each year bestowed
increasing care upon her promising boy, who retu ned
the boundless affection with which his mother rega.ded
him. She was his trusted friend, and he almost worshipped her. But while her death left him deeply
bereaved, the impression of her life and example upon

him was enduring. What was her own character, and what share did she have in moulding her son's character? We cannot answer with precision; but she taught him virtue, truth, religion, and to her influence may be traced the principal traits of his character. Her image was the most sacred and the most cherished of all his early memories. She was a wonderful singer, and she had taught him all the favourite Scottish airs, which he used to sing with enthusiasm. An old soldier of the 93rd, who so long served as messenger at Osgoode Hall, was wont to tell how he remembered the lad coming to him when he was sick in hospital, sitting down by his bedside' and singing to him the old songs until his soldier's heart was all aglow, and his eyes suffused with tears. She had taught him to pray, and to read his Bible. It was her presence that pervaded the home life as an atmosphere; and after her death her very memory seemed a tender and subtle influence, moulding, softening, elevating and building up a nobler and purer manhood. So tender was the gratitude which he cherished towards his mother's memory, that on one of his first visits to the old land he made a pilgrimage to Cork and sought diligently for the grave of her whose sunshine of love had brightened his early life, and helped to make him the genial, domestic man that he was. Unable to find his mother's last resting-place in the churchyard to erect a stone over it, he placed in the church in which the soldiers with their families worshipped, a beautiful memorial window. The subject is "The Raising of Lazarus," and the scene is well delineated by the artist. In the circle above, are the words of the Saviour, " I am the resurrection and the life."   The inscription is as follows:

**This window is placed here by
John Macdonald, Toronto, Canada,
in loving remembrance of his mother,
Elizabeth Macdonald,
interred in the churchyard of this church,
1837.**

This church is no other than the famous St. Anne de Shandon, remarkable for its commanding position, its picturesque appearance, and its lofty steeple whose chime of bells has been immortalized by the pen of the inimitable Father Prout—Rev. F. Mahoney—who was buried in this churchyard.   The well-known ballad is not only exquisite in itself, but is also a rich tribute of fond recollections to his native city, and the " magic spells " of childhood:

> " With deep affection
> And recollection,
> I often think on
> Those Shandon bells,
> Whose sound so wild would,
> In the days of childhood,
> Fling round my cradle
> Their magic spell.
>
> " On this I ponder,
> Wher'er I wander,
> And thus grow fonder,
> Sweet Cork, of thee ;
> With thy bells of Shandon,
> That sound so grand on
> The pleasant waters
> Of the River Lee."

II.

BOYHOOD AND YOUTH IN CANADA.

The days of infancy are all a dream.
How fair, but oh ! how short they seem ;
  'Tis Life's sweet opening spring.

The days of youth advance ;
The bounding limb, the ardent glance,
The kindling soul they bring ;
  It is Life's burning summer time.
                              —*Robert Southey.*

As the rose-tree is composed of the sweetest flowers and the sharpest thorns ; as the heavens are sometimes fair and sometimes overcast ; alternately tempestuous and severe ; so is the life of man intermingled with hopes and fears, with joys and sorrows, with pleasures and with pains.
                              —*Robert Burns.*

Well, then, our course is chosen ; spread the sail,
Heave oft the lead, and mark the soundings well ;
Look to the helm, good master ; many a shoal
Marks this stern coast, and rocks where sits the siren,
Who, like ambition, lures men to their ruin.
                              —*Scott.*

Warriors, and where are warriors found,
If not on martial Britain's ground ?
And who, when waked with notes of fire,
Love more than they the British lyre ?
                              —*Scott.*

BOYHOOD AND YOUTH IN CANADA.

ADVICES having been received of the continued progress of the Rebellion in Canada, Her Majesty's ships of war, the *Inconstant* and the *Pique*, were ordered to Cork for the conveyance of the 93rd to Halifax. The *Inconstant* sailed on the sixth of January, 1838, and reached its destination on the twenth-ninth of the same month, making the passage in twenty-three days. The frigate *Pique* did not put out to sea till the twenty-third, and then encountered one of the most boisterous passages across the Atlantic that could possibly be experienced, and it was not until the fifth of March that she cast anchor in the harbour of Halifax.

Mr. A. M. Smith, of this city, who was one of the 706 soldiers on board, says that he was sea-sick for five weeks out of the six, and that the main-deck was never dry for twenty-four hours in succession. Two men were washed overboard and lost in the passage.

Mr. Macdonald, in after years, gave a poetic description of one of the terrible storms that burst upon them, in which this stanza occurs:

> " I heard a sea break o'er the ship
>   That roused me from my sleep,
> As if some mighty thunder-peal
> Had rent the vessel to her keel,
> And caused her oak-built frame to reel
>   And founder in the deep ;
> Even now I think I hear the cries
> That rose that night and pierced the skies."

Never were tempest-tossed pilgrims more gladdened by the sight of shore than were these passengers of the frigate *Pique* rejoiced to set foot on the soil of British America.

Here young Macdonald attended for a time Dalhousie College. This institution was founded in 1820 by Lord Dalhousie as a seminary for the higher branches of education upon a broad, liberal basis, open to all sects of religion and to all occupations, " to gentlemen of the military as well as the learned professions." The building was erected upon the Parade, and was commodious, but the college had been struggling long for an existence. About this time there was a union with Pictou Academy, and Dr. McCulloch, who had built up that institution, was elected to the presidency of Dalhousie. Associated with him were two other professors, Rev. James McIntosh and Rev. Alexander Romans.

We know little of his student life here, but he seems to have been diligent and faithful in his work during the session which he attended.

His scholarship was general but not accurate. He had attended the Regimental School under a good teacher, who did his duty by him; but the constant change of place, and frequent interruptions must have sadly interfered with the continuity of teaching and with progressive and well ordered study. But his mind was quick and versatile, his memory retentive; he was an eager and constant reader, and already had mastered the elements of an English education, as well as the rudiments of the classics. The opening stages generally show the character, and suggest the issues of the whole journey. The lad missed the inspiration and intellectual stimulant of a mother's love and care, but his father gave attention to the development of his son's mind, and was ready to furnish him with every advantage.

After some months spent on the sea-board, the regiment was ordered to proceed to Upper Canada. Rebellion was rife, and over the land stretched the dark shadow of approaching conflict. The regiment reached Toronto on the sixth of November, which continued to be its headquarters until June, 1843. Here young Macdonald attended the Bay Street Academy, then under the headmastership of Mr. John Boyd. This teacher possessed, in a wonderful degree, the power of developing the minds and quickening the intelligence of his pupils. He was himself a man of more than ordinary ability, the father of Hon. John A. Boyd, who, after rising with distinction through the several grades of the legal profession, became Vice-Chancellor, and is now the Chancellor of Ontario. In the Bay Street Academy young Macdonald worked hard and successfully, progressed rapidly in his studies, making his mark as an active, alert, thoughtful young fellow, with a practical turn of mind, full of enthusiasm, and not easily daunted.

Among his fellow-students were a goodly array of well-known, and even prominent Canadian names, and the soldier-boy distinguished himself among these in more ways than one, but chiefly in the study of languages, having won several prizes, and carried off the medal in classics. The object aimed at in this Academy was not merely information, but preparation for actual life. He was not shut up in a boarding-school, and deprived of the humanizing influences of family life. He lived at home while attending this excellent private school, and many happy days were spent by him on the grounds of the Old Fort. His old regimental teacher speaks of the unusual serious-ness of the lad. He had not known much of the buoyant, elastic, volatile, airy spirit of childhood; nor had he experienced much of the joys of boy-hood. The discipline of the Bay Street Academy was not of the mildest kind. The teacher was a " brisk wielder of the birch and rule." His home life was austere enough, and at times the atmosphere was most depressing, for every misconduct met with cruel punishment.

Of all the changes that have come over this century none is more remarkable than that which has taken place in the relationship between parents and children. It was then the almost invariable practice to rule children by severity; now an opposite extreme pre-vails. There was no gentle mother to plead for the boy, and the fear with which the parent was regarded sometimes made life oppressive; but young Macdonald took the floggings which his stern father gave him as light-heartedly as possible. He made good use of his time and opportunities, and those earlier years were years in which he was graduating for the great work of life.

When the regiment received orders to leave Toronto, Major-General Sir Richard Armstrong expressed the high satisfaction which their conduct had afforded him from the time he had assumed the command in Canada West. He referred to their superb appearance when under arms, their regularity in instruction and the performance of field movements, and the uniform good behaviour of the men in barracks and in quarters. Certainly no such company was ever seen in this city. Wellington once said that the English army was composed of the scum of the earth, but this could never be said of these Highland soldiers. As splendid looking men as could be found in the world, they would march to Church on Sabbath with steady step and in quiet order, each soldier carrying a Bible in his hand, the band accompanying them, not to give martial music on the way, but to assist in the service at the house of worship. They left Toronto amid tre-mendous cheering, the band playing "Auld Land Syne" and "Scots wha hae wi' Wallace bled." Young Macdonald did not accompany them. He cut his cable in the old land and remained to carve out his fortune in this new country. His father continued with the army until June, 1846, when he resigned his position

and gave up the life of the soldier for that of the
civilian. He also came out to Canada, settled in
Toronto, and established a druggist business on Yonge
Street, opposite Shuter. He married again and had
five children besides John and Alexander, the two
children by his first wife. He was a typical Scotchman, with all the eccentricities and peculiarities of the
Highlander, thoroughly honest, stern in his morality,
most rigid in his piety, a strict Presbyterian.

The old military man was one of the right stamp—
honest as the day, transparent as plate glass, well
educated, as is common with the Scotch, and greatly
respected by all who knew him. He lived quietly and
methodically; rejoiced to see his eldest son surrounded
with all the comforts of material prosperity and
advancing in the regard of men; and then, at the
mellow age of sixty-seven, he passed peacefully from
earth to heaven on the 19th October, 1866.

Young Macdonald never lost interest in the regiment to which his father belonged, and in which he
had spent his boyhood days. He always referred
with pride to his connection with it. He continued
to rejoice in its brilliant achievements in the field, and
to follow the fortunes of his many soldier friends of
the regiment. How proud he was that in the Cri-
mean War his old regiment earned the distinctive
title of the " Thin Red Line," and was the only infantry regiment entitled to bear upon its colors " Balaclava." At this terrible charge, when the Turks ran
away, Sir Colin Campbell, the loved chief, rode along
the front and said: " Stand steady men! There is no

retreat from here! Every man may have to die where he stands!" The regiment answered, with a cheer, "Aye, aye, Sir Colin, and if needs be we will do that!" No wonder when the Russian cavalry came dashing against that thin red streak, tipped with a line of steel, the impetuous rush was broken by the splendid front of Gaelic rock. and rolled back in defeat. So, during the Indian Mutiny, they behaved with their old-time valour when at Cawnpore, Captain Lumsden fell as he was waving his sword and calling to his countrymen, " Come on, men, for the honour of Scotland !" and Adrian Hope expired in the prime of his young manhood, with the whispered word to his aide-de-camp, "Say a prayer with me ; " and the most difficult and daring achievement of the centuries—the relief of Lucknow—was accomplished when Sir Colin Campbell, the gray-haired chiefain, with his force of only 4,000 men, opposed by ten times that number of regularly-trained soldiers, supplied with all the munitions of war, and holding an almost impregnable position, yet stormed and carried one fortress after another, and finally brought away in safety every living man, woman and child shut up in the residency. No wonder Mr. Macdonald was proud of this regiment which, more than any other, is endeared to every Scotchman because of its untarnished name and glorious record of achievements. In July, 1881, the title of the regiment was changed to that of the 2nd Battalion Princess Louise's Argyll and Sutherland Highlanders.

Mr. Macdonald was to the last interested in keeping

up the character and dignity of this corps, and adding if possible to its greater lustre. When visiting the old land he would go almost any distance to see his beloved regiment. He loved to make mention of the bravery of his soldier-friends, among them William McBean, who, by exemplary good conduct, bravery and zeal, rose step by step from a private soldier until he received the brevet of colonel; and died in June, 1878, as a Major-General, receiving the honour of a full military funeral. "Others," he writes, "laid them down to die on the heights of Alma; some before Sebastopol; others rest near Balaclava, with which place as the 'thin red line' their name is imperishably associated. Others found their resting-place in the Black Sea; others at Lucknow; others at Cawnpore."

Shortly before his death, while the movement for the formation of a Highland Regiment in Toronto was in its infancy and beset with many difficulties, he gave every encouragement to Mr. Alexander Fraser and to the other ardent young men who were promoting the scheme; and it is not too much to say that to his ready and practical counsel, as well as to the enthusiasm with which he entertained their views on the subject, was due, to a very considerable extent, the confidence which inspired them from the very beginning, that the citizens of Toronto would stand by them and that their efforts would be crowned with success. It can be easily understood, therefore, how it would have rejoiced his heart had he lived to see such a regiment an accomplished fact, and to witness its splendid bearing and steady movements as it passed in review to receive its colours at the hand of Mrs. Merritt, on that famous morning in the Queen's Park, in the presence of the Governor-General and suite, and the congregated citizens of Toronto, who are now so proud of the "Kilties," as they love to call the gallant 48th Highlanders. With all this he did not love war. But he loved and shared the martial spirit of his unconquered and unconquerable race; and while he was a man of peace, a true follower of the Prince of Peace, the prowess and bravery so closely allied with the heroism found on the field of battle, as well as in the less glittering and humble walks of life, entered largely into his character. He believed that the cultivation of the military spirit developed courage which lies at the root of all manliness and the lofty ideals of duty.

> "So close is glory to our dust,
> So near is God to man,
> When duty whispers low, 'Thou must,'
> The youth replies, 'I can.'"

3

III.

STARTING LIFE—CONVERSION.

" Within Thy circling power I stand,
    On every side I find Thine hand ;
    Awake, asleep, at home, abroad,
    I am surrounded still by God."

Our lives are albums, written through
With good or ill, with false or true ;
And as the blessed angels turn
    The pages of our years,
God grant they read the good with smiles,
    And blot the ill with tears.
                          — *John G. Whittier.*

Whatever progress may be made in science, art and literary culture, Christianity will be still there, as what these rest against and imply ; as the indispensable back-ground, the three-fourths of life.
                          —*Mathew Arnold.*

YOUNG MACDONALD'S school-days closed with his fifteenth year, when he left his father's house to plunge into the " world and wave of men," and entered upon the duties of a junior clerk in a mercantile establishment.   Of his entrance upon business he thus writes :

" It was in April, 1840, that the Rev. Mr. Leach, pastor of St. Andrew's Church, took me into the place of business of Mr. John Thompson, of this city, a member of his congregation, to see if he could find an opening for me.   Here Mr. Leach was unsuccessful.   From that we went to the business house of Walter Macfarlane, the " Victoria House," on the corner of King Street and Market Place.   Here also Mr. Leach failed, neither of these gentlemen at the time having any opening for a lad of fifteen.   He then, without my knowledge, corresponded with the house of C. & J. Macdonald & Co., Gananoque, then one of the most important concerns in Canada, and arranged for my entrance into the house.   Neither member of the firm ever having seen me, or having heard from me, I was taken entirely upon his recommendation. Here I attended the ministry of the Rev. H. Gordon.

" Thus it came to pass that at the very threshold of my business life I was placed under obligation to two early missionaries of the Church of Scotland.   To the first I was entirely indebted for the situation which determined my subsequent course. This position brought me under the pastoral oversight of the second, and thus began a friendship which extended throughout their lives.

"If there is one thing of greater importance than another to a young man entering upon life, it is that he should do so under such conditions as will furnish him with the best illustrations of all that is implied in upright and honourable transactions. Under just such conditions was it my rare good fortune to begin my business life in the firm to which reference has been made, where during my two years' residence not one transaction, I venture to say, ever took place which would not bear the closest scrutiny. The partners in the firm were the Honourable John Macdonald, and his nephew, William Macdonald."

Who can tell how much this early association with business men of sagacity, activity and perfect reliability had to do with his own character for integrity and that high standard of mercantile honour which he always maintained? It was also his good fortune to find in his fellow clerks young men of energy, ambition and active force, who have since made a deep impress upon their times. Among these were J J. C. Abbott, who afterwards became Premier of the Dominion, and John Bell, the well-known solicitor of the Grand Trunk Railway. It is no small thing for a young country that its ablest sons should thus find recognition and gain positions where their gifts and capacities can be used to the best advantage.

After a stay of two years in Gananoque, he returned to Toronto, and on the 30th May, 1842, entered the establishment of Mr. Walter Macfarlane, known as the "Victoria House." There are turning points in every life, and in the house of

Walter Macfarlane young Macdonald was to reach the crisis that was to give shape to his whole future life, and in which must be found the secret of his success. In the house itself there were fifteen young men, and Macdonald was the youngest. He had not been long here before one of the most assuming of the clerks ordered him to take out a parcel. It was a large one, and had to be carried for a mile. It was a terrible mortification, and he at once replied that he had not come there to carry parcels. Without further ceremony the clerk found his way to the employer, and said in loud tones, "That boy refuses to take these parcels out." "Oh, very well," was the reply, "tell him to go about his business." The boy's determination was taken in a moment; it was to eat humble pie, and, quick as thought, the parcel was picked up and he was nearly out of sight before the message from his employer could reach him. His situation was saved, and his future, to some extent, decided.

Several of the young men were very fast and very unreliable, enemies alike to their employer and to themselves. Some of them were moral young men— one only was thoughtful and pious. Into the room with this young man the boy was put as a companion. He found it irksome to room with one whose fixed purpose seemed so different from his own. Young Macdonald then went to bed, and rose without prayers. He had been religiously trained, and during his school days had kept alive an intensely devout spirit, but for two years he had been living among prayerless young men; he had imbibed their worldliness, and now in the city, had determined to drink more fully into the spirit and adopt the habits of the ungodly.

"Eternity," he writes, "will reveal many strange things, and doubtless among others, will show the strange way in which I was led to that house, to that room, to that young man, and back to God, from whom I had wandered."

He says : "There are incidents which often occur, too trifling to excite attention at the time, yet, as one sees afterwards, big with results and destined to change the whole of one's after-life. The establishment I was entering was the most extensive retail dry goods concern in Upper Canada. My home was to be under the roof of my employer, and I had assigned to me a room, large and lofty, in which there was a young man who was to be my room-mate. It was not long before I found, very greatly to my surprise, that he was a Methodist. I say surprised, for had it been possible for me to have had anything to say in the matter I would have willed it otherwise—not that I had anything against the young man, nor was there any reason that I should think of him other than kindly, but hitherto I had never been associated with any other than Presbyterians, and had always looked upon Methodists with a kind of mistrust. I cannot well describe my disappointment when I found myself associated with a room-mate who was my senior by two or three years, and a Methodist. Each, in church matters, went his own way ; he to the old rough-cast church on George Street, where worshipped the British Wesleyans ; I to St. Andrew's, on Church Street. As to the structures, the churches externally and internally were as different as they well could be. The St. Andrew's Church, for those days, might with great propriety be said to be a pretentious building. It was built of brick, and plastered to imitate stone ; had a handsome spire, an ecclesiastical appearance, while the location was central and commanding. The other was as unpretentious as a church building could well be; size, about 35 x 60 feet; rough-cast; the whole structure worth probably from $2,000 to $2,500, as plain as wood and rough-cast could make it, and accommodating from three to four hundred people."

The young man here referred to was Mr. T. S. Keough, and the acquaintance ripened into a warm and lasting friendship which coloured the whole of his career. In his daily journal he records that he had determined to "see life;" had begun to delight in various amusements on the Lord's Day and to seek the acquaintance of the irreligious. But his plastic nature was to be changed and his entire religious life shaped through the influence of a faithful companion. No wonder he continues:

"It seems fitting just here, to notice how much the happiness and well-being, the misery or wretchedness of our lives depends upon the companionships which as young lads we form. Indeed, as I look back upon the past, I am persuaded that greater in importance than even home-training, all important as that is, as regards the future of the young man, is the selection which he makes of his companions. If the selection is in every way desirable from the standpoint of God's Word, he may be said to be placed in circumstances of safety; if, on the other hand, he is thrown into close company with those who disregard God's Word, His day, His house, he is placed in circumstances of the greatest peril; all the greater, if such companions are kind-hearted, genial, and unselfish, as such young men so often are; circumstances which may so shape his life as to mean ruin, and ruin only, of soul and body, the blighting of every prospect, the dissipating of every fondly cherished hope.

" Taking my own case as a fair example, what might the result have been had circumstances been different ? I find myself in a room with a stranger, one whom I had never seen, but with whom I had much of my time at least to be associated, without a relative on this continent, so far as I knew. What more natural than that we should go to the same places, do the same things, mix with the same company ? Certainly no better than other lads of my age, and possibly not much worse, I was ready most assuredly to offer no violent objection to anything which meant fun, and would not have been unwilling to have " seen life."

" What if the inclinations of my young friend lay in that direction, what if he was in the habit of spending his evenings in some saloon, of visiting the play, of going to the opera, nay, what if he were in the habit of visiting those abodes which lead down to death ? Would he have invited me to accompany him ? Would I have gone ?

" How wonderfully does God lead us ! What safeguards does He throw around us ! What barriers does He set up to save us from breaking through, lest we perish ! How He leads us in ways which we had not known ! How He directs our steps and brings us under the power of influences of which we had never dreamt, that our own happiness may be secured and His own glory promoted. In none of the hurtful ways to which I have referred was the influence of my friend to be exerted. Here I found a young man who had given his heart to God, singularly pure in his life and in his conversation. Without cant on the one hand, without gloomy misanthropic views on the other, thoroughly consistent among those who were careless. If we were to be companions it must be upon the lines upon which he was walking."

Let us see what the result was. On a Sabbath evening in the early autumn of 1842, he was found for the first time in a Methodist chapel. The preacher was the Rev. John C. Davidson. The. pulpit, like everything else in the church, was severely plain. The choir sat within the communion rail. The leader was Mr. Booth; Alderman Baxter, then a slender young man, was a member—his father, strangely enough, being the leader of the choir in St. Andrew's Church. The singing was very good; none better was there in the city. He was much pleased with the service, and as there was no evening service in St. Andrew's he found himself going each Sunday evening to the George Street Church ; yet doing this without the remotest intention of transferring his allegiance from the one church to the other, or ever dreaming that he was to live or die other than a Presbyterian. In like manner the week evening services on Monday and Thursday attracted him, there being neither preaching nor a prayer-meeting service during the week at St. Andrew's.

"The case therefore stood thus: I attended two services weekly of the church to which I belonged— the Presbyterian—and though not connected with it by membership was fully resolved never to leave; and three weekly services in the church to which I did not belong—the Methodist. The senior preacher on the circuit was Rev. Matthew (afterwards Doctor) Richey. When it is claimed that he was the most eloquent preacher in the city, the statement is one which will not be questioned. He was an Irishman; he must have been then about forty years of age, of fine presence, voice so full, deep and musical, that it might well be said to be phenomenal; faultless as a reader, it was a rare treat to hear him read the Word of God. His pulpit efforts were marked by a solemn and devotional spirit; his prayers were in striking contrast to that hasty, irreverent manner which characterizes the approaches of so many in our day, to the throne of grace. Little wonder was it that his name at that time would attract as many as the building would hold, and more."

Mr. Macdonald was greatly charmed with the pulpit ministrations of this highly gifted man. He attended a special meeting which was held during the last week of 1842, and was closed with a watch-night service, the first of the kind he had ever attended. The service was in charge of Dr. Richey. Mr. Macdonald says: "I remember the sermon well, as being one of great impressiveness. About three minutes before midnight the preacher, in his devout way, said: 'We will spend the remaining moments of the old year upon our knees before God, in silent prayer.' Everything was new to me, the death-like stillness which reigned throughout the church was descriptive of that solemnity which everyone seemed to feel; then the overwhelming silence was broken by the deep, full, solemn voice of the minister, as he gave out the lines:

> "'The arrow has flown; the moment is gone;
> The millennial year
> Rushes on to our view, and eternity's near.'"

This service left a deep religious impression upon his mind; and on February 10th there began another series of meetings which were destined to exert a transforming influence upon his character and life. He became interested in personal religion; then powerfully convicted of sin, and sought earnestly the assurance of God's favour. A long struggle with pride took place before he could take the deciding step, and go forward for prayer.

The very night that he surrendered his will and yielded his heart, he was owned and blessed of God. Divine light, and love, and joy were poured into his being, and he received the remission of sins, and justification through faith in our Lord Jesus Christ. In his " Recollections of British Methodism in Toronto," he refers thus to his coming forward as a seeker:

" There are those who object to any manifestations in public assemblies, such as have been referred to. The result of my own thinking on the matter, after an experience of forty-eight years, has taught me that the man who will stand up in a public assembly and thereby show his determination not only to be a Christian, but his desire to secure the prayers of God's people to strengthen him in his determination, is in earnest. That which prevents a man from taking this step is not a conviction that he does not stand in need of God's grace, *but pride*. The step once taken, this pride is humbled, the man has obtained the mastery over himself, he has proclaimed to his worldly associates that he intends to lead a new life. In one word, he has virtually said with the prodigal, ' I will arise and go to my Father.' He is not far from the kingdom; he has gone to meet the Christ who is waiting to receive him.

" Does it need an effort? It needs the effort of his entire nature, and if he is sincere, it will help him a thousand times more than all the promises to consider the matter and weigh its responsibilities. There are thousands of earnest workers in the Church to-day who have to thank God that He, by His grace, enabled them when invited to do so, to stand up and confess Him, to stand up and acknowledge their need of Him, and who, in this way, were helped to find Christ. And there are thousands to-day who regret that when such opportunities were offered, shame prevented them from availing themselves of such invitations."

This was his spiritual birth, the beginning of a divine life, and his whole after life was but the growth, the unfolding of what he then received. This great spiritual event is the key to his character and his work as a man. The end of religion is conduct. Ethical means practical—it relates to practice or conduct. The grace which he then received passed into habits and dispositions, and gave him his many-sided excellences. Shortly after, he joined the Methodist Church, but not without much thought and spiritual conflict. There were the early influences of home and Christian training in another Church; there was the new-found Saviour and the affluent peace that had sprung up in his heart through the agency of Methodism. He observes:

" Here was a young lad, eighteen years of age, too young to be noticed; certainly too young to initiate any change in Church life, attracted to a Church against which he was strongly prejudiced, drawn from one to which he was as strongly attached, from one to which all his friends belonged. Why was it that he should have become a Methodist, when under ordinary circumstances he should have continued to be a Presbyterian?

"I found myself placed in circumstances of difficulty, conscious beyond doubt that a new direction had been given to my life, through the instrumentality of the Methodist Church; equally conscious that it was my duty that my church relationship must be with the Presbyterian Church. What was I to do? First, it appeared to me that it was my duty to make myself familiar with the teaching of the Presbyterian Church. Having thus resolved, it did not take me long to act; that very day I went to the book store of Hugh Scobie, King Street, and purchased a copy of the "Confession of Faith." I began to examine it with a mind fully made up to endorse all that was contained in it. It would have appeared to me the most profound folly to question aught which it set forth. I expected from it to gather light, and knowledge, and strength.

"I soon found myself in a difficulty. If I was implicitly to accept the Confession of Faith, many passages of Scripture to me were incomprehensible. I closed the book, determined to read no more, but to go for my light and teaching to the Word of God. I bought Dr. Adam Clarke's Commentary, and turned to the article described by him at the close of the Acts, 2nd chapter, as that awful subject, the foreknowledge of God. The article on the 'Decrees' in the Confession perplexed me; the reasoning of Dr. Clarke afforded me no satisfactory solution. The fact was that the wind that bloweth where it listeth had blown upon me, and brought with it the awakening of a new life—a life which had to gather strength and vigour from daily conflict with those who were actively engaged in church life, and from the same source from which they gathered theirs. The conclusion was slowly but painfully reached, that this was not to be obtained in a church whose public religious services for the week, apart from the Sabbath School, were all embraced in the one morning service on the Lord's Day. And thus the step was taken. The severance was made, and I had passed away from the church under whose influence I had seen the light, and to which all my friends belonged."

His new spiritual life responded readily to the doctrines, institutions and ministries of Methodism. He was its child, not by descent, but by real kinship. It met his wants, satisfied his desires, and he was in sympathy with its aims and methods.

On Wednesday, March 15th, he attended a class-meeting for the first time, and with quick insight he perceived its value as a means of grace. The leader was Richard Wordsworth, and the class met in his house on Richmond Street. Mr. Macdonald says:

"The whole thing, to me, was new. To hear men speaking of their unfaithfulness, expressing their fixed purpose anew to consecrate themselves to God's service, and soliciting the prayers of God's people to help them in their purpose; and to hear the leader, a man of experience, who had himself passed through just such mental conflicts, counsel them from his own knowledge of God's goodness, and present to them for their consideration the unfailing promises of God's Word, was something which I had never conceived, was something which I felt was of inestimable value to every young Christian, was something which might, with great advantage, be adopted by all the churches, and which now, after a lengthened experience, I regard as one of the most valued means for the strengthening of God's children in the Divine life.

No better barometer is there by which the spiritual life of the members of the Methodist Church can be gauged than that which is furnished by their attendance upon the class-meeting. If careless and indifferent; if the world preponderates, the class-meeting is irksome. If men are living to God, it is a delight."

He entered the George Street Sabbath School, of which Mr. Alexander Hamilton was superintendent, and soon became a teacher. He bought the Wesleyan standard works, and so studied them that the doctrines and traditions of the Church passed into his life and became a part of himself. He was soon in the full round of religious activity, speaking in class and fellowship meetings, attending prayer-meetings and assisting in conducting them. He was placed on the Prayer Leader's plan, a department of Church work in which the young men went in companies, sometimes singing on the streets, then holding a cottage-meeting near—their field of labour extending from Berkeley Street on the east to the Asylum on the west. While his religion was thus practical and experimental, he was giving close attention to study. His young friend, Mr. Keough, greatly aided him; their sympathies and secret hearts seemed to flow spontaneously together; they were bound together by the most sacred ties of sanctified friendship.

Over the George Street congregation he grows enthusiastic, and while he has no desire to detract from the influence of the Canadian Methodists then worshipping in the Newgate Street Church, in helping on the development of Methodism in the city and in the Dominion, yet he says, " Greater far was the

4

power and influence exerted by the old George Street Church."

" It was to the George Street Church that every-other church in the Connexion looked : its action determined the action of the others. The best men in the body filled its pulpit and ministered to its people ; it was from George Street that the church removed to the Richmond Street Church, the Cathedral of Methodism, which, more than any other church of its day, was the centre of great evangelistic gather-ings, and which, having outlived its usefulness, has recently passed into the hands of the Book Room Committee to be used for connexional purposes."

About the time of his conversion he commenced a daily journal devoted almost exclusively to his re-ligious feelings and occupations. This biography of his inner life is marked by set phrases for religious things, and a particular type of devotion then in vogue ; but it is characterized by great maturity of thought, and is an affecting picture of the Christian lad struggling against his doubts, temptations and sins, and earnestly aspiring after a higher spiritual life. Wednesday, 11th April, 1843, marks the first quarterly ticket he received. On Sunday, 30th April, there is this record :

" Attended a love-feast for the first time. Felt a great diffidence and backwardness in owning my pro-fession. But at length I broke through every barrier and spoke for Christ, after which I felt relieved and blessed. This made me determined that if I was spared to attend another, I would speak as soon as an opportunity offered itself."

He has preserved in his diary the texts from which

preached many of the illustrious men of that day ; and the boy-critic freely passes his comments upon the discourses to which he listens. In June of this year there is an entry which marks a most important epoch, as it gives the first intimation of his thoughts concerning the Christian ministry. His youthful aspirings are thus recorded :

"Thought a great deal about devoting myself to the ministry. I feel the solemn responsibility of such a work, and almost fear that it is sacrilege to indulge in thoughts concerning so great a vocation. But am thankful to say that I gladly accept God's will should He spare my worthless life, and make me the humble instrument in His hands of doing good to the souls of my fellow-men. I have a burning desire to do good, and devote myself to the service of my Redeemer."

He had belonged to a young men's Bible-class in St. Andrew's Church, which afterwards had taken the form of a debating society. Young Macdonald had been elected its first president. He had thus begun to exercise his gifts of speech. In the prayer-meeting he had ventured now and then upon a word of exhortation, and had acquired a readiness of utter-ance. While conducting the band meetings, his con-victions upon the subject of preaching seemed to increase in strength and definiteness, fostered, no doubt, by friends who discerned his gifts. Besides, his companion, Mr. Keough, had become a Local Preacher, and as they worked together, lived together, read and prayed together in closest intimacy, this fact no doubt helped to give direction to the course of his thoughts. He still continued to be diligent in business, a successful merchant in embryo; his duties were very exacting, his hours long, yet the current of his being was steadily setting in another direction.

On Wednesday, September 23rd, 1845, he preached his first sermon. It was in the Yorkville chapel, the Rev. John Bredin being present to hear and approve or discourage the experiment. He preached for thirty-four minutes, and the effort was so completely satisfactory that on the following Sabbath he accompanied Mr. Bredin into the country, preaching for him at Milligans' and at Thornhill. After some months' trial, he passed his examination satisfactorily, and became a fully accredited Local Preacher. The journal tells of increased activity in the cause of Christ, and while there are such records as these, " Thought of abandoning the idea of preaching;" " Have a dread of unworthy motives;" " O what a responsible office is that of a preacher of the gospel!" still his work does not slacken. But there was sore discipline in store for him—severe searchings of heart, bodily suffering, mental anxiety, dark and gloomy forebodings, and the prospect of early death. Disease seems to have become a finger-post of Providence, and to have directed the current of his life.

IV.

ILL-HEALTH—JAMAICA.

Sorrows are often like clouds, which, though black when they
are passing over us, when they are past become as if they were
the garments of God thrown off in purple and gold along the sky.
—Henry Ward Beecher.

Heave, mighty ocean, heave !
And blow thou boisterous wind !
Onward we swiftly glide, and leave
Our home and friends behind.

—S. Graham.

Talk not of wasted affection ; affection never was wasted.
If it enrich not the heart of another, its waters returning
Back to their springs, like the rain, shall fill them full of
    refreshment,
That which the fountain sends forth, returns again to the
    fountain.
—Longfellow.

" IT is well said," observes Carlyle, "in every sense that a man's religion is the chief fact with regard to him." The subject of our memoir has passed the crisis of his being and become a "new creature in Christ Jesus." Having received the new life from above, he gives all diligence to nourish and strengthen it. For this grace, though miraculous in its origin, is yet subject to natural laws in its progress. We find young Macdonald diligently using the appointed means of grace, engaged in visiting the sick, attending prayer-meetings and preaching the Word. He has strong spiritual conflicts; he knows what it is to wrestle in agony with his bosom-sin and to face with courage the daily temptations of life. His diary shows a remarkable elevation of religious faith and feeling; yet there is constant self-reproach for indulging in things seemingly innocent. His conscience is awakened to the evil of vanity, and he resolves to fight his enemy down to its lurking-place. What is written in his diary is rather for God's eye than the eye of man, yet through it we get a deeper insight of his inward humiliation and his spiritual conflicts. How valuable such records are! Marcus Aurelius is one of the most beautiful characters in history. He was an example of goodness in high places; yet the record of him, on which his fame as one of the best of men rests, is the journal of his inward life, his " Meditations."

From his Journal :

" January 22nd, 1846.—By the blessing of God I intend to redeem the time from idle conversation, to set a guard over my lips. How much have I lost by inattention to this duty.

" February 16th.—Felt more humbled and my pride somewhat checked. Much annoyed in spirit about my carelessness, my foolish tempers and dispositions.

" March 8th.—Felt a disposition to vanity, when a lady expressed delight on hearing my sermon yesterday. What a hurtful thing pride is ! May God enable me to overcome it in all its aspects and features !

" May 2nd.—Unable to preach. Got Brother N. to supply my place at Dundas Street.

" May 5th.—Had some thoughts to-night of death, namely, that it is because we do not love Christ supremely that we are afraid to die.

" May 5th.—Felt a want of spirituality, and consequently of devotedness and zeal. Thought much upon the necessity of being as spiritually minded in and about my business and among my shop-mates as I would desire to be when endeavouring to instruct others in the way of salvation."

These extracts show that he had a keen sense of indwelling sin and a longing to be Christ-like, as well as an ardent desire to devote himself to the Master's service for the advancement of His glory and kingdom. At this time the Rev. William Harvard was Superintendent of the Circuit. He proved to be a wise, faithful and kindly pastor, and took a deep interest in Mr. Macdonald's welfare.

" Wednesday, June 15th.—Had some conversation with, and advice from, Rev. Mr. Harvard, who apprised me that, if we were both spared until next District Meeting, he intended bringing me forward as a candidate for the ministry."

Next comes a period of declining health and of deep depression of spirits. He was troubled with irritation of the bronchial tubes and weakness of the lungs. There is an undertone of gloom and melancholy; only now and then do his natural buoyancy and lightheartedness reassert themselves. He seems to be living as in the very shadow of the grim spectre. He makes record of every departure of acquaintance and friend, and is ready to exclaim :

> "Oh, what is life ?
> 'Tis like a flower that blossoms and is gone."

His own mind is absorbed with the idea that he is given over to die.

"September 7th.—Lay awake all night thinking on death, scarcely closed my eyes.

"January 1st, 1847.—Realizing the uncertainty of life, and desiring that in case of a sudden removal from time to eternity the property which I have received from my Heavenly Father should be disposed of in a way which will conduce most to His glory, I bequeath to my father my Bible and Wesley's Notes on the New Testament, and direct that the rest of my books and goods be sold, and the proceeds, with other sums of money, to be applied to the liquidation of the debt on the Richmond Street Chapel. May this New Year upon which I have been permitted to enter, be the best in my life ! May every unholy disposition and temper be sanctified ! May I be enabled ever to see my way clearly before me, and may I be rendered an instrument of good in my day and generation."

His health did not improve. His lungs were inclined to be tuberculous, and he had occasional spitting of blood. Still he worked on with Mr. Macfarlane, in whose employment he had been for five consecutive years, and was engaged in study and systematic reading, writing his sermons with considerable care, and preaching as often as his physical strength would permit. One of his companions at this time was Mr. Sanford Fleming, then a young engineer from Scotland, who has since, through our most stupendous public works, made himself known in every part of the Dominion.

From his Journal :

"Saturday, June 6th, 1847. At the annual meeting of the Canadian Conference a union was effected between that body and the British Conference."

Dr. Alder had been sent out to adjust, if possible, the differences existing for the last seven years, and Mr. Macdonald, as one of the officials was present at the first meeting called to lay before the Board the articles of the proposed union. He thus speaks of the representative of the British Conference :

"Dr. Alder was about medium size, stout, florid, thoughtful face, large head, great profusion of hair, impressive appearance and manner; in addition to his being an excellent preacher, he was a skilled diplomat. In the public Sabbath services which followed, he took no part beyond reading the hymns and Scriptures, both of which he did faultlessly. His message was delivered to a hostile company, and he knew it; admirably did he do his part of the work."

He further says :

" In that great company of officials Dr. Alder had not one friendly hearer, not one who was in sympathy with the movement, not one who desired it. The meeting was protracted to a late hour. Many threats were made. Rather than go into the union they would form an independent church or join the Primitive Methodists. One thing was clear, no Canadian Methodist would be allowed to preach in the Richmond Street Church ; they would lock the doors, they would forcibly prevent any minister of that Church from occupying the pulpit.

" Meantime much writing had to be got through, the proceedings of the evening had to be put in shape ready for the next meeting. Who was to do it ? One had no time, another had no inclination, another gave a flat denial."

Mr. Macdonald undertook to do the needed work. It was done. The meeting was held, and the act of union consummated. The next record in his diary is :

" Attended a union meeting of both circuits, and was extremely pleased with the happy feeling that seemed to influence all present. The appointments were put upon one general plan for the more efficient and amicable working of the whole."

Of this union he thus speaks in his " Recollections of Toronto Methodism " :

" The first Sabbath came and went, as did the second and following Sabbaths, and no doors were locked, no ministers ejected from pulpits, no independent congregations formed, no further negotiations carried on for a union with the Primitive Methodist Church. The union was of God, was crowned with His blessing, and was the first step toward that larger movement which has eventuated in consoli-

dating every branch of the Methodist family into
one united and powerful Church, whose healthful
influences are felt from Newfoundland to Japan,
never, let us hope, to be again dismembered by
trifling differences, but to go on baptized from on
high, and fitted by the consecration of its wealth, its
influences, and, above all, by the devotion of its
people, to do its share, side by side, with the great
army of the living God, as found in the other
churches, in the evangelization of the world."

Had Mr. Macdonald's health continued, he would
undoubtedly have entered the ministry of this
Church, a work for which both his natural gifts and
his spiritual aspirations seemed to qualify him. But
that Providence, which so strangely and beautifully
makes all things work together for good, was ordering otherwise. He was now booked as a victim of
consumption, and his physician advised him at once
to give up all labour and study, and go to the West
Indies. Accordingly we find this entry: " July 21st,
1847, my declining health rendered it necessary to
give up all work, and I left Mr. Macfarlane's employment." He speaks of his employer with the highest
respect, and felt grieved at parting from him. The
feeling was reciprocal, for Mr. Macfarlane gave him
testimonials of the most satisfactory description, paid
him several pounds more than his salary, and handed
him a handsome Bible, the gift of his two youngest
children. Early on the morning of the twenty-second
of July we find him on the wharf bidding farewell to
the friends that have accompanied him to the ship,
and taking passage on the Niagara steamer. He

proceeded to Buffalo, thence to Albany, where he spent the Sabbath. Here he attended a class, made the acquaintance of the superintendent of the school, and addressed the children.

Next day he sailed down the Hudson to New York, where he spent two or three days, and then went on to Boston. With his soldierly instincts he turned his steps to the Navy Yard, and was impressed with its extent and importance. He also visited Lowell, to see the great cotton, woollen and print manufactories. From Boston he took passage to St. John, where he surprised Rev. Dr. Cooney and family with his presence. He preached in the Centenary Church to a large and attentive congregation. Here, also, he met the Rev. Samuel D. Rice, who was going to Upper Canada, and he gave him his keys to select from his library, in Toronto, such books as suited him, the amount to be placed to his credit till he should hear from him again. He found the atmosphere of St. John foggy and oppressive, and after a short stay went on to Frederickton, thence to Chatham Head, Miramichi, the residence of his friend, Mr. A. Fraser, with whom he remained for nearly a month. The recollection of his pleasant visit, in this beautiful home, remained fresh and green in his memory to the end of his days. Another fortnight was delightfully spent at New Glasgow, in the home of Mr. James Fraser, another brother, whose parting words were: "Never hide your circumstance from me, and if you ever stand in need of assistance, my help is ready." The young man was greatly pleased with the attentions paid to all the

observances of religion by these friends of his father's
family, and he speaks of many happy seasons enjoyed
in prayer while officiating at their family altars. From
New Glasgow he went to Halifax and stood again,
after an absence of nine years, upon the spot familiar
to his boyhood. He found the place greatly altered.
At Dalhousie College he saw a number of his old
school-mates; some he remembered; others had grown
out of his recollection. He says, "many pleasing
associations were recalled as I passed each spot which
I had so often trod in my boyish days. When I was
here I was without God and had no hope in the
world." His thoughts and hopes, his purposes and
aspirations have all been changed by the transforming
power of divine love. He preached in the Argyle
Street Chapel, occupying the pulpit in which the Rev.
William Black, the eminent apostle of Methodism in
the Eastern Provinces, had often preached. Of the
congregation he says : " It was the largest I have yet
addressed ; very respectable and exceedingly attentive." Furnished with a number of letters to Jamaica
he took passage on board the brig *Commerce*, bound
for Port Maria. The wind was favourable, and next
day they lost sight of the North American coast. The
voyage was exceedingly disagreeable, and attended
with danger, as they narrowly escaped being cast away
on the leeshore. This is the account :

" Early on the morning of the seventh day after our
departure from Halifax, the captain knowing that we
were within a comparatively short distance of the
Bermudas, judged it expedient to lay to from 1 to 5 a.m.

The morning was squally, a high wind blowing. About 9 a.m. land was seen bearing south-east, distance about ten miles. During the whole of that day the wind blew fresh from the east, accompanied by frequent squalls. Next day the wind shifted to the south-west, increasing in violence, the sea also running very high. About four in the afternoon our storm-stay-sail was carried away, and a considerable quantity of water was taken in over our lee-bows, which threw the vessel on her beam's end, and a heavy deck load prevented her from rising. She now made leeway rapidly, when the captain thought it prudent to throw a portion of the deck-load overboard, which being done, she immediately righted and seemed relieved. As the evening advanced the winds and waves increased in fury, and rendered it a season of painful anxiety to all on board. They were apprised that the situation was one of extreme danger, the vessel rapidly nearing a reef of rocks among the most dangerous in the world. The sea was running high, and the wind blowing so furiously as to prevent us from carrying sail sufficient to bear up against it. The gloom of night, and the fury of the surrounding elements were rendered still more alarming by the appearance of the vivid light on Gibb's Hill, seen occasionally from the top of a mighty wave. Then, indeed, did our case appear hopeless. The captain at once crowded on all sail, being determined that either the masts would be carried away, or that we would escape the danger by bearing up against the wind. Happily, through the assistance of a kind Providence, after struggling hard for about seven hours, the light bore from us east north-east, and shortly disappeared. It was a wonderful deliverance from ship-wreck and one of the narrowest escapes from a watery grave, for had we gone ashore we must all have inevitably perished. Much praise was due to the captain, who with such decision and self-possession met the emergency."

After leaving the Bermudas, the passage was tedious, being about twenty-three days before they saw Jamaica. The last three or four days they were passing St. Domingo and Cuba. These islands present a high, mountainous appearance, and the view from the deck of the vessel is one never to be forgotten. What a picture of loveliness! Lofty mountain ranges towering majestically beneath a tropical sky. At length they descry on the far horizon the dim outline of a lovely isle, St. Jago, Jamaica, gem of the Antilles.

> " The Hesperian isle from distance dimly blue,
> With gradual beauty opened on his view."

They were detained for six days off the island by having simply got a few miles to leeward of their port, where the current was running at the rate of several miles an hour, while the breeze was scarcely sufficient to shake the sails. He thus had ample time to drink in the enchanting scene, as Montgomery sings of this charming land :

> " When first his drooping sails Columbus furl'd,
> And sweetly rested in another world,
> Amid the heaven-reflecting ocean smiles
> A constellation of Elysian isles ;
> Fair as Orion as he mounts on high,
> Sparkling with midnight splendour from the sky,
> Thy barque beneath the sun's meridian rays
> When not a shadow breaks the boundless blaze ;
> The breath of ocean wanders through their sails
> In morning breezes and in evening gales,
> Earth from her lap perennial verdure pours,
> Ambrosial fruits and amaranthine flowers ;
> O'er the wild mountain and luxuriant plains
> Nature in all the pomp of beauty reigns."

They landed at Annotto Bay, and by daybreak next morning Mr. Macdonald, with letters to the most influential houses in the island, and accompanied by his sable guide, was on his way to Kingston, thirty miles distant. It was a delightful trip, and nothing could be more exhilarating. The beauties of nature, constantly before his eyes, enraptured him. He remembered that in the land he had left, the melancholy rustling of the falling leaf was heard in the forest, and bleak winds, the forerunners of winter, were whistling around the farm dwellings, and comfortable fires blazed upon the hearthstones, while here "eternal summer reigns." It is the month of November, yet the people are clad in thin, white apparel, and the trees are laden with the choicest and richest fruit. He admires the bamboo huts of

THE TWENTY-FIVE FOUNTAINS, WEST INDIES.

the negroes, and the picturesque villages along the way.

5

After leaving the town of Annotto Bay, which then, as now, possessed great length without breadth, consisting of one long narrow street, over which there are three or four bridges several rivers, or rather the Wag River, emptying itself by several streams into the sea, they passed a number of large and beautiful sugar

SCENES IN THE WEST INDIES.

plantations, with their picturesque buildings, mills and aqueducts. He found boundless delight in the scenery, the climate, and especially the vegetation. There were trees of every kind, the beautiful sugar cane, the great and principal staple of the Island; the silk cotton tree spreading its ample branches on either side for forty feet; the trumpet tree and the tall cocoanut, the graceful bamboo and the rich mango, cactus hedges, logwood copses and banana walks. The ample foliage of these trees, endless in their variety, afforded a grateful shelter from the burning rays of the sun. The distant views of the mountains, almost Alpine in their proportions, with their lofty summits shrouded in clouds, enchanting glens and ravines with rivers foaming along, forming graceful and feathery cascades; the natural arbors made by vines, moss and ferns, and flowering shrubs crowned with bright blossoms, every form of sylvan life; the endless streams of water beautifully clear; the orange, the mango and other luscious fruits growing so plentifully that he could pluck them as he passed along; all made up a unique and intensely romantic journey, and left upon his mind a vivid and lasting impression of perfect beauty. Kingston was reached in the afternoon, a city of 40,000 inhabitants, the chief commercial city of the Island. He confessed to a disappointment at its straggling appearance. Here he takes train to Spanish Town, the old capital Santiago de la Vega of the Spaniards, for three centuries and a half the capital of the Island. When the train halted at the station, he made his way along its clean and well-paved streets until he stood before a door which bore a plate with the inscription, Rev. J. G. Manly.

From his journal :

"I stood at the door of a gentleman to whom I was an utter stranger, yet if he had not been in Jamaica, I might not have found my way thither. Mr. Manley had been in Toronto, where, I was informed, he suffered from ill-health, but had found the climate of Jamaica greatly to benefit him. I had concluded that

if the climate had had such a beneficial effect upon
him, it would surely be helpful to me.   This was the
main reason for my coming to Jamaica.   Although I
had not the pleasure of his acquaintance, still we
were mutually acquainted with the same kind friends
in Toronto.   He was a minister of the same Church
to which I belonged, and would consequently entertain kindly feelings towards me.   I had left Toronto
under the same circumstances that had compelled him
to leave, and had come at the suggestion of the same
kind friends who had strongly advised him to visit
Jamaica.   And chiefly, I had come because I believed
the good Providence of God had directed me thither.
I rang the bell, a coloured girl came to the door; I
sent in my name, and remained in the drawing-room
for a few moments until the Rev. gentleman appeared.
He received me with kindness, but with apparent
caution.   After a few words had been interchanged,
I presented my letters of introduction, one from his
intimate friend, Mr. J. G. Bowes, the other from the
Rev. E. Evans, Superintendent of Toronto West Circuit.   He at once introduced me to his wife, sent for
my luggage, and insisted on my making his house my
home.   It is impossible for me to speak in language
too strong of the kindness received from these estim-
able people, and it will not appear strange that an
attachment was formed that can never be forgotten."

By the aid of his friends, and the letter which he
had brought with him, he obtained a situation at
£150 per annum in one of the best houses in the
Island, the firm of J. Nethersole & Co., Kingston. He
observed a difference, not only in the class of goods
required for the West Indian colonies, but also in the
class of customers.   The blacks he found were extremely susceptible to slight, and jealous of any pre-

ference shown. They were exceedingly fond of dress, and would buy the most costly materials. He found, too, that whenever a European acted with proper decorum and respect toward them, it secured their confidence and esteem. He soon became a popular salesman with the natives. He at once united with the Church, attending the Coke Memorial Chapel. This is a noble Gothic edifice built on the Parade, the chief architectural ornament of the city, and accommodating a congregation of 2,000. It bears the honoured name of the pioneer of Wesleyan Missions, who landed in Port Royal in January 19th, 1789, preached several times in Kingston, established a cause and had missionaries sent to the Island. He assisted the pastor, Rev. M. Young at the Watch-night service, which was crowded ; and was struck with the custom of the blacks when the moment arrived which ended the old year, of setting up a most doleful sound ; one old woman declaring to him that she heard the old year go out with a *whizzy, whizzy, whizz*, and the new year come in with a whizzy, whizzy, whizz. He formed many delightful acquaintances in Jamaica, and had pleasant intercourse with the Wesleyan missionaries. Among them Rev. H. Bleby, Superintendent of Wesley Chapel, another noble church edifice on Thames Street, capable of accommodating a congregation of 3,000 ; Rev. James R. Westley, a devoted young minister, the first missionary whom he met, and whose ruddy appearance seemed to commend to him the salubrious climate, but whose career, alas, was suddenly ended. He was seized with yellow fever, and a week later thousands followed the remains of the almost idolized young pastor to the grave. Rev. Henry B. Foster, the author of " The Rise and Progress of Wesleyan Methodism in Jamaica," who laboured on the Island as a missionary during an unbroken period of forty-five years, and other devoted men who were seeking to extend and deepen the influence of Christianity on this lovely Island.

But on the other hand, the depravity and licentiousness of the people filled him with shame and sorrow. He makes this bare, unvarnished statement of fact, that the great majority of native girls over fourteen or fifteen years of age were the mothers of children born out of wedlock, the evil being so common as not to bring even a blush of shame to the cheek of these unhappy, unholy matrons. Many Europeans, moving in respectable society, were living in a state of concubinage, with a troop of illigitimate children growing up around them. His whole nature burned with indignation that these evils, which were a disgrace to to the Island, should be looked upon with indifference by the Colonists. He had longings for home, and as the warm months approached, he felt the relaxing effect of the heat. The physician who attended him thought that he might return to Canada with comparative safety, and accordingly he determined to take the first vessel that sailed for Halifax.

Before leaving Jamaica, he wished to see something more of the beauty of this radiant queen of the West Indies. He made a pilgrimage to St. Anne—the garden of Jamaica, where Rev. Martin Young, with his family, had gone. He describes the scenery through the Bog-Walk as singularly bold and striking, among the grandest he had ever witnessed. The Rio Cobre, a small winding river, runs between two immense mountains, whose heights break the clouds and cause them to discharge their burdens beneath, so that it rains heavily here almost daily. In some places the mountain sides are literally perpendicular, the ravines almost vertical, forming wonderfully grand views; while in striking contrast to this scenic grandeur, is the gurgling or placid waters that flow beneath. Streams of exquisite beauty abound, and rolling fields of emerald verdure, with clusters of deep-hued mango foliage, tree ferns and flowering shrubs. Indeed, the Spanish Xaymaca means the country of springs and forests. The groves are not less interesting than the rivers.

> " Waters whose rills o'er ruby beds and emeralds flow,
> Catching the gem's bright colours as they go."

He visited Linstead, "a nest of sensuality," near which, he says, "is the famed Rodney Hall, where many a poor negro has groaned under the lash of the house of correction. It looks like some horrid inquisition—a den of cruelty, in which deeds of darkness and blood have been committed." He greatly enjoyed the rugged climb of Mount Diabolo. It is one continued ascent of seven miles, the road in some places extremely dangerous, but the view from the summit repaid the climber. There, southward, nestled St. Thomas in-the-Vale, surrounded by mountains—the

Vale itself once a mountain lake, drained by some
great convulsion of nature, many hundreds of feet
above the level of the sea—away northward the

MOUNTAIN SCENE, WEST INDIES.

Parish of St. Anne, bamboo cabins, rugged ridges, and
peaks of the Blue Mountains, varying in shape, height
and verdure—the whole tropical landscape dotted

with villages and vast estates. The majority of these estates were, however, abandoned, and the beautiful residences presented a forsaken appearance. The Colony, at this time, was in a deplorable financial condition. The halcyon days of the sugar industry were ended. By the action of the Sugar Duties Bill, passed by the British Parliament in 1846, which equalized the duty on British Colonial sugar with that of slave-grown sugar from slave colonies, there had come great agricultural and commercial depression. The blacks had passed their stated apprenticeship and had received their freedom in 1838. The immediate effect of emancipation upon Jamaican industry was disastrous.

When the Emancipation Act was passed in 1834, the estates had been greatly impoverished, and were beginning to yield much less than they had previously done. The majority of the planters were crippled with heavy debts to English houses. The nearly six millions of pounds sterling awarded to them as compensation for the loss of their slaves went, for the most part, directly into the hands of their creditors, and they were left without resources, with over-worked estates, old, worn-out machinery, and scarcity of labour. Right upon the heels of this came the adoption of the free-trade policy, which reduced the price of sugar one-half to the English consumer and made correspondingly less the planter's profits. In slavery times the English Government had protected Jamaica by heavy differential duties on foreign sugar ; now, abolition had cut down the labonr supply, the Sugar Duties

Bill had diminished the chance for profit in sugar-growing; the planters were unable to compete with the supply from other slave colonies, and at once abandoned their heavily-mortgaged estates. The result was the throwing of thousands of poor people out of work, and a large proportion of the labouring population upon their own resources. No wonder the Colony was in such financial depression. Happily there has come the "awakening of Jamaica;" but still the resources of that fertile, radiant queen of the West Indies are undeveloped, and its commercial importance but dimly realized. He spent a Sabbath at the Mission House, at Beechamville, on the top of a mountain which formed one of many, enclosing a beautiful vale beneath, in which was a large and populous settlement. The religious services on the Sabbath commenced at day-break and continued, with but a few moments intermission, until five p.m. The Chapel was capable of seating a congregation of 1,200 and was well filled. He noticed that the proportion of men in the country congregations was much greater than in the city, where in an audience of 2,400 or 2,500 he had frequently counted not more than 100 or 150 males. He returned more than ever disgusted with the torrent of licentiousness which seemed to sweep unchecked over the land. Luxurious nature seemed to encourage idleness and looseness in morals. The last evening in Jamaica was spent at Spanish Town with his good friends the Manly's. This friendship he counted among the many blessings of his life, and it was a great gratification to him when the Rev.

Mr. Manly returned to Canada, where the friendly intercourse was renewed, which continued to the end of his life.

He had seen, in its length and breadth, this glorious Island—one of the brightest gems in the imperial diadem ; had traversed its lowlands, climbed its heights and sauntered among its hills ; he had rejoiced in its balmy air, its sky of unsullied blue, its sub-tropical waters of turquoise and emerald hues; he was impressed not only with the salubrity of its climate, but with the fertility of its soil, and the unsurpassed beauty of its scenery. This visit gave him an exceptional know-ledge of the affairs of the West Indies, so that through-out his public life he was anxious to create and foster a reciprocal trade with these fair and fertile isles.

He returned to Halifax via Cien Fuego, Cuba, by the brig *Nancy.* He had a delightful passage, the time being spent in reading the whole of Byron's works, many of Shakespeare's plays, and in writing poetry himself. He took a keen delight in versifica-tion. Poetry was an unfailing resource to him ; and he had already tried his prentice-hand at verse. We shall, in a later chapter, produce some of his thought-ful poems, for he not only had a genius for rhythm, but also possessed that vividness and activity of im-agination which makes poets. His poetic lines at this time are unequal, occasionally marred by a false accent or redundant syllable ; but there is about them a delightful limpidity and smoothness; they evince hopefulness and cheer, and are mostly of a contem-plative and religious character. These are some of the themes of his early efforts: "The Irish Famine," "A Storm at Sea," "God is Love," "Hope," "A Sabbath Day in Cien Fuego," "To Rev. J. G. Manly and Lady," "Farewell to Jamaica."

Mr. Macdonald arrived in Halifax, May 15th, 1848, and after spending a few days in the city, went to New Glasgow, where he remained a month or more under the hospitable roof of his friend, Mr. James Frazer. On the 6th July he was in Toronto again. He found the city much improved in appearance, but sadly prostrated in all its business energies. Some of his friends had crossed the Jordan of death; others he was glad to meet again, clasp their hands, and exchange expressions of confidence and esteem. At once we find him resuming his accustomed duties; returning to his old class, taking charge of a select Bible class in the Richmond Street Sunday School, and ready to enter the wide-open gates of golden possibilities.

V.

COMMENCING BUSINESS.

Seest thou a man diligent in his business : he shall stand
before kings, he shall not stand before mean men.

—*Prov.* xx. 29.

To be honest as this world goes, is to be one man picked out
of ten thousand.

—*Shakespeare (Hamlet).*

Study economy. Do not let your house be too big for your
income. At the outset go to sea in a small but well made bark ;
you can sail a three-master when you have gained experience
enough, and can command the necessary capital.

—*Rev. Samuel Osgood, D.D.*

I hope I shall always possess firmness and virtue enough to
maintain what I consider the most enviable of all titles, the
character of an " honest man."

—*George Washington.*

COMMENCING BUSINESS.

IT is a well-known fact of history that the Hon.
W. E. Gladstone, Prime Minister of England, the
illustrious statesman and leader of the Liberal party,
was in youth on the eve of taking religious orders.
In like manner, the merchant-prince of Toronto came
very near becoming a minister of the Gospel. Without doubt he regarded the Christian ministry as the
highest ideal of human usefulness; but the state of
his health was a sore detriment to his prospects for
entering this field of service to God and humanity.
His throat was still troubling him, as it troubled him
through life, and for the present there seemed nothing
left him but to re-enter business. This would not
prevent him from exercising his gifts as a local
preacher, and thus fulfilling the great call of life.
For well has Lowell sung:

> " God bends from out the deep and says
> I gave thee the great gift of life ;
> Wast thou not called in many ways?
> Are not my heaven and earth at strife ? "

And are not the wrongs and evils in society, the sins
and sorrows of individual life, a Divine call to use
our best gifts and acquirements in righting wrongs
and endeavouring to bring heaven and earth into har-

mony ? The man who is unworldly, who has the good of his country and of his fellows at heart, will, by the very force of his own elevated character, uplift others. There is no power on earth like the power of a holy, consecrated life, and everyone who is leading such a life is a minister of God to his fellows, and no matter what his occupation may be, is, by his own saintliness of character, lifting others to higher altitudes.

Mr. Macdonald, in entering the mercantile profession instead of the responsible office of the ministry, did not cease to be a prophet and commissioned messenger of heaven. There is an exalted, as well as a low and grovelling idea of trade. The sole object of business is not profit and worldly aggrandizement True, some modification of the selfish principle may be said to lie at the root of all human action, and nowhere is this so marked and undisguised as in a profession whose direct and avowed object is the getting of gain.

At the same time, the world has always admired those who have been distinguished as honourable merchants. It was said of Tyre, the crowning commercial city of old, that " her merchants were princes and her traffickers the honourable of the earth." It has always been the use made of the wealth acquired in trade that has been the object of commendation and honour, rather than the mere success in accumulation. The true merchant makes no claim to benevolence or patriotism as his ruling motive in trade, but he does profess absolute justice and honour. The morals of trade are of the strictest and purest character. While the direct object is gain, profit, individual benefit, yet no deviation from truth is allowable; there must be unblemished and inviolable integrity. There is no class of men from whom the golden rule of "doing unto others as we would that they should do unto us" is more strictly demanded than among merchants. Mercantile honour is a most delicate thing, and will not bear the slightest stain. The man who, in business, is found to equivocate, is a marked man, while incorruptible integrity is almost uniformly the accompaniment of success, as it always is of sterling character. True it is that in the manifold operations of commerce there are many temptations to acts of dishonesty, more frequent perhaps than in other occupations; and it must be confessed that, in not a few instances, poor human nature is found to yield to them; yet rigid truthfulness is the rule which controls the actions of the honourable trader. Whilst, then, the selfish principle lies at the foundation of trade, there is no reason why the merchant himself should not be active in benevolence and in all Christian virtues; indeed, that his whole life should not be a benediction to others.

John Macdonald possessed in an eminent degree all the qualities which make a merchant prince. The corner-stone of his character was an earnest religious belief; and while his piety was of a rich and ardent type, he had also an integrity as firm as a rock, and an honour as unsullied as the stars.

There are few events in a merchant's life more important than that which introduces him into active business on his own account. As a clerk he had been popular among customers for his alertness and courtesy. He was frank, generous, energetic and upright, instinctively shunning evil practices and associates. An eager and constant reader, he had improved his mind, mastering many solid works; yet his chief schooling had been among men, and in efforts to solve the daily problems of life. Returning to Toronto, somewhat improved in health, he re-engaged with Mr. Macfarlane for a short period, when an opportunity opened for him to go into business for himself.

He secured a store on Yonge Street, west side, one door south of Richmond Street, which he made known as the Large 103. It was a three-story building, and had abundant accommodation for a dwelling-house; but there was no other place of business on the street at the time. He had the offer of a good place of business on the principal thoroughfare, at a rent of $1,000 per annum, but he reasoned thus : " I am commencing business, not on my own means, but on a credit which I am obtaining chiefly from the confidence placed in my character. A larger place would require a large stock, a large staff of assistants, a large expense, while a large interest account might make me dependent permanently upon my creditors. I should also have to contend, at great disadvantage, with those whose means would enable them to buy more advantageously than I could." He resolved, therefore, to take the smaller store. Mr. Macdonald details rather amusingly his efforts to open an account with some of the

Premises in which JOHN MACDONALD *began business in October, 1849,
known then as 103 Yonge Street, 2nd door South of Richmond
Street, West side.*

leading houses. It was little more than twelve months since the crisis of 1847. Men had lost heavily by overtrading, and a more cautious policy was being pursued. Although each of the business men he approached would have been willing to open an assorting account with him, not one of them would give him a stock of goods. One house had just succumbed to the terrible fall in the price of produce, and the senior partner of the firm, unable to bear the terrible reverse thus brought upon him, had gone into a field adjoining his own house, and put an end to his existence. The first wholesale establishment upon which he called was the one doing the largest trade. This house blandly declined to entertain his account, although selling to hundreds of men whose accounts proved so bad that in a very few years the whole fabric fell with a terrible crash. The next firm received him kindly enough, but with the same blank refusal. The third refused, assigning as the reason that their imports were only sufficient for their own regular customers. He called upon three or four other firms, with no better success.

"Little," he says, "did they know or think that the young man, whose account they had thus declined, was not only going to obtain credit, but to succeed not as a retail man only, but, in a few short years, become a direct importer, contest with them for the trade of the country, and do it successfully. Little did they think that, before one year, instead of his pleading with them for credit, they should be soliciting him for his trade, and that before ten years his trade would become as large as theirs, and his credit as good, and his means as ample."

He succeeded in obtaining a credit with the wholesale establishment of Bowes & Hall, and his first in-
voice amounted to £461. His assistants were a young
lad of thirteen, and a young man who had been in
business on his own account. Two days were con-
sumed in checking, marking and arranging the stock.
The first thing he did was to go and effect an insurance upon upon his goods. The next thing was to get
circulars printed, setting forth the place in which he
was to be found, and what he had to offer. On the
third day he took down the shutters, and looked
proudly at his name over the door, in connection with
which might be read: "Staple and fancy dry goods."
He had many friends, for during six years he had filled
a situation in one of the largest establishments in the
city, entering it as a boy to take the cash and carry
parcels, and steadily working his way up until he
occupied the first position in the house.

As soon as he announced to the public that he was
a competitor for a share of their patronage, among
those who gathered early about him to encourage and
help him, were the friends he had formed under Christian associations. They were glad to wish him success in his venture, small and unpretending though it
was. His capital was meagre, but he was not ashamed
of small beginnings. The amount of his stock was
small, but he made the most of it. He had placed
fixtures on one side only of his shop ; and on the
other were shrubs and flowers, tastefully arranged and
displayed in such a way as to give the place a full and
well-stocked appearance. On the 27th of September,

1849, he opened business. The amount of cash which he took on that day was £14 17s. 9d.; on the 28th, £10 17s. 7d.; on the 29th, £9 16s.; on the 30th, £10 4s. 1d. On the 28th he paid Bowes & Hall £14 10s. 2d.; on the 29th, £11 0s. 1½d.; on the 30th, £9 15s. It was refreshing to see how his creditors rubbed their hands, and eagerly inquired whether he did not want anything else. But three days had elapsed, and the firm felt that he was going to succeed. If success could be attained on lines of industry, application and integrity, he was bound to attain it. By the third of December, a little over two months, he had paid this firm £478 2s. 8d., or £6 12s. 10d. more than his original purchase. In that time, also, he had bought from them, in addition to his original purchase, £1,287 7s. Very soon his business began to be talked about, and the houses that had refused to give him credit were anxious to offer him lines of goods. He felt, however, that the house which had assisted him was entitled to the benefit of his account, and resolved that, as far as possible, he would do business with that one firm. He gave his business all his attention; early and late he was there, and from the first day it might fairly be called a prosperous business. When the month of March came, he determined to take stock, and see what had been the result of the season's trade. He did not, after the manner of too many, take it for granted that he was doing well; he was going to test it.

He had been looking forward to the prospect of having his own home, but had determined that until his means would warrant the maintenance of a wife he would remain unmarried. The result of this stock-taking assured him that by prudent management he could maintain the expenses of a home and have an amount of comfort and happiness which was impossible for him to enjoy, situated as he was. He was in his twenty-sixth year, and as soon as possible after his books had been balanced, he was united in marriage to one in every respect worthy the alliance.

He had won the love of an amiable, beautiful and intelligent young lady, the eldest daughter of Alexander Hamilton, Esq. Eliza Hamilton had been brought up in a devout Methodist home; she was of a sweet Christian disposition, and well fitted to be a true help-meet. On May 3rd, 1850, they were happily united as husband and wife. As soon as the marriage ceremony was over, amid the many prayers and blessings of their friends, the bride and groom started out for their new home over the store. There was no honeymoon tour to interfere with business pursuits, and next morning bright and early he was at his place behind the counter.

He felt that he had no right to expend in travel or in furniture the money that belonged to others, and better still, he had no desire to do so. He had no wish to make an appearance other than became his means and his prospects, and in these respects he was seconded by his young wife. There was in the new home no lack of anything absolutely necessary to the wants and the comforts of a young married couple; but there was nothing for the mere purpose of ornament or luxury. One room alone received special attention—his library. In this was a book-case in which were several hundred volumes of books, for he had commenced to purchase books before he was eighteen years old, and before he was twenty-two his library was worth about $300. Mr. James Jennings was his principal clerk, before entering business for himself. He was a Sunday School teacher at the time, and on one occasion he asked permission of Mr. Macdonald to consult one of the Commentaries in his library. "My library is at your service at any time," was the answer, and from that time forward he insisted that on Sundays Mr. Jennings should dine with him, and avail himself of the advantages of his books.

These were happy days. He was full of exuberant hopefulness, and there was the audacity of buoyant young effort.

> "Through long days of labour
> And nights devoid of ease,"

he was toiling on with the purpose of making his mark in the business world. He aspired after a brilliant mercantile career. It is well for the young merchant to aim high

> "Who aims a star,
> Shoots higher far than he who aims a tree."

He possessed boundless resource, had a fine capital of ambition, good sense, energy, a trained mind, and virtuous habits. He was happily united to one who sympathized with him in all his efforts. Cowper has sweetly sung :

> " What is there in the vale of life
> Half so delightful as a wife,
> When friendship, love and peace combine
> To stamp the marriage bond divine ?
> The stream of pure and genuine love
> Derives its current from above ;
> And earth a second Eden shows,
> Where'er the healing water flows."

All day he toiled with effort, strength and will, and at night in the "*douce intimité*," of his young wife, talked over his affairs and cherished prospects, or gave his spare moments to reading, and turned fragments of time to golden account.

Before the commencement of the fall trade, Mr. Macdonald determined to take stock again, though he had been only ten months in business. When he had balanced his books, he arrived at the following results : His sales had amounted to £3,186 14s. 2½d., and after deducting expenses, he transferred to the credit of profit and loss the sum of £300 8s. 6½d. He advertised extensively and judiciously, never exaggerating in the least degree, but using his talent for versification to bring before the public the valuable goods at No. 103. His son, Mr. J. Fraser Macdonald, has shown me a copy of the *North American*, published in Toronto by William McDougall & Company, bearing date of June 9th, 1855, in which is found the following advertisement :

THE LARGE 103 YONGE STREET,

TORONTO,

JOHN MACDONALD,

Respectfully invites attention to his very large stock
of seasonable dry-goods, etc., etc.

The advertisement ends with a poem on Reformation
in Trade, the closing lines of which are :

> " The bonnets, for instance, which a few years ago
> Would cost you a dollar and a quarter or so,
> A much finer style you now can procure
> For less than a quarter of that sum, I am sure.
> Nor did you then think the terms very hard,
> If you bought a good print for a shilling per yard,
> But now you may purchase for half of that price
> A cloth quite as good, and a style just as nice.
>
> Will you call at Macdonald's, if only to try,
> From his well-sorted stock, how cheap you can buy ?
> And we venture to say, when you look through his store,
> You will wonder you never have found it before.
> 'Tis a three-storey house, with the front painted white,
> Which makes its appearance both graceful and light,
> With very large figures that you plainly may see,
> Describing his number as one hundred and three."

His business for the first nine months was something over $12,000 ; for a like period from March 1st,
1851, to January, 1852, it was over $16,000. All
the while his capital was increasing, and he was
now in a position to dictate terms with the firm
from which he bought, who were ready to offer him
inducements to continue his trade with them. He
was also in a position to buy wherever he pleased,
and felt that he could now do so without doing any
injustice to the firm that had first given him a start.

When the business of Taylor & Stevenson was
established, Mr. Macdonald became one of their principal customers. One of the partners, Mr. C. C. Taylor,
was a young man about his own age, of good address,
active and pushing, his intimate friend and companion,

and the firm gave Mr. Macdonald the special privilege of selecting from the invoice-book desirable and cheap lines of goods before their arrival, which were laid aside for his examination and approval. He was not slow to secure those lots which paid him extra profits. The arrangement was mutually advantageous, as Mr. Macdonald became their most valuable customer, bought from them largely, paid them promptly, sold their goods quickly, which yielded him a good profit, and enabled him to add to his capital. After a year or so he began to job, not that he laid himself specially out for that business, but a friend who was about commencing business came to him, thinking that he could depend upon being well and honestly treated. This was no other than William Gooderham, who became a steady customer, and a friendship was ripened which continued unabated to the end of life.

Hitherto the jobbing business which he had done had been either with those who took an interest in him and desired his success, or those who, coming into his shop, were led to make a parcel in some of the lines he had to offer. Now he resolved on taking the road and seeing what impression he could make on small traders in the country. He got his samples carefully prepared, taking with him only lines which he knew would be considered cheap by even the closest buyers, hired a horse and buggy, and on a rainy morning in the month of May, 1852, went forth dreaming of the future. That day he took orders to a considerable amount, and returned, feeling that his journey had been a success. He felt that all he wanted was capital, to enable him to do a jobbing trade as large as any house in the country. He possessed a thorough knowledge of his business, understood the requirements of the country, was energetic, could buy well, and knew that with means he could soon out-distance houses of reputed wealth, that had been long established. For a little a feeling of restlessness and impatience came over him, but it was only for a little ; and then came the determination to work and wait. It was a wise one, and well for him that he had not sufficient capital, until he had acquired the experience to employ it wisely. It was a blessing that he was unable to attempt a large trade, until he had been taught the perils of a small one, and for this he was thankful in after years. Though he never inherited a dollar, yet the means came with the experience. His wealth was gradually acquired, and a wise and overruling Providence continually blessed the labour of his hands.

His success in the jobbing confirmed his purpose. He would be a wholesale merchant, and that ere long. He had made this resolve, and waited anxiously for indications which would warrant him in taking steps in that direction. His shop was enlarged ; the staff had already grown to four ; the shelves on both sides were well filled, and the basement turned to account for reserve goods. Yet the pressure for room continued, and nothing remained but to take part of the upstairs and convert it into a room for stock. Immediately above the stairs were the words, " Wholesale upstairs."

He was now firmly established, was doing well, and always at his business. He employed no book-keeper, but when his store was closed he posted up his books, and made out his accounts. About this time came a pressing request to endorse a note. He quickly made up his mind, and answered, " No." That answer was for his entire business career. Had he yielded to this first request he would have been ruined; he would have done the friend who made it no good, and would have lost his friendship. He took his own decided course—kept his friend ; and, still better, was able to assign to others that he had refused this friend. Here was a breaker which lay early in his course ; he steered skilfully through it, and felt that he had got his craft out into deep water, where there was less danger than near a rocky coast. Nor did he carry money in his pocket. When he wanted money he took it out of his till, and never did this without making an entry of it, and charging it to his own personal account.

Alert, vigorous, ambitious, with natural business talents, an experienced salesman, anxious to secure confidence and customers, he now began to feel the pressure of increased business responsibilities.

But his activity and earnestness were not confined to his dry-goods store. Though not physically strong, yet he was abundant in labours for the spiritual good of those about him. In the Richmond Street Church, of which he was a member, he found ample scope for various forms of Christian labour. He was the super-intendent of the Sabbath School, and a leading official

of the circuit. He was in demand on the neighbour-
ing circuits for sermons and missionary addresses,
and he thus acquired that readiness, fitness and zeal
in Christian work which distinguished his whole
career. His success in business was steady, and with
the increase of means he exhibited a growing spirit
of large and wise liberality.

In the midst of all this activity, a deep shadow fell
upon his heart and home. His beautiful young wife
was sinking into an early grave, and after a brief
married life of four years, consumption seized her as
its prey, and she was thus early "crowned and
blessed." She left behind two children, the first a
perfect little human flower, named Jessie, unfolded
her tender life only just enough to "smell sweet and
blossom in the dust;" the second survived—the
gentle and beloved Amy—who grew up to lovely
womanhood, when she, too, passed on before her
father to the "house of many mansions." These
sharp family sorrows chastened his spirit, but they
were not allowed to interfere with his duties, or his
wonderful activity and zeal.

Mr. Macdonald was a born merchant. He was
ready in resource, and thoroughly enjoyed the stir
and strain of commercial life. His plans were far-
reaching, and they were pushed with resolute self-
reliance, tireless energy, and unwavering faith. He
was ready to seize upon a situation with quick and
comprehensive grasp. He was one of the first to see
the advantage of separating the dry-goods entirely
from other departments of trade, and here his marked

individuality cropped out. Just as in complicated trades, the work is divided into a number of processes, and the division of labour effects a saving of time and material, as well as gives increased dexterity to the workman; so he perceived that with moderate capital, and with a small stock of goods, greater skill and success could be secured in a particular department by having his attention directed exclusively to that work than to have it range through many other departments of trade.

He had achieved success in the retail business, and he saw before him a wider field, where he could carry on the same business on a larger scale in the whole-sale. The story is told of John Jacob Astor, that while yet a stranger in New York, and in the narrowest circumstances, as he passed by a row of houses which had just been erected and were the talk of the town, he said to himself, "I'll build one day a greater house than any of these on this very street." He accomplished the prediction. So John Macdonald saw before him in the wholesale business a broad field of enterprise, and with that far-seeing spirit which anticipates the future, he grasped the assurance of success. Shakespeare says, "We must take the current when it serves, or lose our ventures." The time and tide, without which the best powers and strongest purposes do not avail, soon came to him, and we find him fairly launched upon an extensive trade.

VI.

WHOLESALE MERCHANT.

Labor is the true alchemist which beats out in patient trans-
mutation the baser metals into gold.

> *—W. Morley Punshon, D.D.*

" Business is what it is made to be."

We have not wings, we cannot soar,
   But we have feet to scale and climb,
By slow degrees, by more and more,
   The cloudy summits of our time.

> *—Longfellow.*

Still let thy mind be bent, still plotting where
And when, and how, the business may be done.

> *—Herbert.*

" Not slothful in business, fervent in spirit, serving the Lord."

> *—Paul.*

WHOLESALE MERCHANT.

FROM the moment Mr. Macdonald commenced business for himself, small trader though he was, he had in him the constant presentiment of a wide career. The characteristics which afterwards distinguished him in his widely-extended sphere, at once manifested themselves. He was remarkably energetic, active, and attentive to business. He had tact, promptness, order, hopefulness, straightforwardness and honour. He was genial, courteous, large-hearted and liberal. His integrity won for him respect and confidence; and his business capabilities and success led him to contemplate enlargement. His force of purpose and enthusiasm were amazing, and the results which they brought him were natural and inevitable. He knew there was a high career before him; he felt it in his veins like new wine, and this incited him to larger schemes and to take in a wider horizon. A gracious Providence was marking out a path for him, and soon we find him entering upon an extensive wholesale business. The first difficulty was to get the retail business off his hands. Mr. Marmaduke Pearson, who had been a partner with Thomas Thompson, Sen., in the firm of Thompson & Pearson, was, however, just then proposing to enter business for himself. He was ready to take Mr. Macdonald's business, purchase his stock, and assume his liabilities. Accordingly, in 1853, our subject moved to more capacious premises on Wellington Street, in the centre of the business portion of the city, and nearly opposite the present premises of the firm. He made arrangements with Mr. James Frazer, of Nova Scotia, to go to Great Britain and buy his goods for him for one season, obtaining from him, at the same time, a letter to the well-known Glasgow firm of William Kidston & Sons, who shipped all Mr. Frazer's goods. He was enabled to make an arrangement with this firm which lasted over many years, and which proved highly satisfactory to both parties. Mr. Macdonald was wont to express to his friends the sore disappointment which he felt at his first interview with the senior partner of this great firm. The unpretentious looking little office, a few dying coals in a small grate, and the surroundings generally, seemed to suggest anything but great wealth, with luxurious environments. However, when he learned from mercantile circles the standing of the house and the high estimation with which it was regarded, both on account of the extent of its transactions and the honourable principles upon which they were conducted, especially when he had succeeded in obtaining an open credit of several thousand pounds, matters assumed an entirely different aspect, and that little office shone with a brightness which carbon could not give. The arrangements made with this house enabled him to purchase his goods at first hand and save his discounts; and, although he paid this firm well on to £100,000 in commissions, yet it was money well laid out, since no goods had ever come to Toronto better bought than his. From the start, the other houses found it difficult to compete with Mr. Macdonald, both on account of the quality and the prices of his staples. A strong friendship also sprung up between them. Mr. Macdonald named his eldest son after the great ship owner, merchant and banker, whose acknowledged worth of character, sound judgment, enlightened and judicious views on all commercial matters, steadfast Christian principle and abounding liberality, made him a man after his own heart. Only one ripple of trouble ever occurred during their long business relations together. His goods were all shipped by the sailing vessels of this firm, and in the season of 1855 the ship *Shandon*, which contained the whole of his importations, was lost, and he had no goods for his customers. What was he to do ? Coleridge says :

> " A bitter and perplexed ' What shall I do ? '
> Is worse to man than worse necessity."

The power of quick decision is part of the outfit which makes a man equal to the occasion. He had the faculty of penetrating at once into the heart of things, and saw at a glance what was the proper thing to do. Decision is concentrated force, and it did not take him long to decide. He was put upon his mettle and would try a *ruse de guerre*. In the emergency he hastened to New York, bought a large stock of goods on credit, and then opened them out, writing at the same time to the Glasgow firm to inform them what he had done. The firm was at first indignant at what seemed to them his rash action, and threatened to close the account. However, they soon came to see that Mr. Macdonald had acted in a prompt, high-minded and judicious manner ; that he was equal to the occasion, of ready resource, and master of his fate in the hour of opportunity. The difficulty was speedily adjusted, the corner was safely turned, and the young merchant found himself upon the rising wave. The loss of the goods turned out to Mr. Macdonald's gain, for he had not only the profit from the purchase at New York, but the gain from the insurance paid him on his sunken goods, for then as now marine insurance allowed ten per cent. above the invoiced cost.

The year 1857 was a disastrous one. Trade was very bad. A commercial panic existed throughout the country. Business houses were failing on every hand. Banks were breaking; money was scarce ; confidence gone. Men knew not whom to trust. In this time of mercantile distress, when every house seemed tottering, banks shutting down, no discounts, exchange scarce, Mr. Macdonald had no bills to meet, no paper to be discounted. He simply remitted as the money came in, and the Glasgow establishment bore the brunt. He was thus enabled not only to tide over the awful crisis, but to keep adding to his capital, and brick by brick, round by round, story by story, built up his colossal firm. He lived economically, had few bad debts, had no overstocks, kept everything well assorted and in good condition. His capital was doubling almost yearly, and he was laying the foundations broad and deep of one of the largest businesses on the continent. He was not only an excellent warehouse man, but he managed the finances himself. His forte was in counting-house management. He was able not only to buy at the lowest prices for cash, but he was also able to dictate terms to his customers. He selected only the best, as his goods would readily sell. He sustained few losses, while the honour and reputation of the house were always maintained. He was especially fortunate in Manchester printed goods; this branch of the trade flourished greatly, and the house, like a strong oak, was year by year striking its roots more deeply, and spreading its branches more widely over the land.

In August 14th, 1857, he was permitted to rebuild his home, and was united in marriage to Annie Elizabeth, only daughter of Samuel Alcorn, Esq. His wife was prudent, affable, devoted, judicious and, like himself, had no extravagant views, so that they lived together very happily in a small house on George Street, until the time came for him to erect a permanent suburban home. The business had now assumed immense proportions, and the firm of John Macdonald & Co. was one of the principal trading houses of Canada, enjoying an enviable reputation for stability and business integrity. In the year 1862, he erected the premises which, with enlargements and improvements, are still occupied. The warehouse is built of cut stone, in Venetian-gothic style of architecture, and is one of the most handsome, convenient and commodious business houses in the city. It is a five-story structure,

John Macdonald & Co's Wholesale Warehouse.
Wellington Street View.

elegant and imposing in appearance. When first erected it far surpassed in size and ornate finish every other business establishment in Toronto; and with all the improvements in warehouse architecture, it still holds its place among the chief architectural ornaments of the business section of the commercial metropolis. The building extends from Wellington Street through to Front Street, and is entered from either street, although the principal entrance is on Wellington Street.

The firm of John Macdonald & Co., from the first, went on modestly, steadily, actively, always keeping abreast of the times; year by year increasing its trade, until at the time of the founder's death it ranked, as it still ranks, among the oldest, as well as the largest, in the Dominion. With one or two solitary exceptions, every firm carrying on the wholesale trade when Mr. Macdonald entered the race, has disappeared, while his own seems founded on a rock. How was it that, commencing with so slender capital, such signal success has been achieved? First, there was Mr. Macdonald's own energetic spirit. His temperament was active, persevering, indefatigable; and he infused the same spirit throughout the house. From the outset of his mercantile career, he embarked on a bold and somewhat original course. He was ready to mark out a new path to success. The custom at that time was to sell goods at a certain advance upon the sterling cost. This advance was supposed to cover interest, exchange, duty and profit. Mr. Macdonald took his stand against this custom, and although he

stood almost, if not entirely alone for years, he refused
to sell goods on the sterling, but put on a round advance,
and offered them at a certain, definite price. He believed that the old mode offered room for deception,
and tempted the wholesaler to dishonesty. He believed that it was the more open and honest way to
sell his goods in the currency of the country, and with
no dating ahead. The old system has gone out of
vogue, and all the wholesale houses of any standing
in the country have simply followed Mr. Macdonald's
example.

This house, too, was one of the first to adopt the
system of distinct departments, each department having its own buyer and its own staff of salesmen. Mr.
Macdonald was a thorough organizer, and with keen
foresight he saw that a great impulse would be given
to the whole business by dividing into departments
the more important articles of trade. This would
give the heads of these departments increased responsibility. It would make each staff of assistants more
active and spirited, and promote a healthy rivalry
in the departments. Recognizing the division of
labour, as a means to the best results in almost every
kind of employment, he saw that continued application to a particular department of goods would make
experts in that special line, and that, other things
being equal, experts make success. Along with his
own quickness and shrewdness, his honourable dealings and integrity, he gathered about him associates
of like character. His knowledge of character was
marked, and his employees were young men of stirl-

ing qualities, who seemed to catch his own energy and his generous, frank manner of doing business. He would have nothing of trickery or over-reaching, of lying or fraud of any kind. In his diary of 1873 we find the very basis of his success in what he calls:

"HOW TO ADD TO YOUR BUSINESS LARGELY EVERY MONTH, EVERY WEEK, EVERY DAY."

"Buy well.

Keep your stock well and constantly assorted.

Be attentive and courteous to the humblest customer.

Have a perfect organization of your staff.

Let every man attend to the business for which he is best fitted.

Fulfil every promise you make to customers.

Execute every order with promptness and fidelity.

Study the interest of every customer, as the best means of securing your own.

Be up to the requirements of the age.

Advertise your business.

Do it regularly, truthfully, thoroughly.

Keep no drones about you.

Keep none about you who are not true to your interests.

Earn a reputation for upright dealing by practising it.

Be prompt in the discharge of every engagement.

Maintain over the whole a ceaseless oversight, and conduct the whole with untiring energy.

> Conduct your entire business on the princi-
> ples of God's Word, which contains the
> grandest commercial maxims in exist-
> ence.

> The observance of these simple rules will
> secure continuous prosperity, continued
> confidence, ultimate wealth, and a stain-
> less commercial choracter.

These were the high principles on which he continually acted, and they secured the desired results.

For some time after the custom of employing commercial travellers had become established in Montreal,
and had been generally adopted by the trade, Mr.
Macdonald continued to employ no travellers. Not
that he had any objection to these " ambassadors of
commerce," but he preferred that customers should
come to the warehouse and select for themselves.
For many years he maintained his business with not
a single representative of his house on the road. But
the custom had taken such deep root, and become
so essentially a part of the trading system of the
country, that in the end he gave up his own peculiar-
ity and adopted it. The reasons for his holding out
so long against the custom may be found in the following reminiscence of their first traveller, given by
one of the firm, Mr. Paul Campbell :

" In the year 1867, commercial travelling being
well established in Montreal, and several houses in
Toronto having adopted the system, Mr. Macdonald
was induced to try it. At that time the mileage of
railroad was limited, and it was thought best to send

out a team and equipment, so that the many places removed from railway communication might be visited. An expensive equipment, a fine pair of young lively horses (they proved too lively) and a rig were bought, and an old country traveller of experience was engaged. The traveller engaged was a Mr. J., who, although a man of ability, had one failing more common in the early days of travelling than now, but this fault was unknown to the firm. On a bright morning the traveller, his horses and his samples left the warehouse with the hope of success on the part of the firm, and many promises on the part of the traveller; but promises and excuses were the only resultants of that trip. He would strike a town, and straightway something hurtful would strike him. He was fertile, however, in excuses; they came thickly in, explaining his want of success. He reached Collingwood and put up at a well-known hostelry kept by the genial Charley C——. The patience and forbearance of the firm being exhausted, he was requested to return, and a few days after he entered the warehouse much demoralized, stating that those horses had finally parted company with him about Holland Landing, after nearly killing him. There was in the employ of the firm at that time, as cashier, a gallant young officer of the Queen's Own, who had distinguished himself on the field of Ridgeway, Lieut. F. H. He at once volunteered to go after the horses, but returned two mornings afterwards a wounded soldier again, with an arm in a sling, and otherwise badly battered, also minus the horses. They proved too much for the infantry officer. In the end they were brought home by Mr. Bond, of this city, and for a month or so afterwards there came in little mementoes in the way of bills for damages done to various vehicles and other property, which were quietly settled. The equipment was sold, and the house became famous afterwards for advertising " no travellers employed, no goods sold on the sterling, and no dating ahead."

Mr. Macdonald's first partner was a Mr. Lyle. After the first two or three visits to Great Britain by Mr. Macdonald himself, Mr. Lyle undertook the buying for the house, and bought well and satisfactorily for many years.

One of the gravest emergencies that ever came to any business was when three of his chief clerks— the buyer, the warehouse man, and the book-keeper, went out from him to establish a new firm for themselves. The action came as a complete surprise to Mr. Macdonald. The new firm would compete for his best customers, and though it had not the capital of the old house, yet the partners were accomplished salesmen and tireless workers, with all the buoyancy and ambition of youth. But the old master, with his boundless resource, marvellous business powers, and with the immense energy, promptness, courage and decision that had always characterised him, rose superior to the emergency and, surmounting the difficulty, gained the flood-tide, and still distanced all competitors. The trade went on increasing as if there had not been a jar ; but this circumstance led him to adopt the department system, although for a few years the entire management fell largely upon himself.

Mr. Macdonald always entertained a very high conception of the dignity and responsibility of a merchant, and ever sought to impress upon young men the necessity of cultivating in all business relations a character for honesty and integrity, as well as of making the best and noblest use of their opportunities. His business in the mercantile world gave weight to his utterances, and in an address to the students of the British American Commercial College, on the "Elements Necessary to the Formation of Business Character," he says :

"There are certain conditions which are essential to success in business. These, in addition to a sound mind in a sound body, may be summed up in three words—time, place, circumstance. No one, for example, would think of locating himself in a desert for the purpose of carrying on business. He must be where there is a population—a population which needs what he has to sell—a population which can pay for what it buys.

"It is a common saying that the percentage of successful business men is not more than five per cent. Others with, I think, greater accuracy, claim that it is not higher than $2\frac{1}{2}$ per cent. It may be somewhat startling to affirm that it is possible to reverse these figures, so that with the most favourable conditions, and the untiring application of sound business principles, the percentage of failure might not exceed $2\frac{1}{2}$ per cent., while the percentage of success would necessarily be $97\frac{1}{2}$ per cent. But you will readily take in all that this implies ; without my going elaborately into details, it implies, for example, that the supply ought in no case to exceed the demand ; it implies in each the maximum amount of ability exerted under the most favourable conditions.

"I am going to refer now to elements that are absolutely necessary to the formation of a business character, as forming the foundation upon which it must rest, and which, if lacking, will imperil the safety of the whole.

"I am going to look into the remote past and see if I can find any axioms whose force has been acknowledged and acted upon by the wise and thoughtful ; and whether these axioms maintain the place in our day which they did in the past, and whether they are likely to remain unchanged in the future. The elements to which I would refer are two. The first *Truth*, the second *Honesty*. And the axioms which I find as having reference to these are :

" First, '*Buy the truth, and sell it not* ' ; and

" Second, ' *A false balance is abomination to the Lord.*'

" What is meant by a false balance ? Not the beam merely which is always so adjusted as to place the customer at a disadvantage, but the selling a thing for what it is not ; taking advantage of the inexperience of the customer to secure one's own profit. All this has been declared to be abomination to the Lord.

" That was as it used to be. How is it to-day ? It is the same to day. Truth and honesty are the essential qualities in a bond between individuals, in a treaty between nations ; truth and honesty afford the only real security in the multiplied and ramified transactions of trade ; truth and honesty are bulwarks which protect the nation—more powerful far are they than those behind which are placed bristling cannon and armed men. In one word, they are the pillars upon which the whole fabric of society rests, and are as unalterable and imperishable as is the nature of Him from whom they come. Buy the truth, then, and sell it not.

" I come now to consider the matter of thoroughness. What do I find in ancient records to throw light upon this aspect of the case. This I find :

"' *A workman that needeth not to be ashamed.*'

"Few men master all the details of their calling. Have we not illustrations of this every day? Why did that lawyer lose that case? Want of application and thorough mastery of it. Why did that physician lose that patient? He was weak in some essential element. The sense of this weakness paralyzed his action, and the patient slipped through his fingers. Why did that merchant fail? Because he had never made himself familiar with the minute details of his business. Obtain a thorough mastery of the details of your business.

"I have touched upon truth, honesty and thoroughness. I now come to touch upon energy.

"' *Whatsoever thy hand findeth to do, do it with thy might.*'

"Whatsoever is true, whatsoever is honest, do; but do it with your might. Throw your being into it; be in earnest. Whatsoever is worth doing, is worth doing well; do nothing by halves.

If you think that business success is to be achieved by half-heartedness, or by an energy which is put forward by fits and starts, you make a very great mistake. There is in business, as in everything else, no royal road to success. It is work, work—hard work. It is at it, and always at it. The business world has no room for idlers. There is in it, as there is in all other callings and professions, plenty of room at the top.

"Look at fifty labourers working on some great work, and a keen-sighted man in five minutes will pick out the man who is going to occupy the position of foreman, and that perhaps before the sun goes down. Go into a warehouse or into an office, and you will not be long there before you will pick out the man, or the men, who are of service to that office or warehouse; who are going to make their work felt;

8

who are going to rise. What of the others ? You will never hear of them, nor will anyone else ! Good qualities many of them may have had ; but good qualities unused are like the talent tied up in a napkin—not only bringing in nothing to the owner, but, through the want of energy of him to whom it was entrusted, depriving the owner of his lawful interest.

"I look back again to that period from which we gather the axioms upon which we have been basing our remarks, and I ask whether anything is recorded characterizing results which follow the faithful working out of these principles? and I find this : '*The hand of the diligent shall bear rule.*' I also find this : '*The thoughts of the diligent tend only to plenteousness ; but of every one that is hasty only to want.*

"And is this not so to-day ? Who are the men in our cities who are the leaders of men? They are the diligent.

"See those works rising up resembling a village in their extent, with the hundreds of workmen to whom they give employment ; look for the master-mind under whom the whole has grown up, and you will find in him a diligent man.

"A word or two, then, as to what is essential after you leave this college ; and,

"*First*—Be willing to begin at the bottom ; do not think that when you have left this you know everything. If you have learned the secret of obtaining knowledge in your business, and the spirit which will make you an anxious and a willing learner, you have learnt that which will prove of inestimable value to you.

"*Second*—Be patient. Impatience is the curse of thousands. Remember that Rome was not built in a day ; that you do not find upon the tree at the same time the fragrant blossom and the ripened fruit ; that success is a thing of slow growth.

"On my own grounds there are oaks which twenty-five years ago looked as though they had been there a century or more. Every year they continue to add to their bulk and beauty, by the richness of their foliage and the gratefulness of their shade. Every year they give back to the soil, in their burdened foliage and abundance of acorns, more than they take away, thus adding fruitfulness to their many other qualities. Side by side with them are lofty poplars, planted by my own hand twenty-five years ago. For a dozen years they made annually as much growth as the oak would make in ten years. Then their height was equal to that which the oak had reached in a century. And what then? This, simply, that then they began to decay! The leafless branches presenting no beauty for the eye; the tree itself of no advantage to the soil—nay, a positive disadvantage, extracting, by its greedy and hasty nature, from its virtue, impoverishing and giving nothing back. Be an oak, not a poplar.

"Be patient. Do not begin to think, after you have been in a concern for six months, that you can run the establishment.

"Do not be afraid that the ability you possess will not be recognized. If it is there it will shine out; it will make its effect; it will meet with its acknowledgment; it will produce its results and it will meet with its reward.

"Be patient. You cannot all go into business; you cannot all be merchants. But you can all rise to positions of trust and responsibility. The man who occupies a confidential position in any house, occupies a proud position, one preferred by many because it is in many respects freed from responsibilities which attach themselves to large business obligations. Aim at such positions; for these your training in this college should eminently qualify you.

"But one says, You have omitted speaking of the Bible as a business hand-book.   I have, and the omission has been intentional.

"If you want to pass unscathed through the dangers which beset the path of the young man; if you want to go about your duty free from the allurements of the destroyer; if you want to bring into your daily life a temperament that will enable you to enjoy with continual zest all the blessings of life; if you want to take the highest place in your profession and to make it not only a means of employment, but a means of enjoyment; if you want to secure and retain the confidence and esteem of your fellows; if you want to make the very best of health and wealth and life; if you want to know all that is implied in an honoured and in a happy old age; if, in one word, you want to make the best, and the very best of both worlds, read your Bible.   Not read it only, make it the man of your counsel.   Then, come what will—if the experience of the ages is of any value; if the testimony of the best men living, as well as the testimony of the great and good that have passed away, be of any value, nothing can hinder you from being prosperous, contented and happy."   ·

No place here for the idea that the successful merchant must be dishonest.

> "I grant my bargains well were made,
>   But all men overreach in trade;
>   'Tis self-defence in each profession;
>   Sure self-defence is no transgression."

Mr. S. William Beck, editor of the *Warehouseman and Drapers' Trade Journal*, in a review of this address, says, "If there were any truth in the stupid conclusion that business success implied business guile, the wealth and position won by Mr. Macdonald would have been nothing to be proud of. But the widespread regret expressed upon his death, and the open testimony to his sympathies and his systematic benevolence showed that he was known to be one of ' God Almighty's gentlemen.' His public gifts were splendid, and the part he took in educational and social improvement an active and prominent one. And what of his principles? Well he believed in the usual commercial virtues—foresight, prudence, energy, truth, honesty, application, thoroughness and patience. But with Mr. Macdonald, and with many more besides, business was more than a means of existence, or the road to competence, and honesty more than a policy. The Bible was his business text-book, and from it he took his commercial maxims."

As an employer, Mr. Macdonald took a deep and abiding interest in the young men of his warehouse. He trusted them, put responsibility upon them, and sought in every way to promote their best interests. This interest was heartily reciprocated, and as the result he gathered about him those to whom the reputation of the firm and its success were objects of just pride and keen solicitude.

In 1876, before leaving for Ottawa to attend to his parliamentary duties there, he published a little *brochure*, which he placed in the hands of each of his employees. It is addressed

TO THE YOUNG MEN

OF

THE WAREHOUSE.

———

TO THOSE FIRST,
WHO, CONNECTED WITH IT IN ITS
INFANCY, HAVE BEEN WITNESSES OF ITS GROWTH, A
GROWTH TO WHICH THEIR OWN FIDELITY
HAS MATERIALLY CONTRIBUTED ;

TO THOSE
WHOSE CONNECTION WITH IT,
THOUGH NOT SO REMOTE, HAVE NEITHER BEEN
LESS FAITHFUL OR LESS ANXIOUS
FOR ITS PROSPERITY ;

TO THE
JUNIORS WHO HAVE YET THEIR BUSINESS TO LEARN
AND THEIR MARK TO MAKE ;

THIS LITTLE BOOK
IS RESPECTFULLY DEDICATED BY THEIR EMPLOYER
AND FRIEND,

JOHN MACDOLALD.

OAKLANDS,
February 4th, 1876.

In the Preface, he observes:

"In every large concern, as well as in smaller ones, *confidence* between 'master and men' is absolutely necessary; without it the fabric is unsafe, and its weakness and insecurity may be rendered apparent at any moment.

"Not only is this essential between 'master and men,' but the entire staff must have confidence the one in the other. Upon the completeness and efficiency of the parts, depend the harmony and successful working of the whole.

"Negligence in any one department must to some extent result in injury to the others, as the mistakes of one young man will compromise, in some measure, the reputation of the whole.

"The ambition of every young man should be not only to maintain the good reputation of his house, but to add to it, if possible.

"To impress you with the need of earnest and increased effort in the discharge of your duty; to show you that the interests of the house are to be promoted only by the united and harmonious efforts of all its workers; that the young man of principle must always feel that the absence of his employer is but a motive for greater diligence, I have placed these hurried thoughts together for perusal at your leisure—and, may I not hope, for your profit.

"But I have another object. I am fully convinced that if these thoughts, simple as they be, form the groundwork of your action in the house, they will, especially with the juniors, have the effect of forming character and laying the foundation for success in after life."

He proceeds:

"A business to be successful must be founded upon principles which possess guarantees for development and permanence. These, I need hardly say, involve not only fairness to employees, but interest in them, manifesting itself in desires to improve their position ; high-toned and honourable dealing with customers, taking no advantage where there happens to be an imperfect knowledge of goods, or in any of the many features connected with business transactions ; consulting their interests as much when filling their orders as if they were personally present.

" A business so conducted ought not to suffer by the occasional absence of its head. Were such the case, it would be an evidence either that the watchful eye of their employer was needed to lead young men to do their duty, or an absolute lack of system—or, indeed, of the utter absence of business principle.

" I do not think that I claim too much for our own business in stating that unhealthy inducements have never been employed as a means of its development, and that while all are impressed with the need of untiring earnestness, all are equally aware that the atmosphere of the house is such as secures for the customer the utmost fairness, and, consequently, for the house, a reliable business reputation.

" But some will say such a system can only be carried out by employees of high moral character, whose work is performed from a sense of duty, and who recognize as much their obligations to do rightly by the customers of the house as by their employers.

.   " It is, I think, well known that the young men of this house are of this class ; and I am anxious that they should ever stand in the front rank of the young men of this Dominion, in all matters pertaining to efficiency and fidelity in the warehouse, and to all that pertains to high character out of it.

" Such being the case, there can be no reason why the business should not go on as smoothly and efficiently in my absence as if I were present ; why it should not be marked by the same steady increase, why every customer should not receive the same attention, nor should any cause arise from which any one would have reason of complaint, and, in consequence, the business of the house, or any department of it, suffer in any measure however slight.

"Indeed, I am persuaded that to a young man of high principle the presence or absence of his employer in no measure affects his fidelity; and, did young men but realize this more fully, there would be fewer mistakes in the world; for this principle of fidelity in the discharge of duty lies at the very foundation of all success in life.

"The first point to which I desire to call your attention is that of *courtesy to customers;* upon this I cannot lay too much stress.

"In our house there must be no failure in this point; no one, however small his purchase, must be treated with neglect. In serving your customer spare no pains in completing his list as fully as possible.

"Be at your post in good time. You are aware how much I dislike what is called "night-work," and think that very much of it might be avoided by systematically arranging matters during the day. Our own house has done much to diminish the evils of this system, and I hope to see a yet greater improvement.

"Avoid all extravagant expressions in selling. If the value is good, your customer will not have difficulty in discovering it; prudent men dislike boastful. utterances, as well as the undue advocacy of one's wares.

"In no instance, seek to force upon any customer more than he should prudently buy. If he finds the goods sell, he will repeat; if he finds he has purchased more than he should have done (even if the value is good), he will blame you, and his remembrances will not be pleasant either of you or of the house.

" Cultivate a cheerful disposition ; not only will you feel better yourself, but you will make every one about you all the happier.

" Be energetic ; time is of too much value to be wasted ; the earnest, diligent young man will always find something to do ; if not engaged in selling, in arranging his stock and carrying out improvements in his department.

" I expect heads of departments steadily to aim at making their departments models of their kind, keeping them always well assorted, and free from bad stock ; in short, I should like the departments of the house, for completeness and convenience, to be unsurpassed in the trade.

" I expect heads of departments to be thoughtful and considerate to every one in their room, kindly encouraging the juniors and bringing out of them their best points.

" When the head of a department discovers in a young man anything which should be corrected, let him speak to the young man alone, and never before a customer.

" Juniors are expected to do whatever they are told, cheerfully and readily : no one can ever hope to rise in his business, who is unwilling to begin at the foundation—who, in short, is above his business—who is not prepared for the fag, that advancement may come in due time.

" I desire to see a continuance of that good feeling among all the young men which has so long prevailed in the house, the evidences of which, to me, have been so very pleasing.

" A large warehouse, a large stock, a large capital and an established reputation are all good in their way, but they are not everything ; each is an element of power, and when combined with good management, are agencies by which wondrous results may be accomplished. Yet, great as these advantages are, they may be weakened, nay, frittered away, by what, to many, may appear little more than trifles.

" It will require nothing more than the neglect of the points which I have presented to you as so essential, to impair the facilities of a house, however strong ; to destroy the trade of a house, however well and long established. That being the case, no young man can neglect the interests of his employer without doing him a serious injury. He should realize that if he is not helping to develop his trade by his earnestness and fidelity, he is assuredly impairing it, by his indifference and unfaithfulness.

" I submit these thoughts to you, not that I have any fear that you will be lax in your duty, but with every confidence that the young men of the house will be as faithful and earnest in my absence as if I were present ; that no part of this large business will be neglected ; that every man will be at his post ; that every customer will be faithfully served, and every order carefully filled ; and that it will not require weekly sheets of the comparative sales of 1875 and 1876 to assure me that each department is making all the advancement that it would be prudent or desirable to secure.

" Without a consciousness of your fidelity, I should have hesitated ere I assumed the responsibility of representing in Parliament the commercial division of this great city, with the demands which such a position necessarily makes upon my time, thought and strength.

" Should I be spared to discharge the duties during the period for which I have been elected, I trust that the pleasant relations which now exist between us will have strengthened with time ; that additions will have been made to the staff of the house ; and that the results of your own devotion to its interests will be seen, not only in the maintenance of its reputation, but in the healthful enlargement of all its departments."

> " ' Onward, onward may we press
>   Through the path of *duty ;*
>   Virtue is true happiness,
>   Excellence, true beauty ;
>   Minds are of celestial birth ;
>   Make we then a heaven of earth.
>
> ' Closer, closer let us knit
>   Hearts and hands together ;
>   Where our fireside comforts sit
>   In the wildest weather ;
>   O, they wander wide who roam
>   For the joys of life from home ? ' "

We have only given here the leading thoughts of this singularly happy and practical address. No employer could thus address his young men, who did not enjoy their unfailing confidence, or who had not manifested a deep concern in their welfare. In his diaries are frequent references to one and another of his clerks whom he had called into his office to reprove for certain evil habits, and obtain from them promises of amendment.

Emerson has said, "Trust men, and they will be true to you ; treat them greatly, and they will show themselves great." Mr. Macdonald acted upon this principle. He sought to make the interests of the young men of the warehouse identical with his own. But he would not tolerate indifferent work or half-hearted service ; he would not have around him incompetent men. He was a thorough disciplinarian.

He knew the stern conditions under which success was possible, and he compelled others as well as himself to conform to them.

He was deeply interested in the life of George Moore, the London merchant and philanthropist, and gave a copy of it to each of the young men of the warehouse staff. He always sought to recognize worth and special service done to the firm.

In the year 1878, the trade of the house having grown so much as to necessitate increased accommodation, Mr. Macdonald determined to carry the warehouse through from Wellington Street to Front Street, as he owned the land from street to street. The building being wide, the joists did not, as usual, span the building and rest on the walls, but rested on two rows of iron pillars running parallel to the walls of the building. The iron pillars were cylindrical and hollow, being about half an inch in thickness, while about a foot and a-half from the top of each pillar on which the beams rested for supporting the floor, was a flange which expanded gradually outwards and upwards until it was on a level with the pillar, there being a double surface on which the beam rested. Unfortunately in the pillars for the basement, where the greatest strength was required, the pillars ended at the flange instead of being carried through. This fault, through a concatenation of oversights, was not perceived by the manufacturer or architect, or by the foreman who put them up. There was sufficient strength in these very defective pillars to carry the weight of the floors, but when the goods from the adjacent warehouse were being brought in, the additional weight proved too much for their strength, and they broke simultaneously, like the report of a cannon. They snapped off where the flange joined the pillars, but by a fortuitous circumstance, the large pipes conveying the steam for heating the warehouse ran parallel and alongside of the beam, which rested on the pillars, and this prevented any one of the broken and jagged pillars from falling to the ground. The beam and all the floors fell about a foot and a-half, the beam resting on the broken pillars. Had any one of the pillars fallen to the ground, the floors would have fallen, and the loss of life would have been great, as there were, with painters and employees of the firm, about one hundred in the building at the time. Their exit was rapid. Mr. Macdonald was not in the warehouse at the time. He was much concerned, but pleased and thankful to God that no loss of life had occurred. The iron pillars became so discredited with him, that he ordered them all to be taken out of the entire warehouse and replaced by solid wooden ones. The cost of raising the floors and replacing the pillars amounted to over twelve thousand dollars.

This accident occasioned a great deal of extra labour, and many of the clerks worked night after night for months. To these he gave large additional remuneration for their untiring service. On the Christmas of 1880, the following address was presented by the employees to Mr. Macdonald in beautifully illuminated text.

We, the undersigned, the majority of whom have been for many years in your employment, desire to express to you our grateful sense of the unvarying kindness, liberality and consideration experienced by us at your hands, from our first entry into your establishment to the present time.

When it was decided to organize within the warehouse a Mutual Benefit Society, the movement met with your kind and cordial approval, and most substantial pecuniary support, giving us thereby fresh proof of the deep interest our employer takes in all that concerns the permanent well-being and happiness of his employees.

Nor can we omit to mention here the handsome donation distributed among those who shared in the labour of moving the goods, on the occasion of the accident during the erection of the new building, an accident which, by the merciful Providence of God, was not attended with loss of life or bodily injury of any of us.

In conclusion, let us add that our earnest hope and prayer is, that you may be long spared to see the return of many happy Christmas seasons, and to control and direct in the new warehouse that business which has grown under your wise, liberal and kindly government, to be second to none in the Dominion of Canada.

Mr. Macdonald's system of promotion was from step to step, beginning at the lowest round of the ladder. Mr. Paul Campbell, now one of the partners, was only a lad at the time he entered the warehouse. When the game of lacrosse was first introduced in Toronto, he was one of the principal promoters, and belonged to the first team organized. One morning after a game, he came down to the warehouse, with face badly bruised and otherwise in physical dilapidation. Mr. Macdonald surveyed his battered appearance and said : " Well, Paul, which shall it be, lacrosse or business ? " The young fellow thought a moment, and promptly answered : " Business, sir." The results of his quick decision, in thenceforth giving his sole attention to the establishment are well known. Mr. Macdonald was not in the habit of paying large wages to his hands. He believed in fair compensation and promotion. He had studied somewhat deeply the labour question, and did not believe in profit sharing for merchants. In manufacturing establishments he considered that a share in the profits over and above wage receipts might serve as an additional motive both to capital and labour. But for the sale of manufactured goods the same motive could only operate on a small number of employees, whose mental force and practical experience, combined with strict honour and integrity, would make them competent to manage departments. As a fact, then, he did apply the profit-sharing principle, when he divided his great establishment into departments, and gave ampler compensation and a prospect of partnership to men of experience and intellectual grasp who had risen step by step in the house, and had shown themselves competent to manage these departments. Thus he was in sympathy with the social aspirations of the new era.

The last address to his young men was made a few months before his death, June 22nd, 1889, on leaving for Alaska.   It will be read with deep interest :

" As I am likely to be absent for a few weeks, I have thought that I might address a few words to you before leaving, which might have the effect of proving of service to the business, but chiefly be of lasting benefit to yourselves.

" It will be in the month of October, forty years since the business with which you are associated was founded.   In the month of May, 1890, or in about eleven months, should I be spared to see that period, it will be fifty years since I left my father's house to begin my business life with fewer advantages and opportunities than those possessed by the most of you whom I now address.   As that, therefore, will be my jubilee, I ought, in that long period, to have gathered some knowledge which should be of service to my fellows, specially to those whom circumstances have brought into connection with the house.

" My aim has been to make the concern as perfect in its manner of conducting business, and as advanced as a business house as it is possible.

" To study the interests of those who do business in the house, as well as the comfort, happiness and future of all those connected with it.

" That the house may have failed in securing these ends always is only what may be expected of everything that is human.

" That such, however, has been, and now is, its aim, is equally certain.

" The house, as it is constituted to-day, may fairly be likened to a regiment of the British army.   It has its recruits, its non-commissioned officers, its commissioned officers of various grades, and the discipline

9

that is essential to the prosperity of the one is equally essential to the prosperity of the other.

Let me note these in order. 1st. There are the buyers, the heads of departments. I may, perhaps, unduly exaggerate the importance of such a position, but I state frankly that such a position in this house is a prize of which any man ought to be proud—is such a position as every boy entering the house ought to look forward to as a position which he intended to reach.

The value of such a position to the man himself or to the house depends, however, upon many factors which, if wanting in his character, go very far to diminish from his value to the house, and to impair his own success, and consequently his income.

The factors which I deem so essential in a buyer are good judgment in buying, intense earnestness in selling, personal magnetism in attracting customers, the faculty of introducing goods, and above all, the rendering of a service from the standpoint of conscience rather than as an equivalent for the remuneration he receives. He should serve more customers (and when not absent purchasing), sell more goods than any one in his room. He should have perfect control over his men, and firmness enough to have all his instructions to his staff faithfully carried out. He should himself be a pattern in everything which he enjoins, so that he has the respect of those under him, and if he cannot secure this, then it is manifestly evident he is unfit for his place.

" Manners have so much to do with a man's success in such a position, that, if lacking, it is difficult to say what would compensate for the loss. These remarks, in very many respects, are equally applicable to every traveller. We come next to the Seconds in the departments. Here again, I claim, a position of which any young man might be proud.

" All the qualities which I have spoken of as being essential to the buyer, are equally needed in the second, who has to take the place of the buyer when absent in the markets. He is the next in authority in the room ; and unless there were some strong reasons which would render promotion undesirable, would naturally take the position of buyer, should such a position from any cause become vacant. And so we go step by step until we reach the boy who enters the house as a junior at a salary at the rate of fifty dollars per annum.

" Following out the same figure, that of a regiment, in referring to the goods in the warehouse, so in like manner the discipline which is essential in the army is needed in the warehouse. What would the commanding officer think of a soldier who came on the ground five minutes or one minute after the regiment had fallen in ? Only this, simply that he would be confined. What would be thought of a soldier who would take out his watch when on duty to see when the parade would be over ? Why, he would expose himself to discipline. It should be so in the warehouse. Intense devotion, unselfish service, faithfully rendered, should characterize every member of the staff, from the very humblest to the very highest.

" I want to notice a few points which are essential to your success ; and

" 1st. It is essential that in following any business there must be a strong liking for it. If, for example, there should be in the case of any of you a feeling of indifference as to whether you follow the dry goods business or ranching, or some branch of mechanical industry, be assured, in such a case, that you will fail utterly in making your mark in the dry goods trade, and you would make but a poor rancher or a poor mechanic.

" If you want to be a dry goods man you must throw your being into it, otherwise you will never be anything but a poor hand, will never command anything in the shape of a prize, and will never secure a situation where your place could not be filled, perhaps better filled, in any five minutes of any day.

"2nd. But the great factor in your success, or, indeed, in the success of any man, is to be found in *the fidelity with which you render your service.*

" What does the faithful man care whether the eye of his employer is on him or not! What is there which gives him so much pleasure as the success of the business with which he is connected ? Nothing, indeed, is there which brings such unbounded pleasure to a thoroughly faithful man.

" This principle makes him punctual, affable, attentive, obliging, economical of the time of the house even to minutes, acquisitive; everything about his work is watched. He would not waste a piece of string. He would carefully look after every piece of paper. He would watch the progress which he makes every day, and would only feel satisfied in knowing that every day there

> " ' Had been something attempted,
> Something won.'

" Let me say, however, that fidelity, excellent and indispensable as it is, is not the only qualification needed for reaching the highest results; there must, in addition, be ability and enthusiasm.

" The man at the look-out, for example, may be most faithful—and in what position is fidelity more needed ? —but he might be utterly wanting in the qualities which would ever fit him to command the ship. While, therefore, I deem fidelity as the most desirable of all the qualities for the right discharge of every duty, I would have you not only to be faithful on the look-out, but to strive after those qualities which would fit you to command the ship ; to command the ship not in fine weather only, but in a gale. Have ambition, and follow its lead upon sound and safe principles and you will not be likely to go astray.

"You will perhaps say, "You have drawn a very highly coloured picture." Highly coloured or not, believe me it is true. And, if unhappily you should fail to become successful, which I hope may not be the case, then examine carefully into the cause and I guarantee you will be compelled to confess that it is to be found in the neglect of the very principles which I have pointed out to you as so necessary.

"You will observe that I have said nothing about profanity, intemperance, disregard of the house of God, the breaking of the Sabbath day, the visiting of places of sinful resort, or the keeping of such company as can have no other than hurtful results. I am assuming that all these are wanting in the case of each. If existing, I should have but little hope of the securement of happiness, either in this world or in the next.

"You will perhaps be astonished when I tell you that if my somewhat lengthened experience has enabled me to form any estimate of the proportion of men who so act, that it is not more than one per cent., not more than one in every hundred who is guided by the high motive to which I have referred.

"Nor does this apply to young men in dry goods houses alone. It applies to every trade, to every profession, to every calling, and in this must be found the true secret of the small number who achieve success.

"In a house like this, where the aim is to have only young men of high character, the proportion should of course be considerably higher, but even here I need not say to you that among the workers in this house there is much that is done in no other than in a mechanical spirit, and without that high and noble and lofty inspiration which sooner or later rewards its possessor:

But you will perhaps enquire, Why this address at

this time?   I would say, 1st, chiefly for your own good ; 2nd, for the benefit of the house, in order that its prosperity may be furthered and its efficiency secured.   The house has entered upon a new era.   In four months it will enter upon the forty-first year of its business existence, and the determination is that it must not only be manned by earnest, competent and faithful men, but by that class of men only, that the value of every man will be determined, and every effort made suitably to acknowledge his worth, that incompetent men will discover that unless incompetence give place to diligence and efficiency, their position is jeopardized, and that a place on the staff means that its holder is a real acquisition to the house.

"'But I cannot wait for these prizes,' one may say; 'this advice is all very good for an essay, but promotion is too slow, I cannot wait.'   Of that, every man must be the best judge.   Hence, I have always felt that any man should feel at liberty to change his relationship at any moment, and that the house should have the privilege of dispensing with the service of any of the staff if it sees fit.   This, I think, is the best and safest bond between the house and its employees ; and this, I think, is the surest way to secure satisfactory and unbroken business relationship.

"I am most anxious that the relationship existing between the firm and yourselves should be something more than that which might be defined as a dollar and cent relationship, and I think the best and surest way to secure this higher and more desirable connection, is in each acting from the highest and noblest standpoint towards each other, and for each other's good.   I should like the relations existing between us to be of that high and enviable character that if these became severed, the interest in each other's welfare should not be impaired, so that ought that would secure the advancement of the one would always be regarded with satisfaction by the other. This, I desire to assure you, is my own earnest wish. I have to ask you, if any need should unhappily be found to deal with cases which might involve the severance of our relationship, do not conclude that what is said upon this subject is not earnestly felt, or that such action would contradict this statement.

"So many matters demand my own time and attention and thought, that I do not come as much in contact with you personally as I would desire, and consequently many of the recent additions to the staff are not known to me, but do not conclude from this circumstance that your efforts to promote the interests of the house will fail to reach me. They will all be brought under my knowledge, as will, indeed, any business indifference or inefficiency. My knowledge, therefore, of the part you are playing in the warehouse is greater than you suppose, and nothing will give me greater pleasure than to hear of your continued progress and advancement. And nothing will cause me more regret than to learn that any of you in your departments are failing to give satisfaction.

"To get a right idea of the value of time, of the results of combined effort, and what diligence will accomplish, watch what is going on at an ant-hill, as I myself have done for hours; watch them in the early grey morning, watch them until your eyes will no longer help you, when the sun has withdrawn its light, and you will see such devotion to work, such precision, such order, such method, as can be witnessed in no department of human labour, but which cannot be witnessed without deriving many valuable and important lessons. No wonder is it that the wise man should have said, as an antidote to sloth, 'Go to the ant, thou sluggard; consider her ways and be wise; which, having no guide, overseer or ruler, provideth her meat in the summer, and gathereth her food in the harvest.' (Prov. vi. 6-8).

"How many men are there whose whole destiny is changed by impatience! 'I am not getting on fast enough; I will leave, I can do a great deal better.' In taking such a step, and in reaching such a conclusion, every man must, of course, be his own judge; but let me add that there is scope enough in this house for the very ablest man on its staff—scope enough for the employment of all his energies, opportunities enough of showing what he can do; and I hope there is fairness enough and readiness enough in the house suitably to recognize all such devotion.

"My own sons are part of the staff with yourselves. They entered upon the same conditions, performed the same work, took their positions in the very humblest work of the house, were subject to their seniors, and I would feel compromised and humiliated had they, in such positions, developed any other spirit than that of respect for those placed over them, fidelity in the discharge of their duties, and devotion to the interests of the house. What can I say more which will prove of service to you, keeping in view the principle I have called your attention to? Let me emphasize two or three thoughts:

"1st. Be ambitious. Make up your mind to rise in the house. How high, do you ask? Well, as high as it is possible for you to get. This purpose, rightly formed and properly prosecuted, rarely fails to secure results.

"2nd. Be enthusiastic. I intend this, first, to apply to every head of a department. Do not, I ask of you, be satisfied with anything short of making your department the most complete, the most successful department of its kind in the Dominion of Canada. Avoid any mistakes which have hitherto brought about disaster, which have failed to produce results.

Be diligent yourself, and have no one about you who is not diligent also.

"3rd. Be magnetic. The success of hundreds of men might be traced to their manners. Attract men to you by your earnestness, diligence, attention and truthfulness. Do not deal in extravagant language; your customer will always discount it. Do not think anything a trouble. If your customer fails to find what he wants in your department, take him to another, and, if possible, see that he gets it there. No customer should leave the house without getting what he wants, if it is in stock, and if not, without procuring it for him if he so desires. These remarks apply with equal force to seconds, and every man and boy in the department, office and entering room.

"Of the greater number of you, I may say I know nothing of the manner in which you spend your time after business hours. Let me say how painfully I should feel if any of you were heard using profane language, any of you seen coming out of saloons, any of you spoken of as frequenters of improper houses, and so spoken of as young men of the staff of John Macdonald & Co. I should want to hide my head; I should feel that the house had been dishonoured, and that unless there were a change of habits there would have to be a change of relationship.

"The path of success does not lay in the path of the destroyer or near it. Can I do better than call your attention to the words of the wise man:

"'Enter not into the path of the wicked, and go not in the path of evil men. Avoid it; pass not by it; turn from it, and pass away.'

"If my own experience would in any way prove helpful to you, I would say in a word or two what were some of the points which, as a young man in a situation, I laid myself out to avoid, and what were some of the principles which I determined to follow:

"1st. I resolved never to live above my means, never to go into debt, never to overdraw my account; and in laying myself out to pursue this line of conduct I had no difficulty in carrying it out.

"But you will say, Oh, you found it very easy because you had, in all probability, a large salary. Well, the largest salary I ever had was $440, and this at a time when the absolute charge of the concern in which I was, was placed in my hands.

"I have said I found no difficulty in carrying out my purpose, and a moment's reflection will show you how this was accomplished, when I state to you the character of my expenditure.

"Theatres, operas, saloons, cigars, cabs, horse hire, cost me not one cent. I never in my life saw the inside of an opera house; I never in my life spent one cent in a saloon.

"Rings and breast pins and silver-headed canes cost me nothing; nor did I think them essential or necessary either for my appearance or my position. The simple matter that my coat was old never led me to buy another until I could pay for it; and the same remark applied to anything or everything that I desired to possess.

"I had to dress respectably, and think that I always did, but all the expensive trappings which go to make up the outfit of a dude made no inroad upon my modest income. So, also, all expenditure of which it may safely be said, in the words of the old adage, 'A fool and his money soon parts,' I carefully avoided.

"But you will say, Is it not drawing it very fine to speak about a man's ties, and tight kids, and canes, even if they have a silver head? Surely there cannot be anything wrong in these; they cannot affect my services as a salesman or interfere with my devotion or efficiency in the house? Possibly not, but they may interfere with your pocket and your peace of mind ; let me ask you to take a careful account of every unnecessary thing of this kind which you needlessly buy, add it up at the end of the year, and you will be astonished. Had you been able to exercise self-control, and absolutely not to buy anything which you did not want, you would have had the money which has been thrown away to gratify vanity. But you would have had something vastly better, you would have strengthened those principles which enable you to bring into control every wish that has not in it some useful end, and to keep your desires where they ought to be, in a position which would make them your servants instead of your masters.

"If I were to tell you how carefully I carried out the policy which I am now presenting to you, you would be astonished. But I was forming habits which have proved of life-long service to me. Hence I had always money at my credit; I had always money to lend men, so that when my salary was $120, I could lend those whose income was twice what my own was, what they asked me to lend them.

"I was fond of books, and before I was twenty-two years of age, my library was worth not less than from $250 to $300, and this purchased out of my modest salary.

"Do you ask me how I spent my time after business hours, which business hours, let me say here, extended in summer from six o'clock in the morning until eight o'clock at night, let me say to you that they were wholly given up to the diversified work of church life. In that I found pleasant and delightful and profitable companionship ; I found congenial and elevating work, which tended to the formation of my mind, and to the cultivation of habits, and to the study of God's Word, which have been of life-long advantage to me, which kept me from evil company, from questionable places of resort, and which have left pleasant remembrances worth to me vastly more than gold.

"An employer ought to take an interest, not only in the temporal concerns of the members of his staff, but in their higher well-being. I have not personally given this matter the attention it deserves, and which it ought to have had from me. Will you be good enough, therefore, to accept personally, at this time, these remarks as intended for each one, and will you receive my assurance that the adoption of such a course by you, as the one to which I have referred, cannot work out for you anything but the very best results, not for this world only, but for the next.

"Believe me, that the words are as true to-day as when spoken by the wise man: 'Happy is the man that findeth wisdom, and the man that getteth understanding. For the merchandise of it is better than the merchandise of silver, and the gain thereof than fine gold. She is more precious than rubies, and all the things thou canst desire are not to be compared unto her. Length of days is in her right hand, and in her left hand riches and honour. Her ways are ways of pleasantness and all her paths are peace. She is a tree of life to them that lay hold upon her, and happy is every one that retaineth her. Prov. iii. 13-18.'

"But I think I hear some of you say, 'Could you not have done better, could you not have commanded a higher salary in some other house? It is quite possible I could. I never tried. I was attached to my work, to the house and my employer. Any man who spoke against either the one or the other spoke against me. There is a source of enjoyment greater than that which comes from any salary, however large, or from any position, however prominent, and that is the consciousness that with singleness of eye one's constant aim has been faithfully, efficiently and honestly to do one's duty.

"You will not think it boastful in me to say to you to-day that that consciousness is mine, and that whatever measure of success may have attended my efforts, there is nothing that affords me a purer pleasure than to look back and realize that I never served a man to whom I did not give my undivided energies, whose interests I did not make my own, and in whose success I did not as much rejoice as if I was in that success myself a participant.

"Such a reward, at least, is open to you all. Its value, be assured, you cannot possibly overestimate. Let me ask you to frame your conduct from such a high standpoint, and I earnestly hope that if you are spared to reach my own years, that in your retrospective musings the one thought which will stand out more prominently than any other will be this: 'I am thankful that I am able to say that in all my business relations my one constant and unchanging aim has been to do my duty.'"

Brave, manly and noble words are these, and in every way worthy of being, as they proved to be, the final message of a great and experienced Christian merchant to the members of his staff. If he seemed to possess the Midas-like gift of turning everything he touched into gold, it was because his eye was directed to high aims, and his whole life ran on the continuous lines of integrity, economy, industry and application.

So far from being ashamed of his humble beginnings, he was proud of them.

As the merchant princes of Florence in the height of their power, and when dictating laws to all Italy,

preserved upon their palaces the cranes by which
the bales of merchandise had once been raised to
their attics, so this merchant prince sought ever to
lead young men to the perennial sources of inspiration and help, and displayed nothing of that vulgar
reluctance to allude to the earlier stages of a
remarkable rise from poverty and obscurity to comfort, affluence and distinction.

He was, in many respects, an ideal employer, a
sagacious, enterprising, successful business man, enjoying the unfailing confidence of all in his establishment, as well as of his fellow-merchants, and seeking,
by every means, to exalt the standard of mercantile
honour. Throughout his entire business career he
was an active, living force, a prominent and influential figure, and it has been the rare fortune of but
few merchants to make a more deep and helpful
impression upon their times than was made by John
Macdonald.

VII.

CHURCH RELATIONS.

But as for me, I will come into thy house in the multitude of thy mercy: and in thy fear will I worship toward thy holy temple.

—Psalmist.

O only see how sweetly there
  Our lovely Church is gleaming !
The golden evening sunshine fair
  On spire and roof is streaming.

—German Lyrist.

Love thyself last !   Drink deep
The nectared anodyne of selflessness.

—Edwin Arnold.

For the soul that gives is the soul that lives,
  And bearing another's load
Doth lighten your own, and shorten the way,
  And brighten the homeward road.

—Washington Gledden.

They which builded on the wall, and they that bare burdens, with those that laded, every one with one of his hands wrought in the work, and with the other hand held a weapon.

—Neh. iv. 17.

WE have followed Mr. Macdonald through an unbroken career of business success, until, from humble beginnings, he has, by shrewdness and energy, self-reliance and integrity, become the Canadian dry-goods king; his wholesale firm the largest in the Dominion, and perhaps, in proportion to population, the largest on the American continent. But while thus diligent in business, he was "fervent in spirit, serving the Lord." As a merchant, he was active and alert; as a Christian, he was not less energetic in the Master's vineyard. This activity embraced almost every department of personal and official service in the Methodist Church. He laboured in the Sabbath School, and occupied the pulpit as a local preacher almost every Sabbath; was the leader of a class, assisted at the weekly prayer-meeting, and was zealous in revival services. He was a member of several Boards of Trustees, treasurer of the Missionary Society, a delegate to Annual and General Conferences, and a representative to various ecclesiastical bodies. He took a deep interest in both the spiritual and temporal interests of the local church with which he was connected, while he largely felt also "the care of all the churches." He took an active part in the inauguration of various Church
10

enterprises, and performed the ceremony of laying the corner stone of more churches than any other layman in Canada.

As long as Mr. Macdonald lived on George Street, he was a member of the Toronto West Circuit, of which Richmond Street was the head. He was the Superintendent of the large Sabbath School in this mother church of Toronto Methodism, and was the leader of an important class in the Elm Street Church. He preached almost every Sabbath in some part of the city, or drove out to appointments on adjoining circuits. Mrs. Macdonald frequently accompanied him, and they had occasional "adventures." On one occasion he was like the great apostle, " in peril of robbers." One dark night, as they were returning from Weston, two men rushed upon them, one seizing the horse, the other attempting to lay hold of the driver. Mr. Macdonald, in warding him off with the whip, struck the horse somewhat sharply, so that the spirited animal sprang wildly forward, throwing the man at his head violently to the ground, and then dashed along with all his might, leaving the highwaymen far behind. The horse was utterly beyond control, and ran on for miles until, utterly exhausted, he calmed down. Fortunately the road was clear, and nothing occurred except a severe fright to his wife.

On another occasion, after preaching in Weston, he was returning with Mrs. Macdonald, who carried in her arms her little firstborn child. The night was dark ; Mr. Macdonald drove into the ditch, and all were capsized into the mud. As good Providence would have it, neither mother nor child received a scratch or wound; but these little occurrences somewhat dampened the ardour of his wife in accompanying him to his country appointments.

When Mr. Macdonald removed to Oaklands, he connected himself with the Bloor Street Church, then a part of Toronto East Circuit. The church was known as the Yorkville appointment. The population was small, but the interest was a growing one. He threw himself into the movement, and became an earnest and willing co-labourer, being not only alive to whatever touched the spiritual interests of the church, but also awake to its material prosperity, being a member of the Board of Trustees and a Steward of the Quarterly Official Board. Owing to the distance, he held a Sabbath School in his own house, and gave constant attention to the spiritual nurture of his own children. As the population began to spread northward, he saw the necessity of providing for the religious wants of his own neighbourhood. Ground was secured on Yonge Street, corner of Marlborough Avenue, and a small but comely sanctuary erected. Here he toiled assiduously, visiting the sick, the poor, the wayward, and gathering rich fruit of his labours. He organized a Sabbath School, becoming its first superintendent; and when another could be found to assume this responsibility, he established an adult Bible class. In many instances the seed sown in the minds of these young men ripened into a harvest of true manhood and piety.

In connection with this work he makes the following record :

"Sunday, 22nd February, 1874, Bible class, which about nine weeks ago numbered three, to-day numbered fifty-seven, having grown as follows : second Sabbath, six ; third Sabbath, nine ; fourth, sixteen ; fifth, twenth-four ; sixth, thirty-two : seventh, forty-five ; eighth, forty-six ; to-day, fifty-seven."

The hive was small, but composed of working bees, and the cause grew from year to year. In the communion and worship of this church he partook of some of the richest clusters of spiritual fruit, while his soul was strengthened and gladdened by constant refreshing from on high. Here his younger children were baptized, and his sons and daughters came out and subscribed with their own hand to be the Lord's. He welcomed new-comers to the church, and rejoiced when they were added to its membership. His heart was warmly engaged in every revival effort, and during one of these seasons of religious interest, which lasted nearly a month, in the midst of his manifold engagements, he was not absent from a single service. When the school outgrew the little room in which the work began, he bore the chief burden in furnishing comfortable accommodation in a larger school-room, which is now the Memorial Hall of the church.

The church was two or three times enlarged to provide for the increasing congregations ; and an impulse was given to every connexional cause by the munificent offerings of the Yonge Street Methodist Church.

He cherished kindly relations with the pastors as they came in succession : Revs. W. L. Rutledge, F. H. Wallace, B.D. ; H. M. Manning, George Leach, R. N. Burns, B.A.; George J. Bishop and John V. Smith ; and constant references are made in his diaries to sermons preached by them, and helpful influences received in the sanctuary. The results of his Christian teaching and example in his own neighbourhood will abide continually. He laboured directly for the spiritual good of his fellows, and watched continually for opportunities to reach individuals ; and many intelligent, active, trustworthy church members bear glad testimony to his fidelity in leading them to the Saviour, and confirming them in every good work.

On the Official Board, when church matters were being discussed, his generous nature manifested itself in his thoughtful regard for the opinions and feelings of his brethren. The management of a large business, where one's every wish is a command, encourages sometimes a dictatorial spirit, and often men that are successful in their own affairs are unable to work harmoniously in harness with their brethren. They assume magisterial airs, and wish to be referred to in all things. Not so Mr. Macdonald. He always showed a considerate regard for the opinions of his brethren, and with singular tact would draw out the views of the humblest brother before final action was taken on any matter.

Church Erection.

He was always interested in church building, for he believed that a house of worship in any commun-

ity gave promise of permanent religious influences.
When the Metropolitan Church, that monument to the
energy, enterprise and influence of the Rev. William
Morley Punshon, was to be erected, Mr. Macdonald
became one of the original trustees, and not only contributed liberally of his means, but from its inception
to its completion, gave of his time and activity to the
great undertaking. In his diary for 1873 we find the
following:

"Thursday, April 4th. A day never to be forgotten.
The Metropolitan Church dedicated

The opening hymn, Rev. W. M. Punshon.

The opening prayer, Rev. Dr. Wood.

The lessons, Rev. Geo. Cochran.

The sermon, Rev. Dr. Tiffany, of Newark, N.J.

The effort to collect money, Mr. David Preston, De-
troit. All marked by divine power. $21,000 sub-
scribed.

Evening meeting.

Was called upon to preside. Rev. Dr. Tiffany and
Rev. Mr. Punshon the speakers.

Over $5,000 additional subscribed."

Mr. Macdonald believed that to Dr. Punshon we
were not only indebted for a new departure in pulpit
services, but, also, for stimulating all denominations
to that wonderful extension of church buildings which
are at once the pride and glory of our land. He says:

"The great church-building movement of Ontario
dates from the period of the erection of the Metropolitan Church. If this should be doubted by any one,
let him take the trouble to ascertain the date of the
erection of the splendid churches that adorn Toronto;

let him ascertain when the churches in every city, town and hamlet in Ontario, which are pretentious and modern in their character, were erected, and he will find, with very few exceptions, that they date after the Metropolitan Church. The movement assumed something of the form of an epidemic, and was not confined to the Methodist Church, for it seized all the denominations; and churches began to arise, beautiful in their architecture, commodious in their internal arrangements, and so admirably adapted for church work, with their schools and class-rooms, that it may with fairness be claimed that to-day, Canada, in the number, beauty and arrangements of its churches stands ahead of any country in the world."

Next to Dr. Punshon's influence was his own in this direction, for he not only assisted many of the churches in the city, but contributed also to the erection of others all over the Province, aiding many churches outside the bounds of Methodism. Indeed, whenever appeals were made to him, and he was reasonably convinced of the worthiness of the request, he would give such an amount as he thought the circumstances warranted. He was opposed to excessive expenditures for merely building purposes. He cared not for

> " Storied windows richly dight,
>   Casting a dim, religious light;"

he preferred the plain structure.

He was in such demand at the inauguration of these church edifices that he had preserved no less than thirty silver trowels, presented to him by Boards of

Trustees on the occasion of the laying of the corner-stone. These trowels are of elegant workmanship, and are now heir-looms of the family.

MISSIONS.

From the day of his conversion, he began to think and work for missions. He felt an individual responsibility in the salvation of the world, and to the utmost of his power did he aid in this work, by gifts, prayers and counsel. He was a member of the Missionary Committee of the Methodist Church for more than a quarter of a century, and was its Lay-Treasurer for a good portion of this time. His broad views and earnest spirit, his high sense of the obligation and ability of the Church to extend its labours at home and abroad, made him eager to enlarge the sphere of missionary operation, and take advantage of every opportunity of fulfilling the Master's last command. He not only took part in the deliberations of the committee, but was frequently called upon to make addresses at its annual public meetings. His words were always earnest and inspiring, and he showed a thorough acquaintance with every department of the missionary field, as well as with the workers employed.

He took a deep interest in the complimentary breakfast given to the pioneer missionaries to British Columbia, the Rev. E. Evans, D.D., E. White, E. Robson and A. Browning, in December, 1858, when the Mayor of the city, together with clergymen and representatives of all the Protestant Churches gave, in the old St. Lawrence Hall, a farewell banquet to these first gospel messengers to that infant colony then rising upon the western slopes of the continent.

On May 8th, 1868, he presided at the farewell breakfast given in the Richmond Street Church to the Wesleyan missionaries to the North-West, Revs. Geo. Young, D.D., E. R. Young, P. Campbell, and Geo. McDougall; on which occasion he said that their appointment would add the last link that was wanting to complete the chain of missionary enterprise which would now stretch across the continent. Presiding at the forty-third anniversary of the Missionary Society, held in Guelph, in the November of that year, he pleaded the cause of Red River and the Great Lone Land; and maintained that there was wealth enough in the Methodist Church to send the gospel to every pagan in British North America within twelve months. At this meeting, Mr. Macdonald introduced a resolution to increase the minimum allowance to missionaries from $450 to $500, which, after some discussion, was adopted.

He was anxious to see Canada represented in the foreign field, and, with Dr. Punshon, was one of the prime movers for the establishment of the mission to Japan. His diary of Thursday, October 10th, 1872, bears this record:

"Missionary Committee at St. Catharines. Subject of mission to Japan introduced. Committee decided to commence it, and entrusted the matter to the Committee on Consultation and Finance in Toronto."

Concerning the establishment of this mission, Mr. Macdonald thus writes:

" It was at the Missionary Committee, held at St·
Catharines, that it was resolved definitely to enter
upon the Japan mission. It had been brought before
the Committee, held in the preceding year, and failed;
and now met with considerable opposition. At a
favourable point of the debate a slip was handed to
Dr. Punshon, on which was written : ' If tried now, it
would carry.' He wrote on the slip, and returned :
' The chief difficulty is the man, if we had him I would
be more hopeful.' This paper, so full of significance,
is still in my possession. It being the last subject of
debate, he said : ' Brethren, let us pray to-night about
this matter ; we will then be better able to judge in
the morning.' The morning came, the matter was
brought up, and the Church, through its Missionary
Committee, had committed itself to the establishment
of a foreign mission. How wonderful have been the
results of that action ; how the fears of all the
brethren who opposed it, conscientious as they were,
have proved groundless ; how it surpassed all the
sanguine expectations of those who promoted it ; how
it has stimulated the great missionary enterprise of
our Church ; how it has led to the formation of our
invaluable Woman's Missionary Association ; how it
has intensified the missionary spirit in all the sister
churches, is matter of history."

At the last meeting of the Board which he ever
attended, held in London, he pressed upon the Committee with great earnestness the duty of establishing
a mission on the islands of Martinique and Gaudaloupe,
and saw in such a mission possibilities of large usefulness in promoting the enlightenment and Chris-
tianization of the entire group of West Indian Islands,
that peerless zone of jewels in our nation's diadem.

METHODIST UNION.

He took a deep interest in the union of the different branches of the Methodist household, and an active part in the negotiations which led to the union of 1874, as well as that larger union of 1883, which gave to the Dominion from "sea to sea" a united Methodist Church. From the time that lay delegation was introduced into the councils of the Church, he was an influential member of the Toronto Annual Conference, and a delegate of all the General Conferences held.

FRATERNAL DELEGATE.

At the first General Conference of September, 1874, he was appointed, with the Rev. John A. Williams, D.D., fraternal delegate to the General Conference of the Methodist Episcopal Church of the United States. These representatives proceeded to the Baltimore Conference, in May, 1876, and were most heartily welcomed.

Mr. Macdonald was particularly happy in his address, at the close of which, in response to a question by Dr. Reid, one of the secretaries of the Missionary Society, he raised a storm of applause by stating that the average contribution per member of the Church which he represented was $1.85 per member.

GENERAL CONFERENCE.

He was always a prominent figure on the floor of the General Conference. Ready in debate, wise in counsel, warm in sympathy, and with largeness of

vision, the princely merchant, the large-minded statesman, the genuine philanthropist, the munificent friend
of Missions, the devoted Christian, was always lis-
tened to with interest, and his opinions carried great
weight among his brethren. He was inclined to be
conservative in all church matters, and was greatly
opposed to the revision of the Hymn Book. At the
General Conference of 1878, he pleaded for the old
Wesleyan Hymnal. The points presented were:

" 1. I am persuaded that if any such changes had
been foreshadowed as the Committee recommend, the
Hymn Book Committee would have had its powers
defined.

" 2. The $25,000 or $30,000 which the Methodist
people have invested in hymn books at this period
of depression is another reason.

" 3. The reference to profit by the Book Room is,
to my mind, somewhat mercenary. Mr. Wesley's
idea was that the books should be cheap. If our
hymn books had been cheaper than they have been,
our hymns would have been more widely known.
The aim should be with the book in use to cheapen
it, so as to bring it within the reach of the poorest
of our people.

" 4. I implore the Conference, on behalf of the half-
million of persons in Canada who sing these hymns,
to spare them as they are, and not sweep away from
us the last vestige which binds us to the men to
whom, not ourselves alone, but the world is so much
indebted. I do this in behalf of the Methodist people
of Canada, who have not asked for revision, and do
not want it.

" 5. The argument, to my mind, has nothing in it
that the Church is no longer what it was since our
union with the New Connexion body. I will readily

accept any hymn which the brethren of that Church will add by way of supplement; but they, I am sure, no more than others, desire the spoiling of the old book which, next to the Word of God, has been made a means of grace to many millions. If there is anything in the argument, it will have as much force at some future day, when possibly the Methodist Episcopal Church and Primitive Methodists, and the Bible Christians may, with us, be all united in one common bond.

"6. The Hymn Book, as we have it to-day, is the result of careful revision, the perfected work of our founder, the strongest evidence of which is its having remained unchanged for a century. During that time it has spoken to the hearts of millions, with a power which no other book ever written, God's Word alone excepted, has ever spoken. It has to-day all the power it had when compiled; it is as fresh and as precious to the Church of to-day as it was to the Church of the days of Wesley, and it is a work which is the heritage, not of the Methodist Church only, but of the Church throughout the world. When I think of the changes that have taken place in the arts and sciences, the changes in the thoughts of men and the modes of life; when I think that within the last few years churches have arisen which are exerting a wondrous power in the earth, and that the identity of churches has been lost by being merged into sister communions; when I think that empires have been dismembered and empires created, dynasties established and dynasties destroyed; and then remember that this little book has outlived all that is perishable, is as fresh, as life-giving, as critically correct, as experimentally true, and as precious to the heart of every believer to-day as it ever was, and will be at the last day as it is now, I ask whether or not there is one man in this

Conference bold enough to put his hand upon a heritage so precious, and rob the Church of that for which he can give no substitute ?"

Spite of these hallowed and cherished associations, the Hymn Book was revised, and over three hundred of the choicest modern and ancient hymns added to our Methodist hymnology. Even after the new Hymn Book was authorized and published, Mr. Macdonald struggled to retain the old collection; but he at length yielded, and was brought to see that the Methodist hymnody had lost none of its richness and attractive beauty by the change.

ŒCUMENICAL CONFERENCE.

He was a delegate to the first Œcumenical Conference held in City Road Chapel, in September, 1881, and presented a paper on "The Maintenance of Home Missions to the Most Degraded Populations." Among other observations, he remarks :

" What can be done to better the masses of human beings who crowd together in all great centres of population, ignorant, indolent, vicious and degraded ? Is their condition hopeless ? In this city of London, where there are so many who love and serve God, what sight so sad as to see in such a city thousands of men and women from whom every vestige of all that is good and holy and pure has been effaced, and who, in this city of Gospel-light, seem to have abandoned all feelings of hope for this world and the next; to see multitudes of young lads already old in crime, and who, unless relief come to them, and come soon, will assuredly swell the ranks of the criminal class. Sadder still to see thousands of young girls,

between the ages of ten and fourteen, drifting away
to a doom which appears inevitable; to see flocks of
helpless children growing up to form another generation of the degraded—such of them, at least, as will
survive the hunger and wretchedness, the neglect and
cruelty, to which they are subjected.

Sights such as these, without looking into the gin-
palaces—those sinks of all that is degrading—the
dark lanes, loathsome alleys, crowded lodging-houses,
where thieves and pickpockets and the vilest men
and women congregate, are enough to cause the
deepest pain of heart, enough to beget the most profound thankfulness to God that our own lot is so
different, and enough to lead us searchingly to ask
ourselves, What have we done, what do we intend to
do to make this wretchedness and this sorrow less?
Can these older and more hardened men and women
be saved? these young lads, can they be rescued?
these young girls, can they be snatched from a life of
shame too sad to contemplate? these helpless children,
can they be reached before sin, with its defilement,
has done its work? can the bodies be saved as well
as the souls? A simple glance at the report of the
London City Mission will, perhaps, furnish the best
answer we can give to these questions:

"The achievement of the shoe-black societies, as
well as those of many kindred associations, have put
to rest the question of hopelessness. None are too
low to be raised, none too abandoned to be hopeless;
while the individual instances in which those who
were once neglected street-arabs, vagabonds and
pickpockets, become men holding prominent and responsible positions, demonstrate that positions of
trust and responsibility are open to those who are
found in the ranks of the degraded, and that if determined to live new lives, the past, however dark, does
not bar their future advancement."

But how is this great wave of wretchedness and misery to be checked, and changed into all that is pure, and healthful, and life-giving? God's Word must be in future, as it has been in the past, the great instrument arresting the attention, awakening the conscience, and exciting the understanding to the need of salvation. It must be put into the hands or brought to the homes of those who need it, by agents of unmistakable piety, tact and shrewdness, by those who not only are bringers of the Word, but lovers of the Word, not only readers of the Word, but those who have its truths treasured in their memories and in their hearts. It is but a waste of time to employ anyone in this work who does not love it for its own sake, who has not experienced a change of heart, who has not a love for the souls of men. Herein lies the whole groundwork of the system :

> " The love of Christ doth me constrain
>   To seek the wandering souls of men ;
>   With cries, entreaties, tears to save,
>   To snatch them from the gaping grave."

To-day, as in the days of Christ, " the harvest truly is plenteous, the labourers are few." Taking, by way of illustration, this great city, containing over 4,000,000, and adding to its population some 90,000 souls a year, it has, in connection with the London City Mission, 450 missionaries. But when the masses among whom they labour are considered, may it not be appropriately asked, What are they among so many ? Upon this point the Lord Mayor, while presiding recently at Egyptian Hall, asked, " What are 450 missionaries for this great metropolis ?" And at the same meeting Lord Shaftesbury stated that 1,000 would not be one too many. If we rightly estimate the results sure to follow the faithful efforts of every devoted worker in this field, then we may safely conclude that in this wide world there is not one more full of promise.

If there is a field in the world where more than any other such efforts are needed, that field is the one found in this great city. Here is the deepest degradation, here ample ability to meet it in means and workers. . . . Let the Church unite in sending into this field without loss of time a greatly increased staff of workers; Christian men await but the application to supply you with the means. Better still, let every Christian man and woman in this great city become a worker, not offering words merely, not simply reminding the degraded of their condition, not merely offering Christ to them as their Saviour when the only feelings of which they are conscious are the gnawings of hunger, and the only shelter which awaits them for the night, the canopy of heaven. Let such workers cheerfully minister to them of their substance, giving if it be but a tithe of what they daily spend upon super-fluities, realizing that the poor perishing body needs help as well as the soul. Let every Christian woman of this metropolis take their poor fallen sisters by the hand, many of whom are more sinned against than sinning, many of whom abhor the life, the sad life into which they have drifted, not passing them by as though God had forsaken them, but remember-ing the words of Him who said to an erring one, " Neither do I condemn thee ; go in peace and sin no more"; then, indeed, will results follow such as never have been witnessed in this great metropolis ; and the glad tidings will be wafted to every quarter, and men and women everywhere will be led to labour as they have never done before for those that are outcast and degraded.

11

> " In the long run all love is paid by love,
>   Though undervalued by the hearts of earth ;
>   The great eternal government of above
>   Keeps strict account, and will redeem its work.
>   Give thy love freely, do not count the cost,
>   So beautiful a thing was never lost
>   In the long run."

In a large union meeting held in December, 1881, in the Carlton Street Primitive Methodist Church, to hear the delegates from this great Methodist gathering,

> " One in speech, and one in face,
>   One in honest pride of race,
>   One in faith, and hope and grace,"

Mr. Macdonald, speaking of the " Probable Results of the Conference," said :

" If, then, the ordinary daily intercourse of men may be productive of most important results, if their words, hastily, perhaps thoughtlessly spoken, become active agents for good or ill, what results might one reasonably suppose would follow from the coming together of 400 delegates, representative of twenty-five millions of people, brought together from every quarter of the earth, coming, as many of them did, at great personal sacrifice of time and means,—feeling that a great occasion, the first of its kind, had brought them together in a sanctuary, every foot of which might not irreverently be said to be holy ground, whose aisles had been so often trod by the saints of God, by men whom God had honoured as instruments in reviving pure religion throughout the world, whose dust was resting where they stood awaiting the morning of the resurrection ? In such an assembly, in such an edifice, brought together under such circumstances, where utterances were carefully considered,

where so many of the speakers were men of masterly
minds, whose thoughts were creative thoughts, their
words those of inspiration, where men came to listen,
not in the spirit of criticism, but in a spirit at once
humble and teachable, and where from the opening
services from the able and comprehensive sermon of
Bishop Simpson to the hallowed devotional exercises
which brought the Conference to a close, the Master
of assemblies was graciously present crowning the
proceedings with His favour and His blessing—what
results might be looked for from such a gathering
convened under such circumstances?   Let me say
briefly, that there were results which were immediate
—results which led men to ask what hath God
wrought?   Results of which one may enquiringly
ask, What will the harvest be?   Was it a great thing
to see assembled in one building representatives of
twenty-five distinct branches of the Church of Christ
—many of whose members had upon so many occasions
found it difficult to speak of each other with ordinary
courtesy, to say nothing of brotherly affection; and
had often contended upon the same ground, not so
much for God alone as the maintenance of a sect?
.   .   .   Was it a great thing to realize that the
members of the Conference knew each other only as
brethren?   That the feeling which most influenced
each was the sense that hitherto there had been on
the part of each a large amount of misunderstanding
about each other?   That the differences which divided
brethren were more imaginary than real?   How easy
is it to realize that the members felt that above the
spirit which characterized the Council was the spirit
of that charity which thinketh no evil, which suffereth
long and is kind, which envieth not, which vaunteth
not itself, which is not puffed up, and which led
brethren so sit day after day as members of the same
family, and to part with the kindliest wishes for each

other's welfare.   Now, had there been no other results, would these not have amply repaid all the labour and sacrifice involved in the gathering, sufficient both for the members and others, matter for life-long remembrance?   The utterances of the Council upon the peculiar characteristics of Methodism were clear and unmistakable. . . . Of the results which are to follow, what shall we say?   First, another Council to be held on this continent, where brethren will renew their fraternal greetings, and with an enlarged experience discuss the great matters which will come before it.   Can we not find in the spirit which pervades this meeting, the first of its kind, results which, but for the Council, we had hardly hoped to have seen so soon—a greater interest in each other's work, a rivalry only in seeking to secure each other's good, a gradual growing towards each other, not by any sudden or spasmodic effort, but as the result of exhibiting more fully that charity which is the fruit of the Spirit, and which is the true mark of Christ's followers.   And what we are doing here, is being done at our antipodes. The results of the Council will neither be local nor ephemeral.   They will be felt wherever our language is spoken.   They will be felt as long as time shall endure.   They will be apparent in the great kindliness with which brethren will speak of each other, in the greater tenderness with which they will think of each other, in the gradual but permanent widening of that platform upon which they will stand and work, and as a consequence in the gradual diminution of the number of branches of the great Methodist family, in the hastening of the period when, not in word only, but in deed and in truth, they will all be one, and when it will be said of them, in a sense which has scarcely been possible before, ‘Behold how good and how pleasant it is for brethren to dwell together in unity.’”

VIII.

MANIFOLD ACTIVITIES.

When I think of the agencies which are ceaselessly at work
to make this bad world better, I am thankful that I live.
—*Wm. Morley Punshon, LL.D.*

To serve with lofty gifts the lowly needs
Of the poor race for which the God-man died,
And do it all for love.   Oh, this is great !
—*J. G. Holland.*

We live in deeds, not years ; in thoughts, not breaths ;
In feelings, not in figures on a dial.
We should count time by heart-throbs.   He most lives
Who thinks most, feels the noblest, acts the best.
—*Bailey.*

Life is not as idle ore,
But iron dug from central gloom,
    And heated hot with burning fears,
    And dipped in baths of hissing tears,
And batter'd with the shocks of doom,
    To shape and use.
—*Tennyson.*

ONE would think that the attention which the active merchant gave to his extensive business, and the earnest Christian to his Church work, would have absorbed all his time. But a man of his exhaustless resources and immense energy of character could not fail to make his personality felt everywhere in the community. His activity and Christian work kept increasing. He was constantly engaged in some great, practical, good work. In this he received constant accessions of Divine strength, for no man can persist for years in a course of self-denying labours, prayer and activity unless he is drawing from the Fountain of all grace—our Lord Himself. It was only by the most persistent economy of time, and the most complete surrender of himself to perpetual labour, that he was able to accomplish what he did. He did not enter into investments outside his regular business. He never speculated. The following incident took place when he was a boy. When leaving home, his father placed in his hands the sum of eight dollars. Shortly after, the embryo trader purchased an old watch for a chain which had cost him four dollars, and two dollars in cash, the balance left from his father's benefaction. This watch he sold for the sum of twelve dollars to a lumberman who had just returned from the woods, where he had been working for the company. Upon this transaction he expected to double his money, instead of which he lost chain, money and watch, for the lumberman never paid him a cent. It was a terrible blow at the time, but was one of the best things that could have happened to him, for he saw the danger of speculation, and it was his first and last venture of the kind. His reputation for ability, integrity and zeal in positions of trust caused him to be eagerly sought after to enter upon boards and corporations of trust. But he was cautious, and rarely embarked in such financial ventures. He was for a time a director of the Bank of Commerce, and was largely interested in the Canada Car Company, which required much attention, but brought small profit. With his accustomed sagacity, he saw that he must not scatter his forces in business affairs.

BOARD OF TRADE.

He was, however, active on the Board of Trade. Interested in the commercial prosperity of the city and the province, he devoted much time and judgment in devising plans for promoting and developing that prosperity. These combinations of merchants, manufacturers and traders, to promote the interests of commerce and aid the industrial advancement of cities and nations, are now a part of our modern civilization. His matured judgment, untiring devotion to business, and his unblemished integrity, gave him rank with the most honoured and successful of merchants, and made him very influential in the consideration of all questions pertaining to finance and the industrial interests of the city. He was enrolled among the earliest members of the Toronto Board of Trade, and always took an active part in its proceedings. As late as January, 1889, he presented a paper on the commercial relations between Canada, the West Indies and British Guiana.

In this paper, among other things, he said :

"I have no doubt that there are in this gathering those whose business or inclination have brought them to these lovely islands of the sea. For them, nothing that I can say of their appearance, their products or their people, will be new; but there are others, and I am safe in saying by far the greater number, who have not the slightest conception that within five or six days' journeying from our own city, there are islands so strangely beautiful, so wonderfully productive — islands where perpetual summer reigns, and where—while with us winter has asserted its power, has robbed the forest of its foliage, and the fields of their verdure—there the palm trees bend their graceful forms—oranges, limes, bananas, and sapodillas, and indeed every kind of tropical fruit surround the passer-by, while tropical flowers skirt every road-side, and border many of the great cane fields, whose delicate green with the feathery arrow of the cane rises and bends to every breeze, as do the waves of the sea ; whose lofty mountain peaks rise to the height of 5,000 or 6,000 feet,' and whose low lands present such pictures of loveliness, arising from their great fertility and marvellous vegetation, as are not to be surpassed on the face of the earth. It is under such circumstances that one realizes, to some extent, at least, the vastness and the power of the British Empire, as they thus see it embracing within itself every climate, almost every class of people, and every product of the earth.

"In the month of July, when amid the icebergs of Labrador, in latitude somewhere about 52° 20′ north, and when on that rocky coast at anchor by reason of the fog, the very first object that met my eye when the fog lifted was the ensign of St. George floating on one of Her Majesty's vessels stationed there to guard the interests of her Newfoundland fishermen; and at the close of the year, as I found myself at British Guiana, in something like six degrees north of the equator, and where the mariner ofttimes takes his bearings from the Southern Cross, I found the same ensign floating from British merchant-ships, which had brought there the riches of many lands, over many seas, to take back to as many lands the products of Britain's colonies.

"Steaming from about 52° 20′ north, where our way lay through immense icebergs, sixty of which we would see in one day, and where the hardy Newfoundlander, amid snow and ice, plies his trade; steaming onward and southward to within six degrees of the equator, where the temperature of the ocean is 83°, and where summer perpetually reigns, I found on that great expanse of ocean continuous evidence of the dominance of British commerce. I found in every colony I visited not only that Britain had left upon each the mark of her prowess, but the blessings of her civilization. I felt, as I never had realized before, under circumstances and conditions as opposite as they could well-nigh be, that at each extreme the power and influence of the empire were equally great, and equally great for good. Connected with such a power, I thought upon our possibilities of development; I thought upon our future; I thought upon our destiny. But this was

the one thought which most impressed me—that our
destiny was in our own hands, and not in the hands
of any foreign power, however near or however
great, and realizing this fully, I felt that if in working it out we were but true to those great underlying
principles of truth and righteousness, which are the
guarantees, not only of a nation's prosperity, but of
a nation's stability—if we were but true to our
country and true to ourselves—nothing could stand in
the way of our progress, nothing, by any possibility,
retard our development; for then we should be prosperous and contented at home, and we should be
honoured and respected abroad."

SUNDAY SCHOOL UNION.

An enthusiastic worker in the Sabbath School, a
teacher or officer in it during the larger part of his
life, he took a lively interest in the Sunday School
Union. He was always ready to aid Mission Sunday
Schools in new and remote districts, and believed
them to be fountains of blessings. He was ready to
second every measure that would promote the efficiency of Sunday Schools. He often acted as chairman
of these Sunday School Teachers' Associations, and
gave addresses at their anniversary meetings.

THE SABBATH.

He loved and honoured the Sabbath, and every
encroachment upon the sanctity of the Lord's Day
met with his vigorous and constant opposition. In
the unceasing warfare that has to be kept up against
the enemies of God's Day, Mr. Macdonald could
always be counted upon either as a soldier to fight or

a general to lead. He believed that the domestic, political and religious life of a nation was advanced by guarding the Day of Rest, and sought to enforce the rights and obligations of this day, not only by speech, but by restrictive legislation.

Every sense of humanity, kindness and justice in him was shocked by the perpetual, unbroken labour of the workingman on the Sabbath Day. In his travels over the continent, or along the rocky coasts of Newfoundland, wherever he found a settlement destitute of public worship on the Lord's Day, he would call the people together and preach to them the Gospel. When he visited the famous Yellowstone Park, he arrived with his daughter at the hotel on Saturday night. Next morning all the guests were out in carriages. Mr. Macdonald and his party alone remained. On Monday morning, as they entered the carriage, the driver said, " Are you the gentleman who refused to go out yesterday ?" " Yes, sir; I am." " Well, you are the first tourist that I have met in sixteen years who refused to break the Sabbath. I have driven this carriage all that time, and could never get a Sunday to go to church."

TEMPERANCE.

The Temperance cause had also his active sympathy. In early life, when drinking habits were all but universal, he became an abstainer and an advocate of total abstinence.

He had words of encouragement for the various Orders, Associations, and Bands of Hope; but he had small confidence in any reformation of the individual that did not include genuine conversion. He believed that as a religious movement the Temperance cause achieved its best results, and so the City Christian Temperance Mission had his constant support. He was also a member of the Prohibitory Alliance, for in his deep and intelligent hatred of intemperance, he sought by every moral and legislative means to suppress this crime of crimes. Would that all our legislators could see the folly and sin of licensing men to sell this poison ! The liquor laws are an unspeakable infamy, and the traffic is one under whose curse the civilized world is everywhere groaning. Our prisons, workhouses, and asylums overflow with the victims of drink. Yet through the power of the liquor oligarchy the iniquity is made lawful, though petitions and appeals to our legislatures fall year by year as " thick as autumn leaves in Vallambrosa."

CITY CHARITIES.

The benevolent and charitable organizations of the city all had his co-operation and support. His hand was on almost every lever of the varied machinery to restore and lift up the fallen : the rescue work, reformatory work, prison-gate missions, etc. One of the most unique and helpful of addresses was given by him to the prisoners of Toronto Jail on the Christmas of 1879 :

" You have seen at many public buildings and at different gates approaching them two boards, and upon each board three words: 'The way in,' 'The way out.' I purpose applying these words to yourselves.

"'The way in.' There are many of you who, when boys and girls, if you had been told that upon this glad Christmas morning you would be the inmates of this jail, would have answered, 'Impossible.' You had other hopes and other purposes. But in an evil hour you took your first step and entered the street of Bad Company. which was directly on the route to 'the way in.' This street has a down-grade and is slippery withal, and of the many who are drawn into it very few find their way out. You remember this morning the first step you took into it, and all the other streets into which it has led you, until you are now in a labyrinth from which escape seems impossible. Away down this street you entered another—the street of Drunkenness; then the street of Profanity, which led into the street of Sabbath Desecration, where God's name is never mentioned but to be taken in vain; wherein is no sanctuary and no Sabbath bell, no modest looks, no quiet demeanour, no peace, no happiness, no rest. This brought you to the street called Utter Indifference, at the end of which stood the jail-yard, and over it 'the way in '—your character gone, clothes gone, friends gone, hope gone; so that many a poor fellow, and many a broken-hearted woman has entered it repeating:

"'Anywhere, anywhere, out of the world.'

"But by this time you are ready to say, 'Never mind the way in, tell us the way out.' Well, there are a great many ways out—through the gate, over the walls, through the window; but these will all be found difficult. And let me tell you, unless you get rid of the thraldom of your own selves, you are better here than anywhere else. The thought I want

to impress upon you is this: Be men and women.
Come to God through Jesus Christ, and though He
knows it all, tell Him the story of it all, and in this
jail repent of your past. The only way out is
through repentance; without it, I have no hope in
any promise you may make. Without the help
which God will grant, you could not stand an hour.

" Perhaps one of you is saying, 'If I were sure
that any person situated as I am had ever become a
reformed man, and a useful member of society by
doing as you say, I would try it.' Let me give you
an instance of one better off than any here, perhaps,
lower sunk than anyone here—the Prodigal Son—
who, when forsaken by his companions, said, 'I will
arise and go to my father.' 'But,' you say, 'he had
a father and a home—I have neither.' The whole
scope of this parable is to teach the readiness of our
Father in heaven to receive us. Can you not trust
Him. We present to you this Saviour; we come to
you this glad morning with the joyous message,
" Unto you is born this day in the city of David a
Saviour, which is Christ the Lord.'"

SALVATION ARMY.

The Salvation Army had his sympathy, and he
gave to the movement his countenance and aid. At
first he thought that the excesses of the Army produced irreverence of thought, expression, and action,
making religion grotesque and familiar; but when
he visited London and other great centres of England
and saw the work that was being done among the
degraded, outcast and fallen, his whole being went
out in ardent sympathy with the work; and when
General Booth made his first visit to this country in

1886, a reception was given him at "Oaklands," when his residence and grounds were thrown open to the Army and their friends, and the General had the opportunity of setting forth the principles and progress of the Salvation Army before many of the best citizens of Toronto.

When the Army were securing their magnificent quarters at King's Cross, Mr. Macdonald assisted them by a contribution of one thousand dollars; and always gave largely and cheerfully to the various schemes of this mighty, evangelizing agency.

BIBLE SOCIETY.

He was an unfailing friend of the Bible Society, so catholic in its character and operations. He was not only a regular contributor to the funds of the Upper Canada Bible Society, but also a director, and for many years one of the vice-presidents. Through the whole period of his career he never wavered or faltered in any step that might promote its welfare, and always cherished the largest conception of the importance of this work. He was also a firm believer in the usefulness of tracts and of religious books, and was an active member of the Upper Canada Tract Society.

GENERAL HOSPITAL.

Among the institutions in whose success he took an unwearied interest was the General Hospital. This institution is not for the treatment of city patients alone, but is open to patients from the various municipalities in different parts of the Province, where they receive the best medical advice and attention which the country can afford. He was Hospital Trustee for the Board of Trade in 1868 and 1869, when the stoppage of the annual grant by the old Government of Canada, and the uncertainty as to the policy which the Government of Ontario would adopt in regard to charitable institutions, left the trustees no alternative but temporarily to close the institution. As soon as it was learned that a grant would be made by the local Government, the building was put in excellent order and re-opened. When Mr. Macdonald took hold of the trusteeship, there was no money in the exchequer; few beds for the sick; the institution crippled, enfeebled, and in bankruptcy. But he took money out of his own pocket to keep it open, sought increased funds, and through his faithful and zealous efforts the benefits of the institution were extended to a larger number of patients and its efficiency greatly increased. During one year he attended over one hundred meetings of the Board, and made a still larger number of visits to the hospital when contagious diseases were in the wards. Each week he went from five to six times around the wards, making himself familiar with the patients and doing what he could for their comfort. He was for some years the Chairman of the Board of Trustees, and in October, 1882, in this capacity he delivered an address to the nurses. The address abounds with valuable suggestions, as the following extracts will show :

12

"You doubtless realize that when men or women are prostrated by disease, they require good air, good advice, *good nursing.*

"All the medical skill they need they have here from gentlemen of high professional ability, and whose labours are rendered without fee or reward, other than the consciousness that they are helping to lessen human misery.

"But patients may receive the best medical advice, they may have the benefit of the best medical skill, and in some diseases, unless they receive the very best *nursing,* they may die.

"Do not underrate your position, then. A nurse, who, from right and pure motives, attends the sick with the care, tenderness and fidelity which ministers to their recovery, is a noble woman, and is engaged in a work for which she will be had in remembrance. In order that you may do this, it is necessary that you should, first, *love your work.* You must have some higher motive than working for so many dollars per month. No one ever made a successful nurse, either in an hospital or elsewhere, who did not feel a deep interest in the work itself.

"In order that such may be the case, go about it pleasantly. If a bright, cheerful, sunny, smiling, winning face is needed anywhere, it is in the hospital."

Young Men's Christian Association.

Full of sympathy with the young, familiar with the circumstances of young men in our cities, Mr. Macdonald could not fail to appreciate the aims and usefulness of such an organization as the Y.M.C.A. He knew that such an agency would be most helpful to young men who had no guidance, no direction, no home influences, no helpful associations; and with a view to improve the moral and spiritual condition of these young men, he with a few others originated this movement in the city in 1852. At a meeting held in Bond Street Congregational Church, in December, 1866, he discussed the value of these associations to the commercial world. Among other things, he said :

"Commerce has attained a magnitude in our day, greater than in any period of the world's history. When the Ishmaelites came down from Gilead to Egypt, bearing spices, balm and myrrh, they came on the 'ships of the desert,' the camels. How wondrous are the transformations produced by commerce even in that land made sacred by so many associations. She is about laying her iron-way for the accomplishment of her purposes to the mountain-city of Jerusalem. What changes have taken place since the days of Columbus. Now the adventurous merchantman sends his goods from continent to continent; our rivers and oceans are filled with vessels from every land. How has science shortened distance, so that what used to take months is now performed in days. Where is the country that is not intercepted with railways, and difficulties at one time considered insurmountable have been overcome with ease ? When a commercial panic takes place we get some insight into the influence which commerce exerts in the world. We read occasionally of firms whose stoppage throws out of employment as many men as are found in the British army, and whose liabilities amount to a sum which one of the merchant princes of Tyre in their days of splendour and glory had never conceived it possible of attainment. Look at the fleets and navy-yards of the world, bonded and other warehouses, the millions of men employed in moving the spices, the

cottons, the flax, the grain, and manufactured goods
of every kind, and we will form some idea of the
power which commerce exerts in the world.   It
appears to be a part of the divine economy that the
products of one country are wanted by another, and
the country having the largest manufacturing ability
is largely dependent upon other lands for agricultural
products, so that neither a failure of crops in the one
instance, nor a suspension of industry in the other,
can take place without being felt by both. Seeing,
then, that these interests are so closely connected,
what a large portion of the human family are identified with commerce.

  " Now, what is the value of the Young Men's Christian Associations to these commercial interests ? What
do they propose to do ? Why, to benefit young men,
the majority of whom are in the marts of trade, by
engaging them in Christian work, getting good themselves, and doing good to others. By the diffusion of
a pure and healthy literature among young men, by
visitation of the sick, by the benefit of Bible classes
and other profitable exercises ; in a word, to provide
a home for young men and make it attractive, introducing them to those whose sympathies are with
them. What an important work this of saving our
young men from the path of the destroyer and leading
them into the ways of pleasantness ! To the young
man himself, how invaluable are such influences in
saving him from bad company and giving him the
best possible education for the stern duties of active
life. Is there any spectacle more beautiful than to
see a young man surrounded by every earthly allure-
ment yet living to God and being able to say amid all
these things, ' O God, my heart is fixed.' "

He rejoiced to see the Association steadily increasing in numbers and in wealth, until it had gained the
prominent position which it now occupies in the city.

When a movement was started for the erection of a building for the Association, he promptly subscribed and greatly assisted in the work. On June 1st, 1872, in presence of a large gathering, surrounded by the leading pastors of the city, as president of the Association he performed the impressive ceremony of laying the corner-stone of Shaftesbury Hall.

In October, 1872, on the occasion of the visit of Lord Dufferin, the Governor-General, to Toronto, a deputation from the Association, consisting of Mr. John Macdonald, President; Dr. Daniel Wilson, B. Homer Dixon, K.N.L., George Hague, John L. Blaikie, J. C. Hamilton, C. A. Morse, William Anderson, S. R. Briggs, W. E. Cornell, R. C. Bothwell, James McDunnough, Thos. J. Wilkie, Secretary, waited upon His Excellency, and an address of welcome was read by Mr. Macdonald.

In 1878 he was a delegate to the International Convention of the Y.M.C.A., held in Baltimore, Md., and was a conspicuous figure in that wonderful gathering When the time came to choose a more central location than Shaftesbury Hall, Mr. Macdonald was one of the leaders in the enterprise of erecting the new and magnificent building on Yonge Street, corner of McGill. At the dedication of this structure, so complete in all its appointments, and so thoroughly fitted for Association work, on the evening of November 3rd, 1887, Mr. Macdonald said :

" The beginnings of most successful men have been humble. The beginnings of this Association were very humble. It was indeed ' the day of small things.'

The Association room was small, about eighteen by thirty-three. The membership was small. The means were small, and necessarily the expenditure was small. But steadily this humble agency kept growing ; kept making its power felt. A bold step was undertaken in the proposal to remove to King Street, at a rent of $200 per annum, with about six times the room which the Association then had. Next came the more thorough organizing of committees, and the need of a secretary, and Mr. Wilkie's connection with the Association, when its increase became marked and permanent. No two names deserve to be treasured more in connection with this period of the Association's history than the names of Wm. Anderson and Robert Baldwin. Now came the still more pretentious project of a building for Association work, and Shaftesbury Hall was the result. Two names are here to be remembered, the names of Mr. George Hague and Mr. Homer Dixon. Next came the Bazaar, in which the ladies raised between $8,000 and $9,000, and from that day onward the success of the Association has been assured. Now comes Mr. Blake's connection with this important work. Indeed, the Association has been the child of the people, and the best evidence that its work has been done well is the confidence with which it has been held by the public. But greater than all the results which we witness in this magnificent building, and all the appointments in connection with it, is the work it has done in character-building for the young men of this city. Very many have been led to Christ through its workers and through its agencies, some of these being among the ministers and others among the Christian workers of this and other cities. The days of which I speak then, ' the days of small things,' were really to this association like the grain of mustard seed, now become a great and stately tree."

In December of the same year he attended a public meeting in Hamilton, and made an eloquent appeal for the erection of a Y.M.C.A. building in that city.

He was twice President of the great conventions held in Canada.

He knew that the future of our country depends upon the young men who are rising to take their place in the Church, in politics and in trade; and that the Y. M. C. A. was one of the most important of all Christian organizations; and to the end of his life he entertained toward it the most cordial affection.

EVANGELICAL ALLIANCE.

The Evangelical Alliance was another organization that appealed strongly to his catholic spirit. Its principles and international character were in harmony with his own love of Christian unity; and his ardent desire was that believers of every name and land should be brought into closer fellowship and co-operation. He was at the formation of the Branch in Toronto, and it secured his adhesion and support. He took a prominent part in its proceedings, and frequently presented its claims before the churches and the public. He was active in the meetings held from year to year during the week of prayer, under the auspices of the Alliance. In October, 1888, a General Christian Conference was held in Montreal, under the direction of that Branch of Evangelical Alliance. One hundred and fifteen delegates from all parts of the Dominion, and representing all evan-

gelical denominations, responded to the invitation of
the Montreal Branch.   Representatives from the
American Alliance and from the parent Alliance in
London were also in attendance.   The conference
continued for several days, with crowded audiences
at each morning, afternoon and evening session.
Papers were read, and discussions held on the most
vital, theological, religious and moral questions of the
day.   On the second day Senator Macdonald gave a
most effective address on " Capital and Labour."

At the close of the conference a Dominion Evangelical Alliance was formed.   The headquarters of
the new organization was to be in Montreal; and in
order to secure the influence and co-operation of
Ontario, Mr. Macdonald was appointed its President.
The honour was unexpected, but though his hands
were full of work, yet he could not decline it.   The
agitation concerning the Jesuit Estates Act and the
appropriation of public funds to this Order followed,
and during the year Mr. Macdonald resigned his
position as President.   But his interest in the Evangelical Alliance never wavered.   He believed that it
was accomplishing a great and glorious work throughout the world in diffusing the spirit of brotherly love
and union among all denominations, and among
Christians individually; in vindicating the cause of
the oppressed, and promoting that peace and amity
which should characterize the relationships of individuals, of churches, and of nations.

IX.

PARLIAMENTARY LIFE.

A life in civic acfion warm,
A soul on highest mission sent,
A potent voice in Parliament,
A pillar steadfast in the storm.
            —*Tennyson's " In Memoriam."*

For some must follow, some command,
    Tho' all are made of clay.
                    —*Longfellow.*

Party has, no doubt, its evils, but all the evils of party put
together would be scarcely a grain in the balance when compared to the dissolution of honourable friendships, the pursuit
of selfish ends, the want of concert in council, the absence of a
settled policy in foreign affairs, and the corruption of separate
statesmen.
                    —*Lord John Russell.*

IX.

PARLIAMENTARY LIFE.

PARLIAMENTARY LIFE.

THE pursuit of politics as a profession is in harmony with the best intellectual tendencies of our age. It is as necessary that we should have in our Houses of Parliament trained and skilled legislators, as that we should have able and professional administrators of the law. Why should not legislation become the business of one's life, just as jurisprudence is the business of the professional lawyer's life? True, the methods of election present serious disadvantages to the study of politics as a science or to the following of it as a calling. A free State must be self-governing, and popular suffrage must be the ultimate sovereign. Hence, the people must be free to call for the services, not only of a class of educated politicians, but also of those who never seriously contemplated a parliamentary career. For this reason politics can never become, like law or medicine, a close profession. Besides, the subjects that call for legislative interposition are so multifarious that no special training, either theoretical or practical, could possibly embrace them all; so that men of exceptional aptitude must be selected irrespective of any preliminary training. Whatever our training, when it comes to pursuits in life,

> Some will lead to courts, and some to camps ;
> To senates, some.

Great interests must be represented by those who are particularly interested in them; and so the rank and file of the Members of Parliament will always be representatives of special industries and interests.

Mr. Macdonald was a citizen of great public spirit, gifted with exceptional insight into public affairs, and as his wealth and leisure increased, he was induced to enter the sphere of legislation. In June, 1863, he became a candidate for the representation of the Western Division of Toronto in the Provincial Parliament. Though a moderate and independent man, he was on the Liberal side of politics.

The requisition inviting him to permit himself to be put in nomination was a very large and influential one, signed by nearly a thousand of his fellow-electors, who expressed their confidence in him as an old resident, an enterprising and successful merchant, a man of ability and integrity, and in every way worthy to represent a progressive and improving city.

Having allowed himself to be nominated, he at once entered the arena, contesting the seat with the Hon. John Beverley Robinson, afterwards Lieut.-Governor of Ontario. He appeared before the electors at meetings, setting forth with clearness and vigour his views; but a personal canvass he would not undertake. He would take no personal means to secure a single vote. With that canvass so exhaustive as to amount almost to a preliminary election, he would have nothing to do. He was ready to fight an open battle, fairly and honestly; but his nature was too sensitive and finely strung to descend to a personal solicitation of support. To his opponent he was generous, chivalric and courteous, and opposed to fraud, intrigues and chicanery of every kind. The result of the election was that Mr. Macdonald was triumphantly returned, the "noble ward" of St. John's alone giving him a majority of over 300. Toronto was lost to the Conservatives, Mr. A. M. Smith, the friend of his boyhood, defeating Mr. Crawford in the east by a majority of over 500, and Mr. Macdonald's supporters giving him almost the same majority in the west. The contest was an honourable one, and he was elected by the independent and honest vote of the people, as a man who would act in the House according to his honest, conscientious convictions.

"What do you think of the House of Commons?" asked Lord Wolseley of Carlyle. The sage of Chelsea answered gruffly, "I think that it is a place in which there are 600 talking asses." Mr. Macdonald entered the House at an interesting period of Canadian history, and he was not a silent observer of the great political drama. He was an original speaker, an effective debater, and took a wide and independent range of outlook. He was not a fighting politician, nor a party man viewing everything from a party standpoint. Compared with many of the parliamentarians around him, he was as porcelain to pottery, being of so much finer material and superior qualities. The degradation of politics filled him with sorrow and misgivings. But he cared for his country, as most men care for party, having no private ends to seek, and desiring only the public weal. There were burning questions under discussion. One of these was the seat of Government: for the Parliament had, since the burning of the buildings in Montreal, been convening alternately at Toronto and Quebec. But the chief question was representation by population. By the constitutional Act of 1791, Canada had been divided into two provinces, Upper and Lower, each having its own legislation of two Houses, and its own Governor. Many abuses had crept in; the Governors really had everything in their own hands, and worked through what is known as the "Family Compact." There was a long struggle for popular rights and responsible government, until the contest culminated in the reunion of the provinces by the Act of Union of 1840. This transferred the supreme power from the Crown to the representatives of the people. The "Clergy Reserves" continued to be a bone of contention until 1854, when the immense land grants were secularized, and the rectorial claims were commuted. But the provinces had been given a fixed and equal number of members in the Legislature. The population of the Lower Province was at first larger than that of Upper Canada. But the rapid growth of the west soon created a demand that this representation should be rectified in accordance with numbers. The disparity between the two provinces, in population, was growing wider and wider; and the call from the British province, for a remedy of these inequalities, became more and more irresistible. The French refused the concession of this principle, on the ground that the apportionment had been made irrespective of numbers. The struggle was carried on with the utmost vehemence, the *Globe* leading, until, in 1857, Mr. George Brown moved in the House that representation should be based upon population, without regard to the separating line between Upper and Lower Canada. The resolution could not be carried, but the antagonism between the two Canadas became so great that legislation came to a standstill; the political machinery could not move; there was a dead-lock. A select committee was appointed to find some solution for existing difficulties, and this committee expressed a strong feeling in favour of a Confederation, which should include all the North American colonies of Great Britian. Party hostilities were suspended, and a Coalition Government was formed with Confederation as its object. Delegates were appointed from the various provinces, and a great conference held. A scheme was promulgated, submitted to the Legislature, and finally adopted. The debate on Confederation, which was opened in the Canadian Parliament, on the 6th of February, 1865, was a long and able one. Every aspect of the question, financial, commercial, political and military, was presented; and Mr. Macdonald made several able and effective speeches.

It is needless to say that the resolutions of the Government were carried. The Confederation Act was passed by the Imperial Parliament, received the royal assent, and Her Majesty's proclamation was issued, bringing the Dominion of Canada into existence on July 1st, 1867. Legally, Confederation was the act of the Home Government, yet the new Con-

stitution would never have been inaugurated but for
the action of the Colonial Legislatures. One of Mr.
Macdonald's main objections was that the scheme was
not to be submitted to the people for approval. The
Constitution would have gained in veneration had it
been the act of the whole community. Strange that
a plan so cordially supported by Parliament should
not have been submitted to the people at the polls.
No doubt the Government lacked courage to appeal
to the country for a constitutional expression of
opinion. Had there been such an expression of public
mind, many difficulties which have since arisen would
have been averted, for the constitution of our great
Canadian Confederation would have been made valid
and sacred by the fiat of the whole people, and not
by their acquiescence alone. As we look back over
the history of the Dominion during the past quarter
of a century, in the light of Mr. Macdonald's spirited
opposition to the proposed plan of federation, it does
not require much discrimination on the part of the
student of political science to observe how remarkably correct were his forecasts of the probable effects
of the measure. The politicians desired it as a way
of escape from the dilemma of dead-lock ; but it is a
question whether Confederation has not increased
instead of lessened these sectional difficulties. And
certainly the financial effects of union, and the increased expenditure attending the working of Confederation, he did not overstate.

In 1865 Mr. Macdonald was re-elected for Toronto
West, and sat until 1867, when the inauguration of

the new Dominion called for the formation of a new
Government. Sir John A. Macdonald, who had just
been knighted, in recognition of his services in connection with the new nationality, was sworn in as
Premier; and in organizing his Government he determined to ignore the old party lines, and have both
political parties represented. To this the Liberals
objected, claiming that the Government was a coalition,
and declaring that the temporary alliance between the
Reform and the Conservative parties should now
cease. Mr. Macdonald received a requisition to stand
for the House of Commons, signed by 1,193 names.
He was opposed by Mr. Harrison, afterwards Chief
Justice of Ontario. Mr. Macdonald occupied an independent and untrammelled position, but the cry
was for union; public feeling was in favour of the
coalition Government, and the union candidate was
sustained. . The contest was conducted with tolerable
good feeling, and without much display of acrimony,
but those were days when practices of rowdyism and
lawlessness were resorted to to interrupt and disturb
public meetings. The hustings was a bear garden.
There was the open system of voting, and the polls
would sometimes be held by the most disreputable
portion of the community, so that, amid howlings and
jeerings, showers of stones and brickbats, and with
blood flowing copiously from wounds received, the
electors recorded their votes.

Mr. Macdonald turned with relief to his business
affairs, until in 1875, a vacancy occurring in the
representation of Toronto Centre, a constituency

13

which had been created in 1872, he was invited to
become a candidate, and was returned by acclamation.
There had been the downfall of the Macdonald Government, and Mr. Mackenzie was at the head of the
Administration.

The existence of party has been characterized as
the very life-blood of freedom.   It seems to be
essential to representative government and to true,
constitutional liberty.   The great evil of this system,
however, is that party politicians are inclined to view
everything from a party standpoint.   While Mr.
Macdonald recognized a parliamentary Opposition as
a necessary and constitutional restraint upon the
Government, yet when his party was in Opposition, he
was always ready to aid in carrying out and perfecting all measures which he believed would promote
the public good; and when his party was in power
he was just as ready to oppose a measure which he
deemed to be injurious to the country.   While thus
an independent Liberal, holding loosely to the ties of
party, and discharging the duties of his trust, he was
recognized as a politician who had no axe to grind,
no favours to ask, no other object to accomplish save
the good of his constituents and the welfare of the
land.   The uprightness and ability with which he
had created and was conducting one of the largest
commercial houses on the continent, was universally
recognized, as well as his unswerving religious principles and high Christian integrity.

During this session an Act was passed which always
afforded him very great satisfaction.   On his motion,

the House was requested to consider the propriety of opening its proceedings with prayer. After some observations from both sides, a committee was appointed, and a report adopted to the effect that prayers should be read by the Speaker of the House in the language most familiar to him, and that members should stand during such service. The practice of the House, established, no doubt, out of deference to the French-speaking members, is the reading of prayers in French and English on alternate days.

The budget speech of this year was the signal for a long discussion of the financial condition of the country, in which Mr. Macdonald took a most active part. He greatly impressed the House by the grasp and practical knowledge of the subject which he displayed.

In 1878 there came another turn in the political wheel. This was the great cataclysmal year for the Reform party. The session was becoming more and more turbulent. The policy of the Opposition, led by that parliamentary wizard, Sir John Macdonald, was a policy of deliberate obstruction, and some unusual scenes were witnessed.

I cannot forbear giving some extracts from a letter from Mr. Macdonald to his wife, which contain a lively description of an event so familiar to many old parliamentarians, when the House sat from Friday at three p.m. until Saturday at six p.m., Mr. Mackenzie then consenting to adjourn until Monday. Lady Dufferin, in her charmingly written " Canadian Journals," and others have given graphic sketches of

the incidents and events of that protracted meeting,
but this letter puts them in a most vivid light. The
debate arose from Sir John Macdonald moving an
amendment to the motion for going into Committee
of Supply, "condemning the conduct of Governor
Letellier for dismissing the DeBoucherville ministry."
The Hon. Luc Letellier, of Quebec, was a Liberal,
while his constitutional advisers were Conservatives.
The high-spirited Governor had performed the
coup d'etat of dismissing the Premier and his col-
leagues, on the ground that his prerogative had
been slighted by his ministers, whose treatment of
him had been of a most unceremonious character.
But it was contended by the Opposition that the
Lieut.-Governor had dismissed his ministers for party
purposes, and in violation of the principles of responsible government. Hence the motion. The ministerial speeches were short, but those on the other side
were long and irrelevant. The events of that dis-
graceful all-night session are here given.

OTTAWA, April 13th, 1878.

MY DEAR ANNIE,—It is now half-past four p.m.,
and we have been sitting for twenty-five and a half
hours. All night, and until half-past eight this
morning, I have been in the chamber. About midnight the House became uncontrollable; the Speaker
was unable to maintain order, and throughout the
night, scenes of wild confusion prevailed. Mr. Hood
and I dined with the Speaker *sans ceremonie*, and
Mrs. Anglin sang for us very sweetly. There appeared

every prospect of our having a division before midnight, but as the night wore on it was evident that such a result was hopeless. When Mr. Plumb, the member for Niagara, rose, matters reached their climax. Members banged desk-lids, playing the "devil's tattoo"; made creaking noises, sang songs, blew whistles, shouted and roared. All order was lost, and confusion rampant. The night wore on. Here and there were groups of men using high words, and excited with drink. I watched the grey light of morning breaking through the stained windows, and changing every moment, as the day gathered strength. Then the gas was extinguished, and in the clear light of morning the appearance of many of the members told of the want of rest through the long night. Breakfast was arranged for at the restaurant, as it was feared a division might be taken suddenly. And so it has been going on all day. Lady Dufferin, Mrs. Stephenson and other ladies from Rideau visited the chamber about three, and stayed for a couple of hours. While they were in, singing began. "Auld Lang Syne," "En roulant ma boule," "Marsellaise," and other songs were sung by several of the members, the House joining in the chorus. As Lady Dufferin rose to go out, someone started "God save the Queen." The House rose and sung it well, and then gave three cheers. Now the day is declining, again the evening shadows are dimly lighting the stained windows, and the long hours will be wasted in a folly that should shame intelligent schoolboys. Some twenty spectators

remained in the galleries all last night, and when it
became known that the House had been in session
all night, the people flocked to the chamber, and
filled the space allotted to strangers. Such a night
and such a sitting I have never seen, and never desire
to see again. What the object is I can hardly find out.
All the speaking is being done by the Opposition,
and it is said that their object is to prevent the result
of the division, which will largely be against them
from being known at the churches to-morrow. Keep
this letter. Very few such instances occur in the
history of a parliament as the one here described,
and years after the matter referred to will not be
without interest. I enclose you a few lines which I
sent to the Premier during the "long sitting," and
with it his reply to me:

> "Will this fight close to-night,
>   Or will it pay to give another day
>   To this matter of Letellier?
>   If this be so, then off I go;
>   I'll do what's fair, I'll find a pair;
>   But if you'll fight till morning light,
>   I only have to say 'all right.'"

The Premier's reply:

> "The fight must close to-night,
>   'Twill never pay to waste another day
>   Even for Letellier—
>   At least, I think so; so don't you go.
>   No kind of pair is half so fair
>   As thine own face.
>   Far better stay and share the fight,
>   Than turn your back, and say 'Good night.'"

On the Monday ensuing, when the question was voted, the division stood 112 to 70. The Reform administration had encountered many difficulties, and Mr. Kackenzie's premiership had been accomplished under great disadvantages.

On the 10th of May, Parliament was prorogued and members left the Capital to enter upon one of the most keenly contested elections ever held. The National Policy was inaugurated. The people declared in favor of protection. The Liberals met with disaster all along the lines, particularly in the cities. Toronto East was carried by the Conservatives with a majority of 700; Toronto West, of 639; and Toronto Centre was carried by Mr. Robert Hay, a manufacturer, by a majority of 490. The friends of Mr. Macdonald still maintain that he would have been elected had not the accident in his warehouse, to which we have already referred, so occupied his attention that he could give no time or attention to the political campaign. We have already said that he would never conduct a personal canvass, but his platform addresses were needed to carry the constituency. Mr. Macdonald accepted his defeat with perfect resignation, and, relieved of Parliamentary duties, he was able to give more fully his time and energies to business, the interest of the Church, and the various objects of Christian philanthropy.

As a politician, Mr. Macdonald always felt and acted as though answerable to God for his parliamentary as well as for his personal life. He mourned the prevalence of corruption among politicians, and often

spoke of the foul and fetid atmosphere in which they
lived at Ottawa. They met together in the great
arena of a nation's fortunes, as jockeys meet upon a
race course, to decide upon the methods they should
adopt to overthrow their opponents; and then would
sally out to corrupt the people with money filched
from their own pockets, or stolen from the public
treasury. He also mourned the deadness of the
public conscience, the moral lethargy of the people,
to the evils that were bringing shame upon the
reputation of the country. There was an apathy
and indifference like the *vis inertia* of a glacier, and
as well try to quicken the march of the *mer de glace*
as rouse the masses to drive out of public life any
one great political party guilty of dishonesty and
fraud. Mr. Macdonald remained for nine years in
private life, until in November, 1887, he was appointed
to the Senate on the nomination of his personal
friend, but political opponent, Sir John Macdonald.
The appointment was a very popular one, as his
native capacity, administrative experience, and practical knowledge of the world were well known
throughout the Dominion. That Mr. Macdonald was
legitimately gratified by the appointment goes without saying. Whether he would have preferred the
roses and raptures of strife in the House of Commons to the lilies and languors of the Upper House
is a question; but he had crowded into the past
twenty-five years the activities of an ordinary lifetime, and it was time for him to think of taking rest.
At the opening of the Senate debates of 1888, we

find him busy in introducing bills of various kinds and speaking to various questions.

But the most important of all was his action on the Sabbath Observance petitions presented to the Senate, when the Hon. Senator moved:

"That an humble address be presented to His Excellency the Governor-General, praying that His Excellency will be pleased to cause to be laid before this House a detailed statement of all petitions, with the source from which they have emanated, from the year 1881 to the year 1888, inclusive, praying for the better observance of the Lord's Day."

The session of 1889 was also an active one. On March 7th, Senator Macdonald delivered a speech on the imports and exports of the Dominion. He was an authority on the subject, and his utterances thereon commanded the respect and attention of the Senate.

On the 8th of April, when the question of discriminating duties against the Mother Country was being discussed, Senator Macdonald, from his long experience as a successful merchant, gave great pertinency to the debate in a very piquant address.

On April 29th, there was brought before the Chamber an Act for the "Prevention and Suppression of Combinations formed in Restraint of Trade," upon which Mr. Macdonald spoke with great earnestness, concluding with these words:

"I have throughout my business steadily refused to have anything to do with any kind of combination, and looking along the business experience of my own life, I find that the men who have been most successful have been those who have had the courage of their convictions to carry on their business on their own principles."

This was the last session that he ever attended. When the session of 1890 opened on January 16th, he was too ill to attend, and on the 4th of February he had passed away.

X.

PULPIT AND PLATFORM.

Character is higher than intellect. . . A great soul will be strong to live as well as to think.

—R. W. Emerson.

Life is not measured by the time we live.

—Geo. Crabbe.

PULPIT AND PLATFORM.

WE select, out of a great mass of Senator Macdonald's sermons and addresses, only a few. They reflect the real character of the speaker, and will be read with much interest. His sermons all show that deep and penetrating insight into the Word of God, which only a thoughtful and constant study of the Scriptures under the guidance of the Divine Spirit could impart.

The Bible was to Senator Macdonald a living book adapted to this nineteenth century with all its wants and sorrows and sins. He studied it in its practical application to our everyday life. He had a fund of scriptural knowledge, and the rare felicity of touching a secret spring in some well-known passages, thereby opening up some fresh vein of edifying thought, or causing some precious truth to leap forth where its presence had not even been expected. He is intensely practical; his themes are not subjects "up in the air," but adapted to strengthen faith and incite to nobler, holier living.

The address is selected from his missionary speeches. There is no marked originality; no new truths are uttered; but it is forcible and earnest. The speaker is carried forward with fervency, and at times he rises to the heights of true, impassioned eloquence.

As these sermons and addresses, a few out of a great number, all carefully written out, are read, it must excite surprise how such a busy man could find time for such thorough preparation. It exhibits not only his great industry, but also the variety and versatility of his intellectual powers, and his fixed purpose to fill up his life with the best and noblest well-doing.

I.

"This book of the law shall not depart out of thy mouth; but thou shalt meditate therein day and night, that thou mayst observe to do according to all that is written therein: for then thou shalt make thy way prosperous, and then thou shalt have good success."—JOSHUA i. 8.

These words were spoken to Joshua by the Lord just after the death of Moses. The occasion is most impressive. "Moses, my servant, is dead." What a world of meaning in this sentence! How our minds are impressed with the thought that God's ways are not as our ways; that no man is so needful to Him, whatever be his record, his ability, his influence, his wealth or position, that he cannot be dispensed with. One would have thought that, if there was any man who was needed at this period of the history of the Jewish people, it was Moses; he who had gone unto Egypt's monarch and had said to him in the name of the Lord, "Let my people go" He had seen His wonders in the Egyptian overthrow; had witnessed the murmuring and rebelling of the people as they journeyed through the wilderness; had often pleaded with God on their behalf, nay, had incurred His displeasure through the hastiness which their ingratitude and rebellion had provoked. He had guided them to the very borders of the Promised Land, but he is not permitted to lead them into it.

What are we to understand by these words? What does prosperity mean? We know what the world means by success. It is the possession of enormous means, no matter how acquired, whether honestly or otherwise, whether by inheritance or by labour, whether by skill or by accident, possession is all that the world looks at; and whether the wealth consists in land, mines, timber limits, the increase growing out of large manufacturing interests, or out of a professional practice, or out of immense sums invested, the world is ready to speak of such persons as successful men. It is well that we should be clear upon the point that such conditions are not the ones implied in this passage.

The world again judges of the measure of success by the position occupied by the individual. Hence, if in addition to his great means he is placed in a position of honour and responsibility, the world speaks of him as being born under a lucky star, as being phenomenally successful. Here again such a condition may be wanting. There may be nothing in the condition of the godly man, so far as wealth or position is concerned, to distinguish him from the mass of his fellows; and yet, viewed from the standpoint of the Word of God, his way may have been made prosperous and he may have had good success. All this must be very clear to anyone who has taken the trouble to think over it. If it meant gold and silver, houses and land, then it follows that everyone who obeyed the command would be seized with these varied possessions; that if this prosperity and success meant high position in the municipality and the State, then these positions would be filled by those who so acted. But as we find that this is not necessarily the case, we must look for some other definition of the phrase. Indeed, as the word success is understood in everyday life, it is applied as often to a bad cause as to a good one. A man breaks into your house, he gets away with his plunder, and it is said that he succeeded in robbing the house. The same may be said of almost every form of wrong-doing in which people effect their purpose without bringing themselves under the penalty of the law. The best definition which we can give of success is 'the favourable or prosperous termination of anything attempted.' We will make a great mistake if we associate it in every case with the possession of means and influence, a mistake only equalled by that which leads us to conclude that where these are wanting there are wanting also the evidences of God's favour and God's approval. The world calls a man who has acquired means, even dishonestly, a successful man ; the Word of God calls him a fool.

Consider what the term success refers to in the case of Joshua. He had led three millions of people into the country of an enemy ; before him lay a river which had to be crossed. What was he to do? Construct pontoon bridges? No. Beyond that, a walled city. Was he to employ battering-rams? No. Behind the walls, the inhabitants. How were they to be overcome ? " This book of the law shall not depart out of thy mouth." That river will prove no obstacle ; those walls will fall down before you, and the people will be discomfited. Yet even these promises would have availed nothing had not Joshua applied the wisdom that God had given him, and implicitly followed the divine teaching. It does not mean that he was to sit with the book of the law before him day and night; but that his entire conduct was to be framed in accordance with the law of the Lord.

How does the text instruct us, as to what is meant by " good success " ? There are those, we have no doubt, who, if they could but realize that, by reading the Bible daily they would thereby secure the ad-

vancement of their worldly schemes, would become
constant readers of the Word. But that is not the
idea contained in the passage. We are not taught
that any ambitious project, any speculative undertaking, any questionable business, any undertaking good
and laudable and even well pleasing to God is to feel
the touch of this wonderful passage unless there is a
putting forth of all lawful means for the purpose of
securing ends that are in all respects lawful. We
may fairly dismiss the idea that it has a relation to
the getting of gain, and may safely conclude that it
means rather that in our undertakings, whether they
relate to the support of our families, or in any plans
consistent with the spirit of God's Word, if we would
to the largest possible extent succeed, the Word of God
must be followed.

What book is this to which reference is made? It
was that book which Moses commanded should be put
into the Ark of the covenant of the Lord that it might
be there "for a witness." The one grand truth upon
which the whole fabric rests is that God has revealed
himself to His people by giving them a law for their
guidance, and has declared that obedience to the same
will secure for them His favour and affection.

I have said that belief in a great Being who has
created and upholds all things by the Word of His
power, is essential to our happiness. God did not ask
His people to accept His bald statement that He was
their God, without coupling that statement with another which none but God could make. Referring
to the exhibition of a power which none but Almighti-
ness could perform, He said : "I am the Lord thy God
which brought thee out of the land of Egypt."

Remember that this book which is now said to be
uninspired, this book which it is said cannot endure
the searching ordeal brought to bear upon it by modern science, teaches supreme reverence to God, loyalty

14

to the sovereign, love to our fellowman, respect for and obedience to parents, the rendering of honour to the aged, aid to the poor, and the observing of everything which is deemed essential to our happiness and well-being.

But if it was important that Joshua should meditate in this book of the law day and night, how much more important for us who have the complete Bible, and that Saviour whom the law only shadowed with its types and figures, that we should meditate therein—we who have the story told us " of all that Jesus began both to do and teach, until the day in which He was taken up, after that He through the Holy Ghost had given commandments unto the apostles whom He had chosen "—told us by men who were eye-witnesses and ministers of the Word from the beginning—we to whom Christ is not far off but very nigh, who have but to accept His invitation and rely upon His gracious promises. Surely, if it were important that Joshua should meditate upon the book of the law, it is more important that we should meditate in addition upon the Gospel. Surely if in his case his way would be made prosperous and he should have good success, this result will not be less certain than in ours. The sailor who is making for his port is dependent upon his chart and his compass. The soldier who is going to battle is guided by his marching orders. The Word of God is more to us than compass or marching orders. It is light in darkness, guidance in difficulty, comfort in sorrow, strength in weakness; it is our stay in death.

Ordering every act of our life by the teachings of that Word, following its counsels, making it in short the rule of our conduct, we cannot but be prosperous, because we shall live in the enjoyment of God's favour and His loving-kindness which are better than life.

II.

"And there were certain Greeks among them that came up
to worship at the feast: The same came therefore to Philip,
which was of Bethsaida in Galilee, and desired him, saying,
Sir, we would see Jesus."—JOHN xii. 20, 21.

More than fifteen hundred years before the events
recorded in this chapter, God had brought His chosen
people out of Egyptian bondage by a great deliverance. The feast to which reference is here made was
the feast of the Passover, commemorative of this
deliverance. To this feast came, among others, certain Greeks, to whose presence and to whose desire
to see Christ we are indebted for the comforting
words found in the verses from the 23rd to the 30th.

We are at the outset drawn towards these Greeks.
They had come to the great city to attend the feast.
They were proselytes, but the main attraction for
them is to see Jesus. There are some who, as soon
as they leave home and go to some great city, feel
relieved from the restraints under which they are at
home, and are seized with a desire to see things
which they would not think of seeing when at home.
Well would it be if they would remember that what
is wrong at home cannot be right away from home,
and that whether known or unknown, the Christian's duty is always to glorify God. But a passion
stronger than that of seeing the sights of Jerusalem
influenced these Greeks. It was to see Jesus. This
was all the more remarkable because of the circumstances of His life. He had no regal splendour, no
outward show; there was no earthly patronage at His
disposal. Let us see if we can discover what it was
about Christ which made those Greeks so anxious to
see Him. Everything relating to Him was at the
time a matter of common conversation—His appearance, His words, His miracles, His claims to the Mes-

siahship. The question among the people was, "What think ye, will He come up to the feast?" When He entered the city, so great was the demonstration that even the Pharisees, who were plotting His destruction, said, "Perceive ye how we prevail nothing? Behold, the world has gone after Him!"

These Greeks, probably, had become worshippers of the true God, from conviction and investigation. It is reasonable to suppose that they had some knowledge of the prophecies relating to the Messiah, and because of this they were anxious to see Jesus. Then it is by no means unlikely that they were familiar with many of the incidents of His life: how lepers had been cleansed, how devils had been cast out, how the dead had been raised by His power. They had heard of His control over the elements, how He even walked upon the waters, and had stilled the tempest. Perhaps His own tender utterances had reached their ears; they may have heard of His Sermon on the Mount, of His conversation with Nicodemus, and with the woman of Samaria. His fame went throughout all Syria, so that there is nothing wonderful in the earnestness manifested by these Greeks to see Him. Even in the prison of John the Baptist, which proved also to be the place of his execution, the fame of Jesus had found its way. There John had heard of the words of Christ, and had sent two of his disciples to ask of Him, "Art thou he that should come, or look we for another?" Surely, then, it was not strange that He who so filled the public vision, whose name was on all lips, to whom the afflicted came in troops to be healed, should have been to those Greeks an object of great interest, and that they should come to Philip, saying, "Sir, we would see Jesus."

We come now to consider the object of this visit— not to be cured of any malady, not to gratify any idle curiosity, so that they might say that they had seen him. They had probably heard the shouts of the multitude, and, possibly, joined in the triumphal procession. We must look, therefore, for some other reason. They came in the spirit in which Nicodemus had come, that they might learn the things pertaining to the Kingdom. How did they come? Nicodemus had come by night. He was a prominent man, equally impressed with the sayings and doings of Christ. His position and his experience gave him greater confidence, and he does not ask any one of the disciples to bring him to Jesus. These Greeks did not belong to God's chosen people. They were strangers in Jerusalem, and hence hesitated. "Where can we find Him?" "How will He receive us?" "Who will go with us?" It appears to us that all these questions would present themselves to their minds. Possibly they inquired who would be best able to bring them to Christ. If so, no answer would be more readily given than this: "Find Philip, he will tell you where and when He can be seen." At any rate, him they sought. Philip goes at once to Andrew, and then Andrew and Philip tell Jesus — in other words, bring Jesus to them. The carefulness of Scripture record is very striking in the description given of Philip. It was Philip of Bethsaida, of Galilee. If not so described, the whole beauty of the reference would be lost — if it had been Philip the Evangelist, for example, or merely Philip, for there were many Philips—but if we turn to the first chapter of John, we at once find the connection: "The day following Jesus would go forth into Galilee, and findeth Philip, and saith unto him, Follow Me. Now Philip was of Bethsaida, the city of Andrew and Peter." This reference to Andrew and Peter is significant, in view of the fact that Philip sought Andrew, and that together they brought the Greeks to Jesus. Christ first found Andrew, he went and found his brother Simon and brought him to Jesus. The next day, it is recorded, Jesus found Philip. Philip finds Nathanael and says to him, "We have found Him of whom Moses in the law and the prophets did write." Here is the key to the incident recorded in the text. We see how his own mind was impressed with the truth that Christ was the Messiah, and how fitting it was that he who had brought Nathanael to Christ should also have been the one who, in connection with Andrew, brought these Greeks to Jesus.

What was the result of their interview? The communication to them, and through them to us, of God's plan of salvation; the declaration to them of those astounding realities, so full of mystery that angels desired to look into them. To them, Christ appears first to have made the announcement of His approaching crucifixion. "The hour is come that the Son of Man should be glorified." He taught them from a figure familiar to us all that it was needful that He should die: "Except a corn of wheat fall into the ground and die, it abideth alone; but if it die, it bringeth forth much fruit." This He subsequently in other words made manifest to His disciples. Then follows the declaration, " He that loveth his life shall lose it; and he that hateth his life in this world shall keep it unto life eternal."

Attachment to His cause must be stronger than love of life. His service makes no provision for lukewarm followers, or for ambiguous positions. How abundantly were these Greeks repaid for the intense interest which they manifested in their desire to see Christ!

What are the lessons of the text? How may they be turned to our profit?

1. Christ should be the object of our search. True,

we cannot see Him as they saw Him—cannot catch the words as they fell from His lips; but they are still spirit and they are still life, and in them and through them we may find that same Saviour. We have the fulfilment of His own promises: "And I if I be lifted up from the earth, will draw all men unto Me."

2. But if we would imitate these Greeks in their sincerity and earnestness, we must attend to this matter without delay. They did not say, " We will see Jesus by and by," or " The next time we come to Jerusalem." They make it their urgent business. They find out Philip and say, " We would see Jesus." We can come to Christ in response to His own invitation, and can hold communion with Him in prayer. Can we afford to be indifferent where they were so importunate ? Are we willing that they should surpass us in wisdom in matters of such infinite importance? Are we willing to do without blessings which they deemed of such value ? Let us imitate their example, and like blessings with theirs will be ours.

Have we any evidence of the result of this interview ? I think we have. We have many references to the manner in which the Greeks embraced the faith. One will suffice. Paul preaching at Thessalonica, as his manner was, stated that "Christ must needs have suffered and risen again from the dead; and that this Jesus, whom I preach unto you, is the Christ." And some of them, it is said, " believed, and consorted with Paul and Silas; and of the devout Greeks a great multitude, and of the chief women not a few."

III.

"And many of the Samaritans of that city believed on Him for the saying of the woman, which testified, He told me all that ever I did."—JOHN iv. 39.

Our text occurs in connection with Christ's interview at the well with the woman of Samaria. More, perhaps, than from Christ's utterances in His public ministrations, do we gather from His conversation with various persons, the objects of His mission to the earth. In His conversation with Nicodemus we are taught the absolute need of the new birth, and the marvellous love of the Father in the gift of His only begotten Son. Next in the order of time, we have this interview with the Samaritan woman..

Christ had left Judea for the purpose of going into Galilee, and must needs pass through Samaria. It was noon when he reached Sychar, and while resting Himself, the woman came to draw water. He asked her for a drink, and the woman expressed surprise that He, being a Jew, should request a favour from a Samaritan. Christ said, " If thou knewest the gift of God, and who it is that speaketh to thee, thou wouldist have asked of Him and He would have given the living water." A gift is that which comes without equivalent, and a free gift is that which is given without asking. Christ stood before her as God's free gift, and the living water, by its refreshing, satisfying and purifying qualities, is a fit emblem of the Holy Spirit. The woman, though thoroughly interested, did not comprehend His meaning, and still refers to the water of the well. Jesus, to divert her, said, " Go, call thy husband, and come hither," and disclosed such a knowledge of her history that the woman said, " I perceive that thou art a prophet." Then she asked Him to settle the question as to the place where men ought to worship. The Samaritans had, to a certain extent, adopted the idolatrous worship and customs of the nations among whom they mingled, men whom the king of Assyria brought from Babylon, Cutha, Ava, Hamath and Sepharvaim. Christ reveals to her the nature of true worship. "God is a spirit, and they that worship Him must worship Him in spirit and in truth," and finally declares Himself to her as the Messiah. Never had He spoken in such direct terms concerning Himself to His own countrymen, not even to His own disciples. The woman believed, and went and told her neighbours concerning the Christ.

We are to consider the character of her faith, and

1st. It was a faith that was *prompt and decisive.* There are many persons who seem to think that a long preparatory course is necessary before they can become Christians. They must begin by dropping one sin and then another, resisting one temptation and another, until they are able to cease doing evil, and begin doing well. This effort at self-salvation the woman did not try. She found Him at the well who had revealed to her the inmost secrets of her heart, who had told her that He was the Messiah, and then and there, without hesitating, promptly and decisively, she accepted Him as her God and Saviour.

2nd. It was a *clear and triumphant faith.* It is quite true that all people were in a state of expectancy about the promised Christ, and the woman says, "When Messias cometh He will tell us all things." But how different His coming from what she expected —not with pomp and observation, not with a great revenue, but as a footsore and weary traveller, asking her to give Him to drink, speaking thus to a woman contrary to the customs of all Eastern countries. Would not unbelief suggest then, as now, Can this be the promised Saviour? And the reply would needs be, "Impossible." Was it not so with His own people? " He came to His own, and His own received Him not." Nay, more, they sought His life on more than one occasion, because He had made Himself equal with His Father. To the Jews who had witnessed His miracles, He was constrained to say, " Ye will not come unto Me that ye might have life." How different with this woman! There had not been the performance of any miracle; there had been no display of popular favour with the multitude; nothing to appeal to the eye or the imagination, but He revealed to her the story of her own inner life; also the fact of His Messiahship, and then and there she accepted Him as her personal Saviour.

3rd. It was a *simple and satisfying faith.* It left no room for doubt or uncertainty. There would have been room for both with many persons. Had she been disposed to reason, she might have said, " How is it, if He be the Messiah, that there are about Him all the evidences of poverty? Why this weariness? And even if He has read my inmost heart, why is it that He is dependent upon me for a drink of water? Could He not command the water to flow? Why, again, had He sent His disciples to buy meat? Could He not easily command the stones about Him to be made bread?" Should not such thoughts have come to her mind, for they had been addressed to Him by the tempter? It was not strange that those who had beheld the five barley-loaves and the two small fishes mysteriously multiply in His hand, until the wants of the five thousand men were satisfied, should say, " This is of a truth that prophet that should come into the world"; but here was no miracle. Here the God-man was waiting by the well; His disciples had gone into the city to buy meat; and although in answer to the request of His disciples on their return, that He would eat, He said, " I have meat to eat that ye know not of," the question might still present itself to her mind, Why was it needful that His disciples should go at all ?   But her faith was triumphant, and it was satisfying. "He told me all that ever I did, surely this is the Christ."

The woman went to the well not expecting to see the Messiah. She went in the performance of her daily work, and there she found Him who was the Saviour of the world. The people went to Capernaum, not that they cared for Divine instruction, but for the loaves and the fishes. The woman, without observing the performance of a miracle, accepted Christ. Of the people who followed Him to Capernaum, the Master said, "Ye also have seen Me and believe not."

4th. *Her faith was saving, and consequently well-pleasing to God.* We greatly mistake that it is only the scholarly and cultured who can believe Christ's record of Himself, who can exercise that intelligent faith which takes Christ as a personal Saviour. This woman, from all that we can gather, was a plain woman, in no way above her fellow-countrywomen ; yet she stands before us exercising a faith which, for its sincerity, its earnestness and its simplicity, is worthy of imitation by every earnest seeker after God—a faith which has given courage to many a a stricken and wearied one, and which, throughout all time, will go on doing its work of helping and encouraging all who, like her, desire to find the Saviour.

5th. *But her faith was sublime.* When we consider that it was only by slow degrees that the disciples became fully impressed by the character of Christ and the nature of His mission, the conduct of this woman, in her ready and unreserved acceptance of Christ, is simply remarkable. His brethren say unto Him while He was in Galilee, "Depart hence, and go into Judea, that thy disciples also may see the works that thou doest. For there is no man that doeth anything in secret, and he himself seeketh to be known openly. If thou do these things, show thyself to the world." Literally, "Do not stay in a small place like this. If you are the Messiah, go to Jerusalem. Go to the capital, that your works may be manifest there." And then it is added, " For neither did His brethren believe on Him." And so, in the whole compass of early discipleship, we shall find it difficult to instance a faith so sublime as that of the woman of Samaria.

We come next to consider the results of her faith, first, upon herself; second, upon her neighbours. To ascertain the results upon herself, we are not to look to her utterances to Christ so much as to her actions. She did not say, with Thomas, "My Lord and my God "; nor with Peter, " Lord, thou knowest all things—thou knowest that I love thee "; nor with Saul of Tarsus, " Lord, what wilt thou have me to do?" Yet, she did what all of these would have done, if her actions are to be regarded as indicative of her gratitude and her trust.

She was so filled with joy that she began immediately to tell what had been done for her. She began to invite others to come, that like blessings might be secured for them. Notice the steps. She left her water-pot. She went her way into the city. She spoke to the men, saying, " Come, see a man which told me all things which I ever did. Is not this the Christ?" In the case of the people who had seen the miracle of the loaves, Christ makes a distinct charge of unbelief, saying, " Ye also have seen Me and believed not." This woman, in her ready, willing and earnest engagement in God's work, shows how fully she had the approval of Christ. What would the men think who were addressed by her? Perhaps, that she was mad. Most people who

are intensely in earnest about the salvation of others'
are deemed mad. That disease is not chargeable to
us, for the simple reason that we interest ourselves so
little about the salvation of others. But her earnestness, her persistency, her changed aspect, her happy
condition dissipated their first impression, and in
consequence many of the Samaritans of that city
believed.

"Come, see a man which told me all things which
ever I did. Is not this the Christ?" They came.
Observe, she did not say, "Go." She is ready to
accompany them. They went. They saw Christ.
They heard His testimony, heard for themselves, and
believed on Him. In this connection, we notice that
scholarly training is not absolutely necessary in
order to declare unto others the way of salvation.
Indeed, there may be great learning, and at the same
time great ignorance as to the plan of salvation.
That which is of most importance this woman possessed, namely, to be able to speak from experience
of the pardoning grace of our Lord Jesus Christ.
"He told me all that ever I did." This was the kind
of preaching which confounded the Pharisees. "One
thing I do know, that whereas I was blind, now I
see."

What does the Church need to-day? This woman's
faith; this woman's singleness of purpose; this
woman's devotion. The Church needs her faith, childlike, yet sublime, prompt and decisive, clear and triumphant. The Church needs her singleness of
purpose. It is as true to-day as in the days of Christ's
flesh, that we cannot serve God and Mammon. The
Church needs her devotion. She wants workers who
can tell and who will tell what Christ has done for
them, that others may be saved. Why are these
wanted? Some there are who have nothing to testify.
They have never passed from death unto life, and

cannot speak of the change. Others fear to speak of what they have experienced. They are cowards, afraid to show their colours.

The lessons of the text: (1) That Christ can be found at any time and in any place. The woman found him at the well, while attending to her daily duties; so we may find Him, whether it be in the workshop, the office, or the home. (2) The diligent employment of our time secures for us the best opportunities for turning our advantages to account. (3) The case of the woman of Samaria should put to rest any doubts we may have about the possibility of instantaneous conversion. Nothing can be more certain than that she went to the well without the knowledge of Christ, and that she went from it, not only as a saved woman, but as the first apostle of Christ in Samaria. (4) It establishes the value of testimony, as a means of bringing sinners to Christ. It is a practical endorsement of the class-meeting as a means of grace, for it means nothing more than a recital of God's dealings with His people. (5) It shows that the agencies which God employs for the accomplishment of His purposes are not always gifted people, the prominent, wealthy and influential, but the simple, the poor, the obscure. Finally, it teaches us that work done for Christ is so far-reaching in its consequences that the results for good cannot be estimated. Many of the Samaritans of that city believed. How many? How many more did they influence? Every day in our reading and study of God's Word, in the public ministration of His house, the wonderful faith of this woman is inspiring others, and with great appropriateness might the words of Christ, spoken in reference to another woman, be applied to her: "Verily I say unto you, Wheresoever this gospel shall be preached in the whole world, there shall also this, that this woman hath done, be told for a memorial of her."

Missionary Address, delivered in the Bloor Street Methodist Church, Feb. 1881.

The objects of our missionary meetings are to present annually a state of our missionary work on the various fields of labour, in order,

1st. That we may realize properly the thankfulness we owe to God for casting our lot in a land of gospel light.

2nd. To present the claims which the heathen world have upon us, as professing Christians.

3rd. To enkindle a greater interest in their behalf.

4th. To call forth that spirit of liberality which God expects from His people.

There can be no right appreciation of our obligations where there is no right conception of God's goodness. In other words, we cannot feel for the darkness of others if we ourselves have not been brought out into the light—no sympathy for them in their sin and misery, if we ourselves have not tasted of the good things of the Kingdom. We must ourselves be able to speak of God's goodness from conscious experience before we long to make it known to others.

These anniversary meetings are, among others, the means by which we make known the claims which the heathen have upon us. No one would turn from his door a famished man who sought bread. If your neighbours in an adjoining township were famishing, you would feed them. Who is my neighbour? He whose story of want and suffering is brought home to me, and whether it be the Bread of Life, or the bread that perisheth, you are bound to furnish him with both according to your ability.

But these meetings are intended to enkindle in our hearts a greater interest in behalf of the heathen.

Sitting by our own blazing fire, in our own comfortable homes, how apt are we to forget that a storm is raging without, and that there are those who are exposed to its pitiless fury. Enjoying the blessings of the gospel ministry, how apt are we to forget that there are those who have never heard the good tidings. To sound in our ears the fact that our fellowmen are perishing, and to awaken in us a deeper interest in their behalf is what ought to be accomplished by our missionary meetings; and, finally, to call out a spirit of liberality such as the circumstances demand, and such as God expects.

On the beautiful tablet in Westminster Abbey, erected to the memory of John and Charles Wesley, are these two sentences, "The world is my parish," "God buries His workmen, but carries on His work." The last has had its illustration in this church; two of its most honoured members have been removed—two of its most earnest, devoted and liberal workers—Mr. Robert Wilkes and Mr. John Bridgland. God has buried His workmen, but He is carrying on His work. And if the work is not only to be maintained, but extended, then greater responsibility rests upon those who remain. The other sentence was the motto of Wesley, and it is only when as Methodists we grasp them in their comprehensive sense and are influenced by them that we are in a spiritually healthy condition. "Who is my neighbour," was the question proposed by one anxious to justify himself. We are accustomed to speak of our next-door neighbour, but Christ, by a beautiful parable of the Samaritan, has taught us that every member of the human family is our neighbour, and that while loving God with all our heart, we should in this sense love our neighbour as ourselves. Specially are those our neighbours whose tale of suffering or of darkness and misery is brought home to us, and who are without the gospel. The mistake which we as a Church are making at present is this, that we are not undertaking new work. Men in the Church, as in the world, need novelty and variety. Nowhere as in the Church is there so much room for this, for its resources are exhaustless. Take a journal which caters to public opinion. Let it day after day devote its articles to the discussion of some half a dozen subjects, investing them with no new interest, and its life would be a short one. Take the best business on this continent and let those who direct its affairs be content, with its present methods of doing business, with the number of its customers and the extent of its operations; let it once be said we will not advance, and it begins to decay. Extension is necessary for its very continuance, and if it is to exist at all it must extend. So in the Church. We ought to realize the difference between attempting too much and doing too little.

Our work in Lower Canada ought to be sustained with increased vigour. Our work in Japan is full of interest, but our men labouring there ought to be encouraged and ought to have their hearts made glad by the sympathy felt at every missionary meeting throughout the country, and all this without abating one particle in the interest felt or the support needed for every really destitute domestic mission. If this is not the desire of God's people, what is the meaning of the tidings which reach us from the points where missionary meetings have been held? One reports twenty per cent. advance upon the receipts of last year; another, thirty; another, sixty per cent. We must advance, or we will most certainly fall behind. We cannot stand still. When aggression ceases, decay begins. We cannot be regarded as a Missionary Church and be regardless of our obligations. The people are teaching those who are intrusted with the oversight of this great enterprise, in saying, as they

15

virtually do by their increased contributions, "There is need for more labourers; send them. Here are the means, send the Gospel to lands which have not yet heard it; we will help you." The Missionary Society is now out of debt. This is a great blessing; but are we therefore to refuse to undertake new work and substitute for the spirit of the gospel the spirit of the counting-house? God forbid. The counting-house says: "Let us have the money if you want the goods," and refuses to do anything in which there is not some pecuniary benefit. The gospel says: "Freely ye have received, freely give." The counting-house studies its own interests; the gospel seeks the interest of others. The counting-house absolutely refuses to have anything to do with any who cannot pay; the deep spiritual need, the hopeless bankruptcy of the children of men, is the powerful motive which the gospel has in seeking their deliverance. The counting-house says: "We can take up new work only as you give us means"; the gospel says: "Go into all the world and preach the good tidings to every creature." But there are points from which the Church may gather lessons from the counting-house. The counting-house says: "To be healthy and active we must extend; inaction means decay." Well, will it be if the Church learns this lesson. The counting-house says: "Success can only be achieved by untiring watchfulness and unwearied diligence." It is so in every department of God's Church upon earth.

Now, what is going to be accomplished to-night? Larger subscriptions? Very good; but not all. Never until God's people are all aglow with His love will they live for and labour for His glory as they ought: never will they do all that in them lies for the bodies as well as for the souls of men.

XI.

LITERARY LIFE.

They are never alone that are accompanied with noble thoughts.

—Sir Philip Sidney.

There are few delights in any life so high and rare as the subtle and strong delight of sovereign art and poetry; there are none more pure and more sublime. To have read the greatest works of any great poet, to have beheld or heard the greatest works of any great painter or musician, is a possession added to the best things of life.

—Swinburne, Essays and Studies.

What a wonderful, what an almost magical boon, a writer of great genius confers upon us when we read him intelligently. As he proceeds from point to point, in his argument or narrative, we seem to be taken up by him, and carried from hill-top to hill-top, where, through an atmosphere of light, we survey a glorious region of thought, looking freely, far and wide, above and below, and gazing in admiration upon all the beauty and grandeur of the scene.

—Horace Mann, Lectures on Elocution.

Books, books, books.

I found the secret of a garret room
Piled high with cases in my father's name ;
Piled high, packed large, where, creeping in and out
Among the giant fossils of my past,
Like some nimble mouse between the ribs
Of a mastodon, I nibbled here and there,
At this or that box, pulling through the gap,
In heats of terror, haste, victorious joy,
The first book first.   And how I felt it beat
Under my pillow, in the morning's dark,
An hour before the sun would let me read
My books.

 At last, because the time was ripe,
I chanced upon the poets.

—E. B. Browning.

X.

PULPIT AND PLATFORM.

Character is higher than intellect.   .   .   .   A great soul will
be strong to live as well as to think.

—R. W. Emerson.

Life is not measured by the time we live.

—Geo. Crabbe.

LITERARY LIFE.

AS a class, literature has done little for business men, and business men have done little for literature. Many of our merchants seem to have an aversion to mental pursuits, just as many literary men have a disgust for business occupations. Few literary men have an intelligent appreciation of business, while the majority of business men are so occupied with the pursuits of life that they give little attention to the cultivation of the mind.

It was not so with Senator Macdonald. In the midst of all his activity as a merchant and public-spirited citizen, he was an assiduous student, finding time for self-improvement and giving attention to general and scientific reading.

While a lad at school, he acquired a literary taste; as a young man, he cultivated the acquaintance of the best English authors in prose and verse; as a mature man, he possessed a knowledge of the poets of the day such as few have the ability to acquire or the capacity to retain.

His classical attainments were of no inferior order. He could translate Latin poetry into English verse. Even during his last illness, one evening as he lay upon the sofa, his son Alexander A., who is Classical Master in Upper Canada College, for his amusement gave selections from classical and modern writers, when his father would give the name of the author, and often, to the surprise of his son, completed the quotation.

As early as 1848 his diary contains such references as these :

"July 24. Finished Pope's 'Odyssey' and the 'Battle of the Frogs and Mice.' Pope is certainly an interesting and instructive writer, and justly merits the great fame which his works have acquired for him."

"July 29. Read to-day Pope's 'Rape of the Lock,' a finely finished picture, and Campbell's 'Pleasures of Hope.' Although there are many noble ideas in Hope, considered generally, yet in describing the hope of the Christian he is notably very weak. There is wanting the faith and beauty which characterize the other sections of his poem."

From early life he shows himself a discriminating reader, and he was constantly laying up stores of valuable information. While a lad providing for himself, enduring hard knocks from the world, living on a meagre salary, he was purchasing good and useful books, and laying the foundation for a large library.

As a clerk, he withstood the almost irresistible attractions of city life and the passing pleasures of society, and the evenings that were not devoted to business or religious duties were spent wholly among his books,

> "Holding high converse with the mighty dead."

He committed to memory his favourite passages of an author, and could declaim poetry by the hour.

Had he been absolved from the necessity of earning
his own living, he would no doubt have received a
full university education.   Had his health permitted,
he would have entered the Christian ministry, and
there found fuller scope for the exercise of his literary
gifts, because he was by natural predilection, taste
and habit, scholarly and studious.

When he first set up housekeeping it was on a very
modest scale.   There was no lack of comfort, but
there were no Brussels carpets, no damask curtains,
and no paintings.   One hundred pounds would have
covered all his bills for the furnishing of parlour,
dining-room, bedrooms and kitchen; but there was
one room whose costly furnishing would have put to
the blush many a lordly home.   It was the library,
which then contained over five hundred dollars' worth
of valuable books.

His library was well read, for he had the habit of
marking his books and the dates of his reading them.

One is surprised with the range of subjects.   He
roamed over the whole expanse of literature—philoso-
phical, scientific, ecclesiastical, poetical, historical and
biographical.   He was particularly fond of biography.
Here great men that have lived worthy lives still give
dignity and sweetness to other lives, living again, as
it were, in minds made better by their presence on
the earth.   He was profoundly interested in the life of
Lord Lawrence, the sagacious man, the intrepid soldier,
the far-seeing statesman, and the vigorous administrator; and with a deep reverence for his character
he penned on the fly-leaf of the volume the following:

"To My Dear Boy Jack,—With the earnest hope that the life of this, one of the most extraordinary men which the century has produced, may lead him to apply the lessons which it is so well calculated to teach, and that he may throw into his life-work the same singleness of purpose, the same fine sense of duty and the same unweariedness of effort in its performance.

"Oaklands, *September* 7, 1883."

He read the largest, most helpful thinkers of the day, and never tired of poring over his books. "A good book," says John Milton, "is the priceless life-blood of a master-spirit." He sought the true and right development of his being by communion with these master-spirits. One is surprised that such a busy man could find time to read and write so much. But when he was not engaged in business or public duties, he was always reading. He had his quiet evening hours sacred to study and the cultivation of his family ties. He had the calm, unbroken hours of the Sabbath, for he never allowed any week-day cares to intrude into his Sabbath rest. He has often told me that when the warehouse was locked on Saturday evening, he never allowed any thought of its work till he entered it again on Monday morning. But especially was he relieved of all burdens of family cares. They were all lifted from his shoulders by his devoted wife, who not only threw sunshine into his home, but made it a serene, restful nook, whose moments of calm were undisturbed by a single household concern.

He was never happier than when in his study, arranging and re-arranging his books, devouring some

favourite author, or writing on some theme. Although
only able to give to literature his *horae subsecivae*,
he was essentially a man of letters, and all the delica-
cies and refinements of diction were dear to him.

In addition to what we have given in these
memoirs, he left behind him voluminous writings, all
dashed off in the odds and ends of leisure, but displaying accuracy in punctuation and all the details of
literary art.

He contributed many articles to the *Methodist
Magazine*, under the able and brilliant editorship of
Rev. Dr. Withrow, who always encouraged him in his
literary projects. He also wrote much poetry, for he
had the vision and the power of bodying forth what
he saw in an artistic form. Wordsworth sings:

> " Oh, many are the poets that are sown
> By Nature ! Men endowed with highest gifts,
> The vision and the faculty divine,
> Yet wanting the accomplishment of verse."

He possessed the deep-lying poetry and emotion of
the North ; he possessed also the "accomplishment of
verse." He used the poet's lyre, touching it with
sweetness and grace. His earlier poems are rather
artificial, yet many of them are marked by force and
fertility of diction. His qualifications as a poet
increased with his years, when all his powers were
developed, and his whole nature deepened and enriched. It was wonderful how he preserved throughout a busy life the high poetic mood.

If, according to Mr. Arnold, poetry is simply the
most beautiful, impressive and widely effective mode

of saying things, then we cannot over-estimate its importance.   And if poets are

> " All who love, who feel
>   Great truths and tell them,"

or, as Mrs. Browning calls them, " God's Prophets of the Beautiful," then we should appreciate Senator Macdonald's unusual facility of thought and expression in verse.   Douglas Jerrold characterized certain prose and verse as " prose and worse."   This cannot be said of Mr. Macdonald's writings, for if not marked by great originality, elegance and energy, they have, nevertheless, naturalness and transparency.   He wrote no large work of sustained merit, but he has written a considerable number of exquisite episodes.   His poems could claim an honourable place in any collection of beautiful thoughts.   Here is a selection which, aside from the significance and dignity of the theme, reveals his character and his modes of thought, feeling and expression :

TRUST IN GOD.

Call it not faith to trust in God
    When ample is your store,
And when to barns already filled,
    The Lord is adding more.

Call it not faith to give your tenth,
    While yet nine-tenths remain ;
And while your offering to the Lord
    Is felt not from your gain.

'Tis when the fig-tree blossoms not,
    Nor fruit is in the vine,
The labour of the olive fails,
    Nor corn is there, nor wine.

'Tis when the flock fails from the field,
  Nor herd is in the stall ;
To trust in God then, that is faith—
  The strongest faith of all.

Below is another noble and suggestive poem, which
sounds a note that will vibrate in every true heart.
It reveals the purity and strength of his diction, as
well as his profound emotional impulse :

THE WOUNDED GREY BIRD.

I watched a little grey bird
  As it flew against a wall,
So stunned, so nearly lifeless,
  I saw it helpless fall ;
It gave one gasp and closed its eyes,
  It dropped its bruised head,
And all this in one moment,
  I thought that it was dead.

Between my hands I held it,
  And breathed upon its breast,
As something whispered to me,
  " Now try and do your best."
And soon I felt it struggling,
  And then a kindling glow,
Which told the crisis over,
  Told of the life's blood flow.

I placed it gently on my knee,
  To catch the sun's warm rays,
So strange to see it fluttering,
  For ended seemed its days.
It gathered strength each moment,
  And then with new delight,
It left me to my musing,
  And soon flew out of sight.

How oft in the great city,
  Does many a brother fall,
Stunned like the little grey bird
  That dashed against the wall.

> And wounded bird and man must die,
> 　　We well can understand,
> If someone out of loving heart
> 　　Reach not forth loving hand.

The following lines appeared in the *Evening Journal*, Ottawa, as the flags were displayed at half-mast at the Capital on the occasion of the death of the Honourable Thomas White, Minister of the Interior, during the session of Parliament in 1888:

"THE FLAG AT HALF-MAST."

> Why flies the flag at half-mast
> 　　Which was mast-head yesterday?
> Has one of the mighty fallen,
> 　　Some great one passed away?
>
> Has the rider on the pale horse,
> 　　The rider with icy wand,
> Touched beating heart, and stilled it,
> 　　Of some leader in the land?
>
> The flag which flies at half-mast,
> 　　As it flutters high in air,
> But reads to man this lesson
> 　　That is taught him everywhere,
>
> That man being here abideth not,
> 　　Is cut down as a flower;
> Is like the grass which "cometh forth,"
> 　　Which withers in an hour.
>
> And so the flag at half-mast
> 　　Which was yesterday mast-head,
> Tells in its mournful floating
> 　　Of a gifted statesman dead.
>
> And reads this solemn lesson
> 　　Alike to grave and gay,
> It may float for you to-morrow
> 　　As it floats for him to-day.

Another poem of a similar nature, though its metre is peculiar, yet reads with an admirable expression and power of interpretation. Mr. Macdonald was greatly interested in the life of the London merchant and philanthropist, George Moore. The reading of this biography was one of the decisive moments of his life. He gave a copy of it to each one of his warehouse staff. It was the subject of one of his best lectures, as well as of this inspiring song:

ON READING THE LIFE OF GEORGE MOORE.

When good men die
Are they forgotten ?
From noble lives
Is nought begotten ?
To make men good, and brave, and strong,
Champions of right and foes of wrong ;
To give men higher aims than self,
To make them think and work for others,
To make them feel that men are brothers,
That deeds are better far than pelf ?

When good men die
Are they forgotten ?
From noble lives
Is nought begotten ?
Nothing to break wrong's grievous fetter,
Nothing to make this " wide world " better,
Nothing to arm men for life's fight ;
Nothing to make the warfare sure,
Nothing to help strong men endure
When battling for the right ?

When good men die
They're not forgotten ;
For from their lives
There is begotten

> The noblest purpose, brave and true,
> To aim at what they dared to do ;
>   To find one's work in others' good,
> To spend the life which God has given
> In waging war for God and heaven,
>   'Gainst vice and all its hateful brood.
>
>   When good men die
>   They're not forgotten ;
>   For all of good
>   Which they've begotten
> Is graven as with iron pen
> To help and glad desponding men.
>   The record this of race well run,
> More lasting far than granite pile,
> Or storied urn in abbey's aisle,
>   And then the Master's glad "Well done!"

An ancient bard sings :

> "The poet gathers fruit from every tree,
>   Yea, grapes from thorns and figs from thistles, he ;
>   Plucked by his hand, the basest weed that grows
>   Towers to a lily, reddens to a rose."

So with our poet-Senator, the most common objects of
nature kindled his imagination, exalted his mind, and
made him a heaven-sent messenger of the truth.   On
his way to Sitka, Alaska, the steamship *Elder* cast
anchor in Freshwater Bay, whose mirror-like waters
reflected a rich, thick border of unbroken forest, and
the dark, deep shadows of a lofty range of snow-clad
mountains.

The captain told him that eighteen years before, a
young Englishman serving on board the Admiral's
ship, the United States steamship *Saranac*, was
killed, and that he had been buried here with military

honours. The Senator determined to find the spot,
and secured a Red man as his guide, for

> "The Indian knows his place of rest
> Far in the forest-shade."

He found the grave in a perfect state of preservation,
and with the inscription clearly marked upon the
headstone.

Mr. Macdonald says, " I found myself unconsciously
weaving the story into the following simple lines."
They are exquisitely graceful lines. It was his latest,
and perhaps most tender poem.

THE SAILOR'S GRAVE.

What mean those sounds of music,
  And the dip of the muffled oar,
As those boats in long procession,
  Move slowly toward the shore?

And why are those men armed
  Who are not bent on prey?
Why this imposing pageant
  In the waters of this bay?

See! The Admiral's ship is flying,
  Its flag at half-mast head,
And that boat with its mournful draping,
  It bears a sailor—dead.

See! His comrades gently bear him
  To his lonely place of rest,
So far from his home of childhood,
  From the land which he loved best.

Hear the echo of the volleys,
  As they fire them o'er his head,
Ere with measured steps they leave him
  To slumber with the dead,

Where the wild, unbroken forest
  Throws its shadow o'er the bay,
Its stillness broken only
  By the salmons' sportive play.

In a land whose snow-clad mountains
  Guard, as sentinels, his grave,
Fit resting-place for England's son,
  For one so young and brave.

O England, dear old England,
  Thy sons lie scattered wide,
Some sleep 'neath palms in tropic lands,
  Some by the glacier's side.

But dear is every spot to thee
  Where'er their ashes lie,
And dear to thee is this lone grave
  By this Alaskan sea.

A very grateful tribute to Mr. Macdonald's poetic
genius was given by the venerable and gifted Rev.
Dr. Scadding in his " Toronto of Old."   Alluding to
the lofty pines that once covered the hills on both
sides of the Don, he tells us how a solitary survivor of
this forest of towering trees was long to be seen
toward the northern limit of the Moss Park property,
and that this particular tree has been graphically com-
memorated by an anonymous writer.   He then gives
Mr. Macdonald's poem, " The Old Pine Tree."   Dr.
Scadding himself assured me that, as soon as he had
found out the author, he made fitting recognition of it
in a later edition of his book, where the poem can be
found.

These poems are full of freshness and naturalness.
He is not like Browning, one of the greatest and purest

teachers of the century—most intellectual of poets—
but so careless about being understood as to be fatally
lacking in lucidity of thought and expression, and
who needs an interpreter to wander with us through
the " Palace Beautiful " of his verse.

If culture is, as Mr. Arnold puts it, to know the best
that has been thought and said, then the subject of
our memoir was essentially a cultured man.

But while he read and wrote much, the Bible was
his favourite, all-absorbing study. This is one out
of many of his diary records :

" Read to-day the books of Nehemiah and Esther
with part of Ezra, and twenty-five chapters of the book
of Job; read largely from Trench on the miracles."

He was not a critical student of the Word of Truth.
The critical study of the Bible may be dangerous, but
it is indispensable. There has been created within the
present generation a new type of scholarship called
the " Higher Criticism." It is just as assiduous in
collecting facts as the old, but it brings to their
examination a more critical method. It sifts, com-
pares, analyzes, classifies ; in short, it works induc-
tively instead of deductively. It has been influenced
largely by the developments of science, and manifests
not only great skill and acumen in arranging facts
so as to reveal their true significance, but is also
marked by the spirit of candour, judicial comparison
and the pre-eminent love of truth for its own sake.
There is a broad, an arrogant and flippant spirit of
Bible criticism that must not be confounded with the
more reverent and devout spirit which, however bold

16

and independent in its methods, yet reverences the
" Law of the Lord." Christianity is not afraid to
throw open the gates of her citadel, and allow the
closest scrutiny of its strength.

The Bible has a human origin, as well as a divine,
for no one asserts that it fell, like the fabled statue of
Jupiter, perfect from the skies. But, after the most
fierce assaults, the great body of its truths abide perfectly uninjured, and it stands to-day as it shall ever
stand, the king of books, the Kohinoor among dia-
monds, man's undying treasure, God's eternal Word,
" which liveth and standeth forever."

It is needless to say that with Senator Macdonald's
conservative turn of mind he did not have much sympathy with the new science, nor with the higher critics.
He was not in touch with them.

He read the Bible largely for his own personal
profit. It was the voice of God to his own soul, and
in its simplicity, its calm authoritativeness, its direct-
ness and living power, it seemed to reach the centre
of his being, and to enter into his inmost life. While
its lofty thoughts fired his mind and excited his
admiration, its concentrated and burning rays of
truth were brought to a focus on his deepest heart.
He read the sacred page as God's message to himself,
and could say with the Psalmist: "Oh, how I love Thy
law; it is my meditation all the day."

XII.

BENEVOLENCE.

He is truly great that is great in charity.

> —*Thomas à Kempis.*

The soul of a truly benevolent man does not seem to reside much in his own body. Its life, to a great extent, is a mere reflex of the lives of others. It migrates into their bodies, and identifying its existence with their existence, finds its own happiness in increasing and prolonging their pleasures, in extinguishing or solacing their pains.

> — *Horace Mann.*

To pity distress is but human, to relieve it is God-like.

> —*Horace Mann.*

Who soweth good seed shall surely reap ;
The year grows rich as it groweth old,
And life's latest sands are its sands of gold.

> —*Julia C. R. Dorr.*

They serve God well
Who serve His creatures.

> —*Miss Norton.*

For his bounty,
There was no winter in't ; an autumn 'twas
That grew the more by reaping.

> —*Shakespeare.*

In giving, man receives more than he gives, and the more is in proportion to the worth of the thing given.

> —*George Macdonald.*

BENEVOLENCE.

SENATOR MACDONALD'S life was one of unusual activity. Indeed, he crowded into the
last fifteen years the activities of an ordinary lifetime. A born merchant, shrewd, intelligent, far-
seeing — yet he was a Christian first, a business
man afterwards. Whether his business yielded him
wealth, honour, social position, he held all as a trust
from God, to be used not primarily for his own
aggrandizement, but for the advancement of His
kingdom in the world. It has been well said that
by doing good with his money, a man, as it were,
stamps the image of God upon it, and makes it pass
current for the merchandise of heaven.

There is danger in the getting of wealth. George
Herbert says :

> " Gold thou mayest safely touch, but if it stick
> Unto thy hands, it were death to the quick."

And even Horace, the heathen poet, has told us :

> " Money was made not to command our will,
> But all our lawful pleasures to fulfil ;
> Shame and woe to us if we our wealth obey,
> The horse does with the horseman run away."

It is one thing to get money, it is another thing to
have money get us.

The attempt to win means, as well as their actual
possession, may be either a blessing or a curse. If

it makes us avaricious and hard-hearted, it is a curse, not a blessing.

Senator Macdonald realized that money is a sceptre —that is all; an instrument of power that is to be held for its uses, not for itself. He had the business habits which makes capital. The strictest economy was his rule. But careful for himself he was always lib-eral to others. He had the sense of Christian steward-ship. He was a man of benevolence, a philanthropist in the highest sense of the word. His whole career was an illustration of the integrity, liberality and public spirit which are indispensable in the character of a great, successful, and philanthropic merchant.

He bestowed upon the needy not only money, but that which is often more difficult to give—time and thought and attention. Of what avail our best gifts if the heart be withheld.

> "To the noble mind,
> Rich gifts wax poor, when givers prove unkind,"

Senator Macdonald loved commercial enterprise as a literary man loves literature, or an artist loves art; but he delighted in the acquisition of property, not that he might increase his own comforts and enjoy-ments, but be better able to promote the comfort and alleviate the condition of his suffering fellows.

Avarice, the love of money for its own sake, was as far from his nature as was dishonesty or false-hood. He believed in and practised systematic giv-ing. He started life on this principle. He says:

" The business man who thus acts, never makes a mistake, never injures his business, and is never without means to give. He is always likely to give in increased measure each year; and has no creditors, for no man is more prompt in his payments, nor enjoys a greater measure of happiness, because he draws it from the purest of all sources. Few men give as they ought to give; few men give in proportion to their means. Giving becomes a habit as does withholding also. It may be laid down as a safe rule that few men are reckoned among willing givers who did not commence giving when their means were small, and who gave then as cheerfully as afterwards when means increased. The world owes nothing to the men who are always going to do some great thing, but who never feel that the time has arrived for the unselfish deed. The man who has no heart to give of his little, will never feel that he has anything to share with others, no matter how great his wealth, or how pressing the cause."

When a lad of sixteen, his employers took a deep interest in Queen's College, Kingston, which was about being founded in connection with the Church of Scotland, of which they were members. His salary then was only fifteen pounds; yet he wanted to do something, and after a little thought he put his name down for three pounds. That was Mr. Macdonald's first subscription—one-fifth of his entire income. This first offering was a life-long service to young Macdonald. He had subscribed the money and it must be paid. This meant that he could not squander his small means, but that he must husband them to meet the engagements as they became due. We have in our possession the receipt for the first instalment paid upon this subscription. It is as follows :

"GANANOQUE, *Feb.* 8th, 1842.

" Received of John Macdonald, jun., ten shillings, currency, amount of the first and second instalments due on his subscription to Queen's College.

" W. S. MACDONALD,
" *Local Treasurer.*"

As soon as he commenced business for himself, he opened a donation account, and from that day forward this account had its place on his ledger. The amounts under this head were small for some time. He felt that he had no right to give away that which belonged to others; but he felt also that while his house expenses and the entire management of his business were conducted with economy, he was in a position to be a giver to some extent, and to that extent no creditor ever had a right to find fault with him. Hear him again:

" Business men sometimes shield themselves from giving by saying that they are in debt, and that in justice to their creditors they must first be just, then generous. Hear these gentlemen talk about their business to someone who is soliciting an order from them, or to some friend, and what do they say? ' Best season I ever had.' ' I have done this month half the amount I did the whole of last season.' ' I expect this year to pay my rent out of my discount.' Or, ' I made an offer to-day for a site for a new warehouse.' While to someone seeking a subscription, an hour after, they will say, ' I can do nothing to-day. I am struggling, you know, to establish a business. By and by I hope to be able to help not only this but other objects.' Or perhaps they rudely refuse to listen to the appeal at all, under the plea that they are too busy, or that they never put down their names for show, but give in such a way as that the right hand knows not what the left does. Poor fools! making wealth and at the same time forging a chain with which it will bind them as its slaves: making wealth to embitter in the end their own happiness, passing through life without gladdening any heart, and without experiencing the luxury of making others happy, or realizing the truth of those most precious words, 'It is more blessed to give than to receive.' How much should that man give to benevolent objects whose business produces no profits? Not a dollar. But why does his business produce no profit? Very probably from extravagance or inattention. Let him attend to his business, let him be prudent, economical, and courteous, and his business will soon show results, and he will soon have means with which to help others.

"How much should a man give whose business is prosperous? That will depend upon his income. 'But,' he says, 'my goods are sold on time and may not be paid.' Let him make a fair and reasonable allowance for a rest; let him estimate what his bad debts are likely to be; let him look at the years that have passed and at the results they have yielded; let him look at the season's business in which he is engaged and estimate its prospects; let him weigh the claims of the object, or objects, for which his assistance is sought; let him weigh also the effect which his help will give, and the loss which his refusal would cause, and then give readily and cheerfully, but no more than he can afford."

He experienced all the annoyances that fall to the lot of the reputed philanthropist. While in his office, scarcely an hour passed that he was not called upon by some agent or some needy applicant for assistance.

Many of these would be wholly unknown to him, without references or introductions of any kind, but he was ready to examine every claim and bestow the needed help. Scarcely a mail arrived that did not bring some appeal for assistance.

Senator Macdonald not only honoured the Lord with his substance, but by personal efforts and unwearied labours he did much for the cause of Christian benevolence.

He kept himself near the poor, in daily contact with distress, misfortunes, and privations; he took upon himself a little of their poverty, like the dust of a journey. Every day was full to the brim with good words and good deeds—what Wordsworth calls

> " That best portion of a good man's life,
> His little, nameless, unremembered acts
> Of kindness and of love."

Every day of his life was a blessing to somebody, for he could say with Alice Cary,

> " I hold that Christian grace abounds
> Where charity is seen ; that when
> We climb to heaven, 'tis on the rounds
> Of love to men."

He found many ways of doing good with his money. He gave constantly, by wholesale and by retail. His bounty descended in copious showers on great institutions; it distilled in gentle dews upon not less needy individuals. He gave munificent sums publicly, but more frequently did his benefactions follow humble want to its retreat, and there he solaced misery and sorrow known only to God.

He gave as a prince to the various forms of church work, in erecting churches, making repairs, paying off debts, furnishing parsonages and replenishing Sunday School libraries. He did not approve of costly sanctuaries burdened with debt,

> " But such plain roofs as piety could raise,
> And only vocal with the Maker's praise."

He not only gave largely to missions, but did all in his power to awaken and stimulate in others a like interest.

He was the unknown almoner who offered through Dr. Withrow and other adjudicators one hundred guineas for the best essay on " The Heathen World: Its need of the Gospel and the Church's obligation to supply it."

Another cause very near to his heart was the Superannuated Ministers' Fund, and his appeals on behalf of this fund were fervent and noble.

No one admired more than he the manly qualities and pre-eminent ministerial gifts of Rev. Dr. Wm. Morley Punshon ; no one rejoiced more than he in the great good accomplished by this loan of British Wesleyanism to Canadian Methodism; and no one contributed more than he to give success to his ministrations and labours in all the great movements of the Church, the endowment of Victoria University, the establishment of a Foreign Mission, and church-building.

When, in October, 1871, the news flashed over the wires that Chicago was in flames, his firm at once forwarded a shipment of goods in behalf of the sufferers by fire. The mayor of the city sent back the following telegram :

" God bless you. It is just what we need. Accept the heartfelt thanks of a suffering people for your very generous donation.　　　　　　R. B. MASON."

Mr. Macdonald also sent further contributions, which were gratefully acknowledged by the Chicago Relief and Aid Society.

He was the founder of the Macdonald Bursary in the University of Toronto. If the facilities of commerce have been multiplied and her gains increased by the discoveries of science and the inventions of art, commercial men have repaid the debt by rich gifts to schools and colleges, and noble endowments of institutions of learning where science can be advanced and art promoted.

Senator Macdonald was one of the original promoters of the scheme of University Federation. During the stormy controversy in Methodism over this question, he never wavered for a moment; and his generous offering of $25,000, along with the generosity of William Gooderham, Mr. Cox and others, gave an impetus to the movement in favour of Federation that could not be resisted. *Festina lente.* Events moved quickly. He did not live to see Victoria College rising in the Queen's Park ; but his far-seeing wisdom was indicated, and the success of this educational movement was well outlined in the Convocation address of Chancellor Burwash at the close of the first year of work under the Federation Act.

A leading layman of the Methodist Church, a constant and munificent supporter of all its institutions and funds, his bounty was not confined to his own denomination. He was engaged in humanitarian work of every kind. Of orphanages and asylums he was a generous supporter. It would be difficult to enumerate all the enterprises and efforts—religious, philanthropic, educational—to which he lent his support and aid. A few weeks before his death he gave $40,000 for the establishment of a hospital in connection with the Medical Department of the University, and in his will he made, in memory of his daughter Amy, an additional provision of $60,000 towards the New Park Hospital.

One of his last appeals was in behalf of the Presbyterian Home for Alaskan Girls, in which he says:

"I cannot describe the degradation that exists, neither can I adequately tell of the transformation which has been accomplished in the existing schools through the instrumentality of faithful, loving Christian men and women.

"If every reader of these letters will send me one dollar, or more if they feel disposed, so that sufficient aid will be furnished to this most desirable and much needed object, I venture the statement that never will money have been better spent, never will it have accomplished better results, never have hearts been gladdened more than will be the hearts of the noble missionaries, their wives and the lady missionaries who are doing such grand work among those Indian tribes to-day. . . . All sums sent me will be forwarded to the various points indicated in these letters in such proportion as with my knowledge of their respective wants I deem best, unless the donors should themselves indicate the disposition of such sums as they may feel constrained to contribute."

Senator Macdonald thus gave largely, constantly, cheerfully, and on Christian principle. He believed that God's blessing attended liberal giving. He built upon the adamantine foundation of fidelity to God and man ; and while his business career extended over two or three terrible convulsions, which shook the very pillars of the commercial world, yet they disturbed not the solid basis of his prosperity.

It is said that during the crisis of '57, Mr. Kidston, the head of the great Glasgow house, came out to Canada to inspect Mr. Macdonald's business affairs. As soon as he opened the ledgers, he saw his "donation account," noted with what strictness and fidelity he was discharging his obligation as a steward of his Maker, and he closed the books, saying, " Mr. Macdonald, we will proceed no further. I am perfectly satisfied ; I have no fear of the merchant who conducts his business on such principles."

In a private memorandum to his eldest son, John Kidston, a partner in the firm, he imparted the information that for some years past he had devoted to charitable purposes one-fifth of his income. No wonder he was recognized as a philanthropist, and that the fragrant memory of his virtues and his charities

"Smell sweet and blossom in the dust."

XIII.

TRAVELS.

Sleep safe, O wave-worn mariner;
  Fear not the night, or storm or sea;
The ear of Heaven bends low to hear—
  He comes to shore who sails with me.

—N. P. Willis.

"Hame, hame, hame,
  An' its hame that I maun be;
Hame, hame, hame,
  To my ain counterie."

Windermere! Why, at this blessed moment we behold the beauty of all its intermingling isles. There they are—all gazing down on their own reflected loveliness in the magic mirror of the air-like water, just as many a holy time we have seen them all agaze when, with suspended oar and suspended breath—no sound but a ripple on the Naiad's bow and a beating at our own heart—motionless in our own motionless barque—we seemed to float midway between that beautiful abyss between the heaven above and the heaven below on some strange terrestrial scene composed of trees and the shadows of trees, by the imagination made indistinguishable to the eye; and, as delight deepened into dreams, all lost at last—clouds, groves, water, air, sky—in their various and profound confusion of supernatural peace.

—Christopher North.

SENATOR MACDONALD was not only a well-read but an extensively travelled man. Like Ulysses, he had seen the cities of many men and learned their thoughts.

Few men enjoyed natural scenery more than he did. He revelled in the works of God. The majestic and the beautiful moved him to intense delight. He did not belong to the globe-trotting fraternity who form hasty observations and with the *cacoethes scribendi*, irresistibly strong upon them, proceed to draw sweeping deductions and offer crude dissertations of a misleading and mischievous character concerning the habits and customs of many lands. He was a careful and accurate observer; he studied both sides of the shield, and sought to acquire an intimate acquaintance with the social, political and economic conditions of the countries which he visited.

It is said that to know a man thoroughly you must travel with him, and see whether he takes his conscience along with him; whether his character remains the same when the restraints of daily occupation, public opinion, home life, and the forces of habit are removed.

In all his journeyings Senator Macdonald preserved his character as a genial, unselfish, appreciative Christian gentleman. However urgent his business, whether

on the continent of Europe, in the far West, or on
the rock-bound coast of Newfoundland, his invariable
rule was to rest at the end of the week, for he considered all unnecessary Sunday travelling as wrong.

The first time he made an ocean passage he found
himself sharing his stateroom with a very prepossess-
ing looking gentleman from Boston. As the night
advanced and he thought of turning in, the question
came up : "Shall I go through my private devotions ?
May it not be an offence to my companion ?" While
thus deliberating in his own mind, what was his surprise and delight to see his companion kneel down and
engage in silent prayer. It was a rebuke to his fears,
and an encouragement to him always to show his
colours. The gentleman was no other than the Hon.
Jonathan Lane, and they became life-long friends.

We have seen how in his young and callow days he
visited the West Indies for his health, and found
boundless delight in the climate, vegetation and scenery
of that "gem of the Antilles," Jamaica. Even then
we notice how he felt the intimate life of nature, her
weird power and charm, her all-penetrating life and
beauty.

He crossed the Atlantic many times, and made extended tours through the countries of Europe. He
wrote much in a pleasant, gossipy manner, and his
descriptions of scenery show not only great delicacy
of feeling, but how deeply nature allowed him to enter
into her secret. His sketches of cities, well known
places of interest, and the customs and life of foreign
people, are very entertaining.

In December, 1861, he made an ocean passage, and spent a few weeks in Great Britain.

In December, 1870, he made a nine days' passage from New York to Liverpool by steamer *Russia*.

In the summer of 1879 he made a pilgrimage to the Old World, accompanied by his daughters Lucie and Amy; and in 1881 he again crossed the Atlantic, taking with him Mrs. Macdonald and the daughters Marion and Annie. These frequent foreign tours gave him an exceptional knowledge of European affairs. While visiting France, Rhineland, Switzerland and Italy, he spent much time in Great Britain. He loved especially his "ain counterie," and cherished the warmest sentiments of loyalty, gratitude and admiration for the land of the hills and the glens. He had drank in with his mother's milk the many traditions of "Auld Scotia," and he passionately loved her shaggy woods, her heathery slopes, her mountains and her green swells of meadow-land. He not only loved the home and haunts of Burns, and the charming seat of Abbotsford, pervaded by the spirit of the great minstrel of the north, but he loved the very character, the *noblesse obligé*, the generous and chivalrous enthusiasm of the Scotsman himself.

The bard of Ayr sings :

> "In heaven itself I'll ask no more
> Than just a Highland welcome."

This was the welcome which Senator Macdonald always found at the very door-step of his native land.

During the same season of 1881, the Senator

re-crossed the ocean by the steamship *Peruvian*, to attend the first Ecumenical Conference, held in London.

In June, 1885, he made another trans-Atlantic trip, accompanied this time by Mrs. Macdonald and the daughters Winnifred and Ethel. He spent much time in the great metropolis, the centre of commercial enterprise, the market of the world. He also passed some weeks in the south of England, and was enthusiastic over the beauty of the Isle of Wight.

The following year he took his children, Lucie, Winnifred and Fraser, sailing by the steamship *Parisian* from Montreal. In a series of letters to the *Christian Guardian* he says:

"Among the many changes which have marked the last fifty years, none have been more remarkable than those connected with ocean passages. True, passages were then made in twenty-one or twenty-two days, but they were so occasional as to be objects of wonder; thirty-five, forty and fifty days were the rule. To cross the ocean in those days was the event of a man's life; the man made out his will (although sensible men should always have their wills made), he bade a solemn good-bye to his friends, and when he returned he was the hero of the hour, a subject of interest and wonder. All this is changed. Men cross the ocean to-day with less concern and less risk than they could have gone from Toronto to Amherstburg fifty years ago, and with so much certainty that they may order their dinner for a certain hour on a certain day and be there to enjoy it."

Reaching the Old Land, he says:

"Glorious England! Not unmindful of your sons, who are proud on every sea to sail under your flag! Not unmindful of your sons, who in every land fight your battles! Not unmindful of the widows and orphans of those who fall in your service. What land is like to thee? Who does not glory at being an Englishman?

"How lovely the country looked! It was in patches only that the hedges had assumed their shiny garb, but here and there the hawthorn blossoms had begun to fill the air with their fragrance. But the whole country was dressed in that tender, delicate, virgin green, which shows so lovely in the early spring-time. Every field has been so carefully ploughed, harrowed and rolled that it looked as level as one's dining-table; not one stump, not one rail fence to be seen through the entire distance. Large numbers of sheep (most of the dams having two lambs) were in the fields, with large numbers of cattle, among which were many Galloways."

Here is a vivid description of the Queen's visit to the Exhibition of that year, and a sight of Her Gracious Majesty, etc.

"One who, like myself, had never seen Her Majesty, could not help realizing that they were about to look upon the head of a royal house the most ancient in Europe, who rules over an empire on which the sun never sets, whose subjects comprise members of nearly every race and every creed on the habitable globe, a prominent place on the Exhibition walls announcing the fact that the area of the British Empire is 9,126,-999 square miles, and that its population is now 305,-337,294 souls.

"And now she comes. She is in a black silk robe,

adorned with black beads, her bonnet of black being relieved by a silver-grey feather. She is passing to hear the singers intone those stirring words of the Poet Laureate:

> " ' Shall we not thro' good and ill
>   Cleave to one another still ? '

And the close of them :

> " ' Sons be wedded, each and all,
>   Into one Imperial whole—
>   One with Britain, heart and soul—
>   One life, one flag, one fleet, one throne.
>   Britons hold your own,
>   And God guard all.'

.   .   .   .

" Here she is, within ten feet of where we stand. Her face is broad and full in features—a regular Guelph. Her face is red, very red. In this respect her photographs convey no idea of her appearance—very short, very stout, yet carrying herself with great dignity, and every inch a Queen. I felt that it was worth my passage across the Atlantic twice told, and all my expenses in London, to see the woman now passing so very near to me. As she passed by the Canadian court, cheer after cheer went up with great enthusiasm ; to every one of which she turned towards the court and bowed to her Canadian subjects.

What majesty in her movements. How fully she recognized that amid all the dignitaries from the Prince of Wales and other members of the Royal family—that amid all the heroes who joined in that procession, who had fought England's battles by sea and land—Admirals, Generals and Field Marshals—men whose faces were bronzed and whose breasts were covered with medals—Napier of Magdala, Seymour and Lumsden—men whom the nation delighted to honour—well did she recognize that, great as these and other men there were, and that much as they had done, that not for them, but for her, did these cheers ascend. She alone acknowledged the compliment— she acknowledged it as a Queen.

Two thoughts struck one as she passed through the Canadian court to make her way to the Albert Hall. First: Here is a woman who has been living amid the manifestations of the loyalty of her people for fifty years, and yet she is not indifferent to the expressions of loyalty of her colonial subjects, but every cheer receives its befitting acknowledgment. Does this not bespeak a Queen? Second: She occupies a position the most difficult for anyone to occupy—viz., that position of distance from all others that no one dare tell her of any weakness; that no one dare chide her for any inconsiderateness; that no one can tell her of any incompatibility of temper. In these respects is it not true that her position is a more difficult one (taking all the circumstances into consideration) than that of any mortal upon the face of the earth to-day, man or woman? . . .

" But she has passed. I have seen the Queen of England, and I am wonderfully pleased that I have done so. What a scene the grounds presented. What changes time has wrought. At one corner of the Exhibition one might realize from the people they meet that they were in the streets of Toronto. Here are men of distinction from China, with their blue silk robes. Here are various castes of India, some all in white, with white turbans gracefully twined about their heads; some all in veils, some clad in many-coloured 'silk robes, sone in crimson velvet braided with gold, some with curiously-shaped head dresses; ladies from India, whose caste in days gone by prohibited them from seeing the face of man unveiled, wandering about and enjoying the scene as did the people of Canada. Verily, the whole was a sight only to be seen in a lifetime—never, in so many respects, to be seen again."

Whatever he touches is done in an incisive and felicitous manner.. There is no haziness in his description—the subject stands out as clearly cut as a cameo.

During his stay on the Isle of Wight he looked up the 93rd Highlanders, lunched with the officers, and revived the sunny memories of early days with his old regiment.

His graphic letters were cut short by a severe illness, and it was a period of intense anxiety to his family. However, through careful nursing and the skill of his physician, Sir Joseph Lister, he rallied, and returned home somewhat recruited in strength.

In the summer of 1888, accompanied by his daughter Ethel, he took a most refreshing holiday, visiting Newfoundland and the Labrador coast.

His letters to the Toronto *Globe* commanded general attention throughout the Dominion, and were read with lively interest. We can give here only a few excerpts:

"How little do we know of Newfoundland? How little of Labrador? We have been accustomed to think of both as having rock-bound coasts, of being lands of fog and fish; of Labrador as being also the home of the seal and the region of eternal ice. Yet Newfoundland is our oldest, and, in very many respects, one of our most important colonies. . . .

"Our first point is Harbour Grace, for which we had a large amount of freight. . . .

"I rode over the mountains to Carbonear. The

population of the place is some 4,000. Like Harbour Grace, almost the entire population sustain themselves by fishing. The road from Harbour Grace to Carbonear is most picturesque. Mountain passes, winding roads, frowning rocks, and patches of green forests of spruce, make up the picture. Carbonear is built upon the slope of a lofty range, with white houses, most of them having small cultivated enclosures.

. . . .

"Our cargo out, and we are off for St. John's. On the base of a rocky promontory, at the left hand side of the entrance to St. John's harbour, stands the Fort Amherst lighthouse, on the right Signal Hill, 525 feet above the level of the sea. The Narrows leading to the harbour are nearly a mile in length ; the entrance to them is about 1,400 feet wide, and at the narrowest point not more than 600 feet. When two-thirds of the Narrows have been passed the harbour turns to the west, and there, completely land-locked with lofty hills on either side, vessels may ride in perfect safety. It was a magnificent sight to see the Admiral's ship, *Bellerophon*, with two men-of-war following, steaming up the Narrows, and casting anchor in the harbour, an English and a French warship being previously in port, thus making a fleet of five warships—four English and one French.

. . . .

"To one from Ontario, everything about Newfoundland is new, and consequently full of interest. The harbours are much alike, all land-locked, nearly all surrounded by bold, rugged and lofty hills. In entering some, the ship makes a complete circle, in others, half a circle ; in some, her course is in the shape of the letter S, so that when once in, it is difficult for a stranger to see, not only how the vessel came in, but how she was to get out. The settlements have about them so much that is alike, that when one has been seen, you have a very good idea of what the next will be like. . . .

" Newfoundland is very well supplied with churches, nearly all built of wood, and in places like Fogo, and even smaller, three churches are often found—one an Anglican, one a Methodist and one of the Church of Rome. . . .

" As we neared the coast of Labrador, although no perceptible change took place in the atmosphere, great patches of snow were seen lying in the gulches, and here and there a place which could not be so accurately described as in the well-known lines :

> " ' It was a cave, a huge recess,
>   Which held till June December's snow ;
>   A mighty precipice above,
>   A silent tarn below.'

. . . .

" Here we entered the Straits of Belle Isle. The sunsets were magnificent, such, indeed, as no artist could paint, such as no pen could describe, making the heavens, even in these bleak latitudes, like a ' sea of glory,' and lighting it up with such grandeur as forcibly reminds one of the words of Jean Ingelow, which could only have been conceived under such inspirational circumstances :

> " ' And far against days' golden death ·
>   She moved where Lindus wandereth,
>   My son's fair wife Elizabeth,'

Leading one to enquire if the death of day be golden, what reason is there that the close of one's life should not be radiant, and why should not one feel that, although clouds and darkness have been scenes in one's life with which they have not been unfamiliar, yet assuredly one may realize that ' at evening time it shall be light.' . . .

"At Blanc Sablon I saw the process by which the cod liver oil is prepared. I was struck with the cleanliness of the process, with the purity and clearness of the oil, resembling amber in colour, and quite as free from odour. I tasted it, and found that it was not only not difficult to take, but was something which one could get to like, and which must be most nutritious. Oil of this quality, I was informed, was worth £30 per tun; seal oil, £16, and finer qualities, £22. . . .

"There is much that Confederation can do—there is much that it cannot do. It can make the colony an integral part of a great Dominion. It can thus give it a prominence which it does not possess to-day. It can make its voice heard and its power felt in the Legislative Chambers of Ottawa. It can rely upon having the interest of the entire Dominion awakened in the development of its great resources. These are results which Confederation would undoubtedly secure; but it cannot bring back to the island the days of extravagant profits and colossal fortunes— these are gone."

On the 22nd of November of the same year he sailed with his youngest daughter, Ethel, from New York, per steamship *Barracanta*, for the West Indies. He not only desired to catch another glimpse of the proud appearance of those isles of the sea, and breathe the balm of their soft southern air, but he was anxious to foster between them and Canada a reciprocal trade. His letters and addresses helped to create a public interest in this trade, and no doubt formed one of the factors which led to the granting, by the Dominion Parliament, of the liberal subsidy to the "Castle" line of steamers now plying between the Dominion ports and the West Indies.

The last journey made to restore shattered nerves and vital energy was to the far Pacific Coast:

> " A clime where glittering mountain tops
> And glancing sea, and forests steeped in light
> Gave back, reflected, the far flashing sun."

Accompanied by his daughter Winnifred, he left Toronto, June 28th, 1889, for British Columbia, *via* the Northern Pacific Railway, visiting Chicago, St. Paul's, Minneapolis, Yellowstone Park, Spokane Falls, Portland and Alaska. His letters to the *Globe*, called " Nine Thousand Miles by Rail and Water," were very voluminous and interesting. Of Chicago he writes :

" We reached Chicago on time, and approaching it I had my first view of Lake Michigan. What a wondrous place ! In the Palmer House is a picture of the city in 1831—two log-houses, a small, rude log-bridge crossing the river near the present site of the Palmer House. A little over half a century— what an extraordinary change !

" It now enters upon its onward course as the second city in the Union, with a population of one million one hundred thousand people. Has the world ever seen a city spring up as this has done ? Was ever a city overtaken by so great a calamity as befell it in 1871, when, in a few hours, miles were laid desolate and property destroyed to the value of about $500,000,000 ? One hundred millions of pounds sterling, or about one-seventh of the national debt of Great Britain. It is from this period of disaster, which would have blotted out the very site of many a city, that its great development dates, and it entered upon that course of advancement of which it is so difficult to foresee the end."

The Grand Canyon of the Yellowstone Excites His Awe and Admiration.

"My first impressions were those of wonder and astonishment; my last and the abiding one was one of awe.

"I speedily realized how feeble had been my conception, and as speedily realized how impossible it would have been that it could have been ought else. I had never seen anything like it, I had never fancied anything like it; while no description, however graphic, could convey to one a description of the picture upon which I was gazing.

"Before me was the yawning chasm, the cliffs rising perpendicularly for about two thousand feet, emblazoned with colours so rich, striking and wonderful as to throw into the shade all the picture galleries of Europe. On the right, the lower falls of the Yellowstone—considerably higher than those of Niagara; beneath, the bed of the river, foaming and dashing in its wild course, receiving the waters of many tributaries, each having its canyon rolling onwards, broadening and deepening, until from a point above the mouth of the Big Horn River until its confluence with the Missouri, a distance of about two hundred and fifty miles, it becomes during a good stage of water navigable for steamboats of from two to three hundred tons.

"Hovering over us were the eagles—a fitting place for the king of birds—sweeping o'er the chasm with a conscious sense of security and an utter indifference of man's puny efforts. Perched upon the very top of the highest crags were their nests, upon which, however, we looked down, the young broods adding to the weirdness of the picture. . . .

"Farewell to the Grand Canyon, worth alone all the trouble, expense and fatigue incident to reaching

it; sight which never can be forgotten; the joy of
having seen it something which can never fade.

CRYSTAL STAIRS, YELLOWSTONE PARK.

"I have spoken with those who have expressed disappointment at Niagara Falls—to those who have
been disappointed in other objects the fame of which

is world-wide. I have never yet seen, nor do I expect that I ever will see, anyone bold enough to express disappointment at the Grand Canyon of the Yellowstone."

Concerning the great river of the Pacific Coast, he says :

"The Columbia has charms peculiarly its own for all who are fond of nature. It furnishes one of those wonderful trips, of which, indeed, there are so many, which never can be forgotten—one of those trips which leaves upon the mind pleasant pictures not to be seen elsewhere, and which never fails to afford pleasure in calling them up after the journey itself has become a thing of the past.

"Some idea of the enormous wealth of the Columbia River, so far as its salmon is concerned, may be gathered from the fact that in 1883 the total pack was no less than 629,400 cases, valued at $3,147,000.

"The river abounds with sturgeon. At one of the landing places there was one which had been caught weighing about 100 pounds, and one of our passengers told me that he had caught one measuring 22 feet. Great numbers of seals, too, we saw during the day, at which the soldiers amused themselves firing with their revolvers, the bullets sometimes striking the water marvellously near them. We leave the Columbia where its great affluent, the Willamette, joins it, and proceed amid beautiful scenery for twelve miles up the latter river until we reach Portland. We had, in addition to Mount Hood, good views of both Mount Adams and Mount St. Helens ; and well it was so, for during our stay at St. Paul, where, in a clear state of the atmosphere, six snow-clad mountains are clearly visible at the same time from the park, the atmosphere was so dense from the smoke of forest fires that it was with difficulty that anything could be seen beyond the range of the city."

He writes glowingly of Vancouver Island and Victoria :

" Victoria, the capital of British Columbia, is picturesquely situated in a beautiful harbour in the south-east of Vancouver Island, its population being from 12,000 to 15,000.

" I was not prepared for the many evidences of thrift and substantial progress which met me at every turn. The streets are wide, and well laid out. The shops and places of business are imposing and attractive. The stocks of goods which are displayed in the windows and exposed in the places of business are such as are to be found in our largest and most important cities. The standing of the merchants is equal to that of any merchant in any of our Canadian cities.

" The climate of Victoria is mild in winter and cool in summer, and I was not surprised to find that in consequence it was a favourite resort for tourists."

From Victoria they took steamer, *George W. Elder,* for Alaska, visiting the different settlements along the route, reaching Sitka August 8th, and arriving back at Victoria August 17th. He took a deep interest in the Indian missionaries, and made an earnest appeal on behalf of the natives of Alaska and the Aleutian Islands.

He returned by the Canadian Pacific Railway. He has this to say of the great Pacific terminus :

" In many respects Vancouver is the most remarkable place we have seen since leaving Toronto. Vancouver as it is now had no existence three years ago. Where great, wide streets exist to-day, was then a dense, un-broken forest. How dense that was and how magnificent were the trees, is manifest by the number and size of the trunks which have not yet been removed. Streets now are being opened 'out, on either side of which the forest remains as it has been for the past hundreds of years ; yet, as we drove by these we were told that the price of a lot of fifty feet on one of these forest streets ranged from $800 to $1,200.

" Well may the people of Vancouver be proud of their park, upon which I trust no encroachments will be made, however strong the pressure may be, for commercial or other purpose."

He was impressed with the mountains, and particularly the prairies.

" And thus we keep rolling over the vast and it indeed seems boundless prairies, feeling the full force of the words of the poet :

> " ' Lo ! they stretch
> In airy undulations far away,
> As if the ocean, in his gentle swell,
> Stood still with all his rounded billows fixed
> And motionless for ever.' "

The long journey is accomplished !

" And now the conductor, passing through the car, cries, ' Toronto,' and in a few moments we are at the Union Station. A few minutes later we are at our own home, wife and children on the verandah to meet and welcome us, realizing that kind of experience that one never tires of repeating, intensified in this case by the fact that perfect health had been the portion of all at home, that not one moment of uneasiness had befallen the travellers, that health and increased delight had been their portion on their journey of 9,000 miles to Alaska by the way of the

18

Northern Pacific and home by the Canadian Pacific Railway."

His closing sentences are:

"And now that I find myself in my own city and my journey over, my verdict is that while loving the United States none the less, I find myself loving my own country all the more. Cherishing nothing, I trust, but the very kindest wishes for my American friends, and the greatest possible success for their country, yet I am proud of my nationality, and fully assured from all that I have heard and seen, that no people on this wide earth have more to be thankful for than have the people of Canada, and, applying the words of the poet to their own country, none should be able with greater sincerity and feeling than they to say :

" ' There's no place like home.'

"It was with these soul-stirring words welling up in my breast that I reached my own door, words which, when applied to Canada, I venture to say every Canadian may with confidence adopt."

Little did the many readers of those interesting letters dream that ere two months had rolled away, Senator Macdonald would have embarked on the journey to that mysterious, unseen land from which no traveller returns.

XIV.

HOME LIFE.

Stay, stay at home, my heart, and rest ;
Home-keeping hearts are happiest,
For those that wander they know not where
Are full of trouble and full of care ;
    To stay at home is best.
           —Longfellow, Song.

        Home is the resort
Of love, of joy, of peace and plenty ; where,
Supporting and supported, polished friends
And dear relations mingle into bliss.
         —Thompson, The Seasons.

Whenever we step out of domestic life in search of felicity, we come back again disappointed, tired and chagrined. One day passed under our own roof with our friends and our family is worth a thousand in another place.
         —Earl of Orrery.

Home is the grandest of all institutions.
         —C. H. Spurgeon.

HOME LIFE.

WE have not sought to present a strictly chronological narrative, but to bring out the character of the man in the various relations and engagements of his life.

We have already revealed in his business and political life those strong and manly traits of personal character which commanded the admiration of all who knew him. But of all the varied features of the life of Senator Macdonald, none were more marked than the intense warmth of his home affections. No portraiture of the man would be of any value that failed to present in their due sequence the personal and family events of those busy years in which he was so occupied with mercantile, parliamentary, social and ecclesiastical duties. He was essentially a family man.

The stream that rushes along at full tide rarely meanders through quiet woods and meadows, and one would have thought that the current of Senator Macdonald's life was too swift to allow him to rest upon its banks. But his main delights were in the midst of his quiet home, and all the hours of rest were sacred to the cultivation of family ties.

The early years of his life, though full of unremitting effort—his intellectual faculties becoming sharpened, and the range of his business knowledge widened —were nevertheless not eventful. There is little of a picturesque or striking nature.

" So runs the round of life from hour to hour."

Yet they were fruitful in influence, for all the while he was not only enriching and beautifying his own character, but building up a home of wealth, intelligence, refinement and piety. The whole atmosphere of that home was permeated by a domestic affection that was quite ideal in its manifestation. Among the images of earliest childhood his mother's shone out as in a picture. Her memory always came back to him with a sort of celestial radiance, and it exerted a mellowing influence upon his own home-life.

In his early years he had sharp domestic sorrow in the loss of his beautiful young wife. But when he again set up the family roof-tree, he had found a most affectionate partner, a true companion and friend. He relied much upon his wife's clear, sound judgment, and he gave her the full affection of his pure, strong, manly nature. It is almost romantic to read in one of his Alaska letters:

" The weather is balmy ; the reflection of the water perfect ; the scene such as no painter could transfer to his canvas or writer fittingly describe. And here I find myself in circumstances calling up in one whatever is in him of the sense of the beautiful, finishing my entry with this remark, ' The anniversary of my wedding day.' "

They were blessed with a large family of children— five sons and five daughters. These were born at intervals of about two years, and as follows:

John Kidston Macdonald.

Annie Eliza, born March 28, 1859, who was married in February 1, 1882, to Mr. Montgomerie Lewis, of London, Ont.

Marion Louisa, born August 28, 1860, united in marriage to James Morrow, Esq., of Halifax, October 19, 1882.

Lucie Elizabeth, born June 6, 1862, who, on December 3, 1889, married Dr. J. A. Grant, son of Sir James Grant, of Ottawa.

John Kidston, born November 4, 1863, the present head of the firm.

James Fraser, born November 2, 1865, who married Mary Eveline, second daughter of Rev. G. M. Milligan, of Toronto.

Alexander Alcorn, born October 22, 1867, who, on the 21st July, 1890, was united in marriage to Annie C. Ballantyne, third daughter of the late George Laidlaw, Esq., of Toronto.

Winnifred Julia, born September 19, 1869.

Ethel Alberta, born July 30, 1871.

Duncan McGregor, born June 6, 1873 ; and

Arthur Nimo, born October 6, 1874.

He was a model *père de famille*, devoted to his children and idolized by them. He played with the boys, participating in all their boyish sports. He was particularly good at the game of marbles. He was the finest shot and generally the winner. Chess was another favourite household game. He sought to make his children happy at home, and provided them with all the means of innocent amusement.

Christmas was a joyous family day, and in the evening that home party was one of the most pleasant of scenes, the father full of high and buoyant spirits and joining in fun and frolicsomeness. Indeed, he considered this the best way of keeping his sons and daughters from the alluring snares of sinful amusements.

As they grew older, he entered into their higher companionships, and shared all their studies and pursuits. He watched with intense solicitude over their spiritual interests, and rejoiced when their hearts were given fully to the Saviour.

Every now and then appears in his diary a record like this:

"Class this evening. John has been going to class for one month."

Returning from one of his journeys, he says:

"Arrived at home about 6.30 p.m. What a joyful meeting. Found my dear wife at the door to meet me. Amy and all the children were there. Never did I feel happier or more thankful."

A man of intense domesticity, devoted to wife and children, he poured out upon them all the love of a tender heart.

When Her Majesty the Queen gave to the world the story of her happy home in the Highlands in the days of Albert the Good, how that revelation of the sweet, pure, domestic life of Balmoral Castle won all hearts. So the chaste home life of the Merchant Prince of Toronto was a model of simplicity, domestic affection, dignity, culture and sturdy piety.

In 1860 he purchased "Oaklands," and made it one of the most delightful suburban residences of the metropolis. The grounds are extensive, and command a wide and charming view. Trees and green fields

with the soft sunshine streaming down upon them,
make a very pretty foreground to the picture of the
city, which seems to borrow enchantment from
distance; its streets and squares spread out, with
many a spire and lofty tower uplifted in the air.
Along the horizon, far as the eye can reach, up and
down, are the gleaming waters of Lake Ontario. The
house itself is embowered in trees and shrubs, and
seems to express the personality of its owner. The
architecture is home-like. Entering the hall, on the
right is the library, a pleasant, airy room, with a desk
in the centre, and book-shelves all around, loaded
with valuable books. Next we come to the stately
drawing-room and the dining-room, both of which
open on the lawn, and command a fine view of the
city and lake. It is well planned, both for convenience and beauty, and on all sides extends a large and
well kept lawn, with parterres and flower beds bright
with blossoms of every tint.

The oaks in their symmetrical beauty have stood
for generations; but the Senator prided himself in
having planted nearly every tree on the grounds.

Every part of Oaklands gave evidence of cultured
taste and of an intense love of nature, and the owner
could say with Longfellow :

> " I hear the wind among the trees
> Playing celestial symphonies.
> I see the branches downward bent
> Like keys of some great instrument."

He took a deep interest, not only in the grassy
lawn, the blooming flowers, the budding and blossom-

ing trees, but also in the birds, their love-making,
their nest-building, their songs. In the melody of
these wild birds he could detect each songster that
sought to "disburden his soul of its music," and could
say with the poet :

> "That's the wise thrush; he
> Sings each song twice over,
> Lest you should think he never could re-capture
> The first fine careless rapture."

A genuine child of nature, in close affinity with the
love of flowers and his love of birds, was his affection
for children. Every summer his pleasant grounds
were thrown open to the Sunday School scholars of
the Yonge Street Church. What a joy it was to the
Senator to mingle among the children on these pic-nic
occasions, and join in laugh and shout and merry
games. It was as if he said :

> "Come to me, O ye children,
> For I hear you at your play,
> And the questions that perplexed me
> Have vanished quite away.
> Ye are better than all the ballads
> That ever were sung or said,
> For ye are living poems,
> And all the rest are dead."

But while he showed great capacity for domestic
love and domestic happiness, there was plainness and
economy in the home life. There was no ostentation,
no luxurious wastefulness and showy modes of living.
Among the mercantile classes, luxury is an all-devour-
ing evil. They allow great establishments to eat up
their gains. Senator Macdonald realized that family
happiness was not dependent on superfluities and

ostentatious display.   There was plentifulness everywhere, but no needless luxuries.   By word and deed
he sought to condemn the prevalent extravagance of
the household.   When useless luxuries called, he had
nothing to spare ; when the poor called, he had to
spare, and was glad to give of his abundance for
their support.

In the home no one could resist the fascination of
his affectionateness and geniality.   He was the most
delightful of hosts.   He knew how to entertain with
grace, courtesy and dignity, and with that prince-
liness which thinks nothing too good for its guests.
Hospitality, like other things, is modified by environ-
ment, and there is danger, from the restlessness, the
pressure, the breathless hurry of modern life, of its
becoming one of the lost arts.   Says Hamerton, "The
friendships of the heart are sacred, and should be
permanent like marriage."

> " The friends thou hast, and their adoption tried,
>   Grapple them to thy soul with hooks of steel,"

sings the Bard of Avon ; while the words of Holy
Writ are, " Ointment and perfume rejoice the heart ;
so doth the sweetness of a man's friend by hearty
counsel."   Senator Macdonald's was a nature that
offered love for love, confidence for confidence, and
his friendship was steady in its flame, and lasting in
its endurance.   Through all the relations and passages
of life it abided continually.

On a great house was this legend carved in stone :
" *Amicis et sibi* " (for my friends first, and afterwards
for myself).   This seemed to be the legend at " Oak-

lands." Indeed, on the stained glass window of the hall, beneath an open Bible, and between the crest and motto of the family, is this inscription:

" Through this wide open gate
None come too soon, and none return too late."

How many hundreds remember his kindness, and love, and hospitality ? "Oaklands" will always live brightly and beautifully in their memory. What a pleasure it was for him to offer the hospitalities of his home to distinguished ministers from England, the United States, and all parts of the world, and to men and women engaged in religious and benevolent work. How many weary and exhausted missionaries have found delightful days of repose, comfort and Christian cheerfulness under his roof, and in that happy family circle have risen from feebleness to strength.

There was one thing that every guest of this household cherished as among his most delightful memories. The service of family prayers was one of the most honoured institutions at "Oaklands." It was the first act of the assembled household. A portion of Scripture was read, a hymn often sung, and then, as a priest of his own fireside, he presented his offering at the altar of the home. The last letter which Mrs. Macdonald ever received from her husband is dated from Victoria, B.C., and this is the closing sentence: "I am grateful for mercies vouchsafed. I want you to read at worship, 1 Chronicles, 29th chapter, from 10th to 19th verse "

XV.

PERSONAL CHARACTERISTICS.

The great man is he who does not lose his child's heart.
                              —*Mericus.*

This is the porcelain clay of human kind.
                              —*Dryden.*

                    Pity and need
Make all flesh kin.   There is no caste in blood,
Which runneth of one hue, nor caste in tears,
Which trickle salt with all ; neither comes man
To birth with tilka-mark stamped on the brow,
Nor sacred thread on neck.
                              —*Edwin Arnold.*

Only what we have wrought into our characters during life
can we take away with us.
                              —*Humboldt.*

A Christian is God Almighty's gentleman.
                              —*J. C. and A. W. Hare.*

PERSONAL CHARACTERISTICS.

WE come now to the most difficult and the most delicate part of a biographer's task, namely, to give an adequate and just conception of the character of his subject. Is it the biographer's duty to portray the weaknesses as well as the excellences of his hero? We think it is. The object of biography is to exhibit character, and the writer has a duty to perform, not only to his subject, but to truth. He is not merely to play the part of the advocate; he is to be judge—to weigh, analyze and discriminate, that he may present a faithful sketch. It is impartial statement that one desires to see, both in history and biography. How can the biographer portray the energy, devotion, fidelity, and activity of his subject as springs of high action, and worthy of imitation, without also acknowledging those blemishes and defects that should become beacons of warning in the voyage of life. Not that these weaknesses should be ostentatiously put forward, but they are to be candidly admitted, wherever they are found.

Many prominent traits of Senator Macdonald's character have been clearly indicated in the narrative already given, but we desire here to present a full length portrait, with all its lights and shadows, that our readers may know what manner of man he was.

In personal appearance Senator Macdonald was tall and rather slender, with handsome, clear-cut and regular features, an agreeable, open countenance, gentle gray eyes, high forehead and light hair and whiskers. Erect, commanding, particularly neat in his dress, of graceful presence, he was a man calculated to attract attention anywhere. He was a well-built figure, and though never robust, yet his wonderful activity gave evidence of considerable physical energy. Though he never wholly recovered from the shock which he received from his throat and lungs attack, yet he enjoyed through life a fair share of health.

In manners, he was a high-bred, dignified, courteous gentleman. "Be courteous" is the injunction of the apostle. Courtesy is the grace of saying and doing things fitly. A courteous man is a man of court-like or elegant manners. Courtesy is not mere surface polish, but part and parcel of the man's inner self, the outcome of a generous nature.

> "Manners are not idle, but the fruit
> Of noble nature and of loyal mind."

Senator Macdonald had real kindliness and generosity of heart, and to him could be given

> "Without abuse,
> The grand old name of 'gentleman.'"

While his voice was pleasant, yet it betrayed his birth and blood. This Scotch accent, not harsh and crabbed, but rich and pleasant, clung to him through life.

In conversation, he was rich, varied and versatile.

We have already dwelt upon the wealth of his mental gifts and resources, the variety and versatility of his intellectual powers, and the accuracy and accumulation of his knowledge.

He had an artistic mind, and the true spirit of poetry was his. He had a love of language and an aptitude for the study of it, and for a business man was highly cultivated in general literature. He felt the influence of the subtle *zeit-geist*, the spirit of the times, and lived fully abreast of the age.

One of the foibles of his truly great and attractive character was his genial egotism. He had the sense of individual worth, and was not unconscious of his gifts. This apparently overweening estimate of self gave to those who were superficially acquainted with him a wholly erroneous impression of his character. George Eliot says: "I've never any pity for conceited people, because I think they carry their comfort about with them." It could hardly be called conceit, for he was ever ready to attribute to a higher source than self all his gifts and all his success. Nor was it pride, which consists in exalting self at the expense of others. He had the true spirit of humility, yet he had that trait in the organization of the Highlander—that show of self-importance in manner which would say with Shakespeare's Henry IV.:

"I am not in the roll of common men."

Along with this inheritance of Scotch blood and training came a certain dictatorial bearing, an imperiousness of disposition. He had an intensely strong

19

will, which could not bear thwarting, an autocratic bent of mind which could ill endure contradiction, and which was somewhat severe toward those who ventured to differ from his views and convictions. Some thought him stern and unapproachable, because he had what was remarked about Burke, "A certain inborn stateliness of nature which kept people at a distance."

Another mark of the Celtic genius was his impulsive nature. His susceptibilities were easily ruffled. He was quick to resent wrong; his self-control was not complete, and in Parliamentary debate he would not hesitate to drive his lance home between the joints of his opponents harness. But there was no venom, no unmanly hate; all was generous and chivalric; he was "lord of a great heart," and like Longfellow's Miles Standish, "He was sensitive, swift to resent, but as swift in atoning for error."

He had much of the *perfervidum Scotorum ingenium.* The flood of loyalty and patriotism rose to its full height in his nature. He was a thorough Canadian, yet he was very clannish, and thought there was no man like the Scotchman. The ancient Roman could utter the proud boast, "*Civis Romanus sum*"; Senator Macdonald could say with exultation "I also am a British subject. I belong to the Anglo-Saxon race." The *Britannica civitas* is a wider and more honored privilege.

He had also the quiet humour of the Scot. Amid the carking, corroding cares of life he kept his heart fresh, yet there was a vein of sadness in his make-up.

Interlaced with his sprightly moods were seasons of melancholy, when everything was clad in the most sombre hues; he was in a state of extreme dejection. This may have had its origin in the state of his health and in the reflective and deeply sensitive turn of his mind.

Another clearly-marked trait in his character was his love of kin. He paid great respect to his soldier-father, and saw that he wanted for nothing in his old age. As he rose step by step he did not shun the society of his kindred, or leave them out of sight; he was the same kind, unassuming, loyal relation. This strong feeling of kinship is shown in the ample provision made in his will for the members of his father's household. This was the chain that bound his children to him irresistibly. He cherished the strongest love toward them. How touching his treatment of the wish of his gentle Amy.

> "None knew her but to love her,
> None named her but to praise."

She had been a great sufferer, and near the end she greatly desired of her father that the property that would have gone to her, had she lived, be devoted to the relief of the suffering. This was the secret of his interest in, and provision for, the University Park Hospital.

He abhorred meanness of any kind. He hated especially that sneakishness "which creeps and crawls and leaves its slime and its odour behind." His eldest son related to me that one morning they were driving down Yonge Street, when they met a man who had treated him shabbily, and was utterly devoid of all honesty. Involuntarily Mr. Macdonald bowed to him, when at once he reined up his horses, and looking the man in the face, he said: "I want you to understand, sir, that that was a mistake, my bowing to you. I do not recognize you, for I regard you as a thorough scoundrel."

He was a man of strong prejudices. He could be easily imposed upon, but he possessed this characteristic of Alexander III., the Imperial Autocrat of all the Russias, that when once a man has deceived him he never trusts him again.

He had enthusiasm. He was an indomitable worker. "*Labour ipse voluptas.*" He had the genuine love of work. He had great system. In reviewing his life one wonders how he could get through so much ; but he had the knack of packing engagements and duties into close compass.

He was thorough, never doing anything in a half-and-half fashion, and he turned every spare moment to golden account. He was like Cicero—ready to consume "even the shreds and waste ends of time," or like one of those of whom a French writer tells, "So covetous of the moments that if Old Time should let his hour-glass fall, they would stoop for the sand, and, by incessant labour, collect all the scattered grains."

His promises were kept to the moment and fulfilled to the letter. Louis XIV. called punctuality the "politeness of kings"; in trade it is called the "soul of business." Senator Macdonald believed it the *sine qua non* of success. He was a man of prompt, rapid action. It was constantly noticed of him that when he was driven up to the warehouse he would be out of the door before the carriage stopped. And he had also the backbone quality of perseverance. He would never slacken until he had planted his banner on the crest of every hill diffi- culty. He had been trained in the school of hard- ship, and the steel thread was woven into the texture of his life. He was a man of determination, and his purpose once fixed, there was no looking forward to what he might be, or looking backward to what he might have been, but a-doing the thing set before him, and doing it thoroughly with all his might. He felt that

> " Life is to wake, not sleep ;
> Rise, and not rest ; but press
> From earth's level, where blindly creep
> Things perfected, more or less,
> To the heaven's height, far and steep."

He was especially a man of integrity. He was absolutely upright and truthful. The least sugges- tion of falsehood or untrustworthiness was abhorrent to him. Without fear or reproach he bore a con- science void of offence toward all men ; alike in home, or warehouse, or legislative halls, he never said a word or did a deed that did not bear upon it the stamp of unsullied integrity. There is nothing we need so much in business life and in public life as the principle of integrity. Unfaithfulness, unrelia- bility is only another name for moral rottenness.

And this brings me to say that religion was the
Alpha and Omega of his being. His life-story could
not be told unless this aspect of his character were
put in the forefront of the narrative. Without this
vital principle, we fail to appreciate the secret of his
successes and the motive power of his actions. His
conversion in the old George Street Wesleyan Church
was the crisis of his being, and the key to his after
life. He was a Methodist, but he was no bigot. Not
the faintest shadow of intolerance or of sectarian
bitterness ever darkened his intercourse with his
fellow-Christians. He would not

> "Melt in an acid sect
> The Christian pearl of charity."

He was true to his convictions. It was well known
where he was to be found on every moral and religious question. He held that no man had a right
to be liberal in the sense of giving away a part of
what he believed to be the truth. He knew the priceless worth of truth, and loved it with all his soul.
As Paracelsus tells us:

> "Truth is within ourselves—
> There is an inmost centre in us all
> Where truth abides in fulness; and to know
> Rather consists in opening out a way
> Whence the imprisoned splendour may escape,
> Than in effecting entry for a light
> Supposed to be without."

To him, divine truth was a living force, applied to
living issues of the day. His life was true. The
Christian religion was not so much a system of doctrines as a grand realization—a blessed experience.

He clung with firm faith to Jesus Christ as a personal Saviour, and loved God with the fulness of childlike affection. He would not swim with the current or bow down in adoration before the idols of the hour; he would serve his God in all the matters which make up the warp and woof of our lives. He believed and realized that the cleansing, purifying, fertilizing tide of the river of God should flow on and on, through all the affairs of the world.

We have more than once alluded to his profound veneration for the Word of God. His reverence for the letter and the spirit of Holy Writ was most marked. He delighted in searching its treasures and pondering them in his heart. He sought to impress upon others that this was the most precious treasure in the world. A young man called upon him who was out of employment, and in despondency. The Senator said to him: "Have you read that striking passage in Joshua i. 8? 'This book of the law shall not depart out of thy mouth; but thou shalt meditate therein day and night, that thou mayest observe to do according to all that is written therein: for then thou shalt make thy way prosperous, and then thou shalt have good success.'" After a little further conversation, the young man said on leaving, "Will you please tell me again where that passage is to be found?" It was given. A few weeks after, Mr. Macdonald received a letter from this young man thanking him for calling his attention to the study of God's Word, telling him that he had taken the Bible as his chart for the journey of life, that he had secured a lucrative position, and was enjoying " good success."

He believed the Bible to be *par excellence* the book for daily guidance. One of his sons had been visiting for some days at the house of his affianced. The Senator feared that he was staying too long, and sent him a telegram. The message was, " See Prov. xxv. 17." The Bible was got; they all gathered around it in great excitement, and read, " Withdraw thy foot from thy neighbour's house, lest he be weary of thee, and so hate thee." His own Bible was well marked. The passage, " Be thou diligent to know the state of thy flocks, and look well to thy cattle," has this commentary by him, " In other words, whatever your business, be careful regularly *to take stock.*" So Rev. xiii. 3, "And all the world wondered after the beast," has this : " See Tennyson's 'Charge of the Light Brigade.' The poet borrows his striking refrain, 'All the world wondered,' from this passage of Scripture."

His own deep personal religious experience, the variety, fulness and soundness of his spiritual life, largely came from his devout study of the Word of God. He had those regular habits of devotion without which the Christian life cannot be preserved. He lived in constant communion with the Father of spirits, believed in the " sweet reasonableness " of prayer, and in answered petitions he had a constant confirmation of the Divine interposition in the affairs of life.

Senator Macdonald delighted to refer, as an instance of special Providence, to the rescue of the six hundred and forty-one persons on board the ship *Kent*, when on fire in the Bay of Biscay, by the brig *Cambria*. He says :

" When all were looking for death—that is, before the *Cambria* hove in sight—Sir Duncan, then Major, Macgregor wrote on a slip of paper, on which was his father's address, as follows :

" ' The ship, the *Kent*, East Indiamen, is on fire. Elizabeth, Joanna and myself commit our spirits into the hands of our blessed Redeemer. His grace enables us to be quite composed in the awful prospect of entering eternity.

" ' DUNCAN MACGREGOR.
" ' 1st March, 1825, Bay of Biscay.'

" Now for the history of this bottle. Left in the cabin, it was cast into the sea by the explosion that destroyed the *Kent*. About nineteen months afterwards the following notice appeared in a Barbadoes (West India) newspaper :

" ' A bottle was picked up on Saturday, 30th September, at Bathsheba (a bathing place on the west of Barbadoes), by a gentleman who was bathing there ; who, on breaking it, found the melancholy account of the fate of the ship *Kent* contained in a folded newspaper, written with pencil, but scarcely legible.'

" The letter itself, taken from the bottle, thickly encrusted with shells and seaweed, was returned to its writer when he arrived, shortly after its discovery, at Barbadoes, as Lieut.-Colonel of the 93rd Highlanders. This paper, now in possession of his son, Mr. John Macgregor, widely known as ' Rob Roy,' through his book, ' One Thousand Miles in the *Rob Roy* Canoe,' and ' The *Rob Roy* on the Jordan,' I saw in his Chambers in the Temple, London. He it was who, when a child of a few weeks old, was the first human being to find refuge in the little craft, the

Cambria, having been caught from his mother's arms by Mr. Thompson, the fourth mate of the *Kent*."

Senator Macdonald, after he had visited the Island of Barbadoes, sent to Mr. Macgregor (" Rob Roy ") a photograph of the very spot where the bottle was found, and of Culpepper House, the residence of the gentleman who found it.

He recognized an overruling hand in his own life, and could sing with the poet :

> " My bark is wafted to the land,
> 　　By breath divine ;
> 　And on the helm there rests a Hand,
> 　　Other than mine."

On June 18th, 1883, there is this record of a

" MIRACULOUS DELIVERANCE.

" This morning as Brady (coachman) and myself were driving along King Street, the horse ' Milan ' started to rear. Brady held on bravely. Presently I saw that a crash against one of the Grand Trunk wagons was inevitable. The crash came, and strangely enough threw me out of my own wagon into it, and, with all but a few scratches, uninjured. The horse kicked and ran with the broken wagon, but it was caught on Yonge Street. I do trust I feel thankful to God for His preserving care upon this occasion, when death seemed so near. Surely there is still for me a work to do."

Another entry, July 13th, of the same year, is as follows :

" While walking down Yonge Street this morning, I hailed a street car, and stepping on to it while in motion, did not perceive that another car was rapidly approaching in an opposite direction. They were together before I had noticed; and so close that I cannot at this moment realize how it was that I escaped being crushed, possibly to death. How wonderful is God's watchful care! I felt that on reaching my office I could not but bow my head in humble acknowledgment of His preserving care. May He ever keep me in a humble, lowly and thankful spirit."

Just the year before his death there is this record:

"Our engineer in conversation to-day on the falling of the warehouse in 1878, said, 'In all my professional life I never saw such a case. How it should have gone so far and stopped without becoming one mass of ruin is unaccountable. And it was only of God's mercy that the building and everyone in it was not destroyed.'"

Thus he delighted to acknowledge an over-ruling Providence, and he believed "that all things work together for good to them that love Him."

> "God's plans, like lilies pure and white, unfold.
> We must not tear the close-shut leaves apart;
> Time will reveal the calyxes of gold."

He lived not only in the spirit of prayer, but in the spirit of sympathy with the Lord Jesus Christ. He sought to follow the Great Exemplar, who pleased not Himself but lived for others.

We have alluded to his benevolence. True charity is a virtue of the heart and not of the hands.

"What the Abbot of Bamba cannot eat he gives away for the good of his soul. He steals a pig and gives away the trotters for God's sake."

Senator Macdonald not merely gave out of his abundance; he held his possessions as a steward, and sought to use them for the benefit of the weak, the needy, and the suffering.

> " Loathing pretence, he did with cheerful will
> What others talked of, while their hands were still."

His great watchword was " duty." " Duty, that which," says George Herbert, " gives us music at midnight." " Stern daughter of the voice of God," as Wordsworth has it.

How he loved the ringing words of Tennyson in praise of duty:

> " Not once or twice in our rough island story
> The path of duty was the way to glory.
> He that walks it only thirsting
> For the right, and learns to deaden
> Love of self, before his journey closes
> He shall find the stubborn thistle bursting
> Into glossy purples, which out-redden
> All voluptuous garden roses.
> Not once or twice in our fair island story,
> The path of duty was the way to glory."

Indeed, in gathering up these sparkling gems that make the diadem of his Christian character, it can be truly said that his dominating desire was like that of Sir Henry Lawrence, who, after the distinguished administrative ability, energy, and indefatigable devotion with which he had discharged the onerous and responsible duties entrusted to him, being asked what inscription might be put upon his tomb, said, " Let it be, ' Here lies Henry Lawrence, who tried to do his duty.' "

Senator Macdonald, in every detail of life, tried to do his duty, and his success in life is a conspicuous illustration of the truth,

> " Honour her and she shall exalt thee."

XVI.

LAST DAYS.

We know when moons shall wane,
When summer birds from far
    Shall cross the sea,
When Autumn's hue shall tinge the golden train ;
But who shall teach us when to look
    For thee, O death ?

                    "Gone !
Taken the stars from the night and the sun
        From the day !
Gone, and a cloud on my heart."

Whatever crazy sorrow saith,
No life that breathes with human breath
Has ever truly longed for death.
                            —*Tennyson.*

            God keeps a niche
In heaven to hold our idols ; and albeit
He break them down to our faces, and denies
That our close kisses should impair their white,
I know we shall behold them raised, complete,
The dust shook off, their beauty glorified,
New Memnons singing in the great God-light.
                    —*E. B. Browning.*

        Death's but a path that must be trod
        If man would ever pass to God.
                            —*Thomas Parnell.*

"I am weary.   I will now go to sleep.   Good-night."
                        —*Meander's dying words.*

    Say not " good-night," but in some brighter clime
        Bid me " good morning."
                            —*Anna Letitia Barbauld.*

To our graves we walk in the thick footprints of departed
men.
                            —*Alex. Smith.*

LAST DAYS.

WITH advancing years, Senator Macdonald's thoughts were turned toward the future. Though he had no anxious dread of death, yet he had reached a point where earth would seem a pleasant place. He had prospered amazingly, his family had grown up around him, honours had fallen thick upon him, higher and wider circles recognized his excellence, he had leisure at his command, and it would seem that he might for years repose amid the fruits of his toil. He faithfully walked with God, and was daily rising in elevation of character. He was using his surplus wealth and spare time in the service of others, and was a mighty factor in the attempted solution of nearly every question affecting the moral and religious welfare of the young nation.

But the shadows were lengthening. His plenitude of virile energy was gone. His diary of 1883 bears this record:

"*December 27th.*—To-day I enter upon my sixtieth year. I seem unable to realize it. Truly, I must now begin to think that I am getting old. How good God has been to me through all these long years that are past; how mercifully He has guided me, from how much that is sad has He saved me; how little have I rendered to Him, other than ingratitude for all his blessings. May the years which remain be more fruitful."

The following year there is this register:

"*November 24th.*—Twelve months ago to-day laid up with an attack of my old complaint, attended by copious discharge of blood; confined to bed for about three weeks. How good God has been to me since then; how much He has taught me; how mercifully He has spared me; how well I am to-day, though not quite well, compared with then; and how much have I to be thankful for on the ground of health compared with thousands. I want a spirit of greater thankfulness; a spirit of greater dependence upon Him; a spirit of greater trustfulness in His goodness, in His mercy and in His truth."

In December, 1885, he writes:

"*Sunday,* 27th.—To-day I complete my sixty-first year. How good, and how gracious, and how merciful God has been to me all these long years; how strangely and how mercifully have I been led; how many have been the blessings of the past year; how many blessings surround me to-day; how undeserved have they all been. Oh, that my spared life may show forth God's praise!"

During this year there was a perceptible loss of strength, and though he was occupied with religious and benevolent effort, and wrote and travelled much, yet the disease from which he had suffered for years did not readily yield to medical treatment, and his whole system betokened decay.

In one of his letters to Mrs. Macdonald while at Victoria, he wrote:

"*August* 17, 1889.

"I thought you would like to hear from us up to the latest hour of our departure. We leave to-night for Vancouver. The climate is pleasant, but with all the rest we have taken here I have not had any other than a languid feeling. I hope the Alaska trip will brace me up a little."

"*August* 30.

"Winnifred and I returned from Alaska, and found all well at home."

"*August* 31.

"Very ill with an attack of indigestion. Remained at home this morning, and felt much better for the rest."

These are the last two entries in his diary:

"*Friday, September* 13, 1889.—Mr. James Good died in his 75th year. Mr. William Gooderham died last night while conducting a service in the Haven. Born in my year—1824—I feel this to be another of the solemn calls that I have had lately. No one in Toronto has been doing more good with his time, means and influence. He has been the city's most munificent giver. How mysterious his death! Who will take his place?"

"Congressman Samuel S. Cox, called 'Sunset Cox,' died on the 10th, in New York. He was taken ill on the 4th. Just a few days ago I met him at the Mammoth Hot Springs Hotel apparently quite well. He expressed a desire to see my letters about Alaska, and promised to send me the census returns of the United States, with the perfecting of which he was charged. He is gone. How sudden! What a void a death like his makes. He was born also in my own year—1824."

20

Thus he was deeply impressed with a sense of the invisible and eternal world, and was evidently meditating on the great change, that the Messenger might find him with his lamps burning and his loins girded.

The months of September, October, November and December were spent much at home, in reading, writing, meditation, and in soul culture.

He read the Bible constantly, with the commentary wholly Biblical, which he had used for two years.

Sunday evening, December 22, he read the whole of the Gospel according to St. John. At the end of the Book is pencilled, "Oaklands, December 22, 1889, 8 p.m." This is one of the last of the markings in his much-loved Bible.

On Christmas day he was able to attend the services in the church, and made his last appearance and last public prayer in the sanctuary. In the evening he read in the Acts of the Apostles, and made his last entry: "Wednesday, Christmas, 1889, 9 p.m.; 15 chapters."

The following day he was taken severely ill. He had complained of uneasiness and an unaccountable depression. In the wholesomeness and purity of his life, he could have said, with Browning :

> " Have you found your life distasteful ?
>   My life did and does smack sweet ;
> Was your youth of pleasure wasteful ?
>   Mine I saved and hold complete ;
> Do your joys with age diminish ?
>   When mine fail me, I'll complain ;
> Must in death your daylight finish ?
>   My sun sets to rise again."

But his disease now distressed him, and weighed on his spirits, and he assumed a wearied, broken-down aspect.

His life was as a finished temple, with the altar fires lit, and the voice of worship ascending ; but he complained that on account of his great weakness, he was not able to pray. He said to his wife, " One of the hardest things I have to bear is that I have not power to pray." To his daughter Lucie he said, " Have you been able to do some little thing to-day to make someone happier ? " He was looking at life in the light of eternity when, instead of being a straight line, it looks more like a line drawn by an anemometer upon the recording sheet, and when the holiest must say :

> " Ah ! but the best
> Somehow eludes us ever ; still might be,
> And is not."

His illness was sweetened by the constant devotion of his wife, and the society of beloved children. His every want was anticipated, and they watched over him with tender, increasing solicitude. He was suffering from a severe internal malady, and in a short time the disease assumed a most alarming aspect. His family physician, Dr. W. T. Aikens, called to his assistance Drs. Grasett, Cameron and Strange, who performed a difficult and delicate operation. The operation was successfully carried out, but Senator Macdonald's condition did not improve. Day after day he became weaker. Fever supervened, he became

unconscious, and about nine o'clock on the evening of
the 4th of February, 1890, surrounded by his family,

" God's finger touched him, and he slept."

Death came to him without pain, without foreboding.
It was like Pilgrim at the Land of Beulah, waiting
for the message and the crossing of the river. The
day he was to cross, "there was a great calm at that
time in the river," and the river was very shallow.
He went quietly down to the gates of death, and
when they opened behold! it was not death, but life.

> " They looked ;
> He was dead,
> His spirit had fled,
> Painless and swift as his own desire."

His death was a shock and surprise to the country,
but everything betokened the love, esteem and profound respect of the people among whom he so long
had lived. A distinguished citizen had finished an
honourable career, a good man had gone to his reward, a public benefactor had yielded his spirit to
God.

His funeral was private. On Thursday morning, the
6th of February, a simple funeral procession, made
up of his family and a few friends, threaded its way
silently to the Necropolis, where all that remained
of Toronto's Merchant Prince was laid away in hope
of the resurrection from the dead.

> " Life's labour done—
> Serenely to his final rest he passed ;
> While the soft memories of his virtues yet
> Linger like twilight hues when the bright sun is set."

XVII.

TRIBUTES.

"'Tis ever wrong to say a good man dies."

IT is scarcely necessary to say that when Senator Macdonald's noble and beneficent life was closed, letters of condolence came to Mrs. Macdonald and the family from multitudes far and wide—from all parts of the land and from beyond the sea; sermons were preached and memorial services held; religious and philanthropic societies and boards with which he had been connected passed resolutions of respect and affection. We select a few out of a number of eulogiums, and they indicate the remarkable place which he held in Canadian life.

The Senate Debates of the Fourth Session, Sixth Parliament, contains the following record:

Hon. Mr. Smith—It becomes my painful duty to announce to this House the death of one of our most esteemed members, Senator John Macdonald, of Toronto. I am sure that every one who hears me will share my regret at this sad event. Where he was best known the regret will be most deeply felt. He was a good citizen, a useful member of society and a man of great benevolence. I deeply lament his loss as a good friend and neighbour in Toronto, and I sympathize with his family in their bereavement.

Hon. Mr. Scott—I am sure that every member of this Chamber who had the pleasure of knowing the late Senator Macdonald will with great sorrow join in a tribute of respect to his memory. During the time that he was a member of this Chamber we all felt that he possessed a superior mind, that he had calm judgment and great equanimity—that he was a thoroughly benevolent and true Christian in all his characteristics. Though allied to one of the political parties of the country, the late Mr. Macdonald never felt himself trammelled by party political views. As a rule, in giving utterance to his opinions in this Chamber, we all felt that he was exercising an unbiased judgment. He was a man who acted from the very highest impulses of human nature. He seemed to be ever anxious to do good. Even in that remote country, Alaska, where his political sympathies were not aroused, he took a deep interest in rescuing the native children of the country from barbarism. He headed a subscription to place the native girls of that country in schools, where they would have the benefit of an education and be protected from the evil influences of the white men. Outside of his public life, Senator Macdonald was deeply beloved. He was a man of very benevolent character; his purse was ever open. God blessed him with great wealth, and he distributed it most generously and liberally. His great charities were most unostentatiously given. It is only now discovered, when he has gone, the very many persons who were receiving from his purse. Not this Chamber, but this country, has sustained a great loss in the death of Senator Macdonald.

Hon. Mr. Howlan—I would accuse myself of very great ingratitude if I allowed this opportunity to pass without paying my tribute to the memory of the late Senator Macdonald. It was not my good fortune to have a lengthened acquaintance with him. He was a gentleman that I am proud to number among my friends. During the past year it pleased God to visit me with sickness when I was twelve hundred miles away from home. No man was more constant at my bedside than Mr. Macdonald, and his lofty sentiments and the breadth of his mind impressed me very strongly with the nobility of his character. He has left few men behind him like himself. He was a man of deep sympathies, profound thought and earnest convictions, and able at all times to express his views, not only with his pen but with his tongue. In the city of Toronto, where he resided, his loss will be greatly felt. He had been reared as a Canadian, not in the lap of luxury, but supported by his own industry, and he will take his place among those who aided in the building up of the Dominion. Long after we have passed away, and another generation takes our place, he will be included among those who contributed by their energy, their ability and their moral strength, to the greatness of the country. Among them no name will be honoured with greater distinction than that of John Macdonald, of Toronto.

Hon. Mr. MacInnes (Burlington)—In rising to address the House, I do so with a feeling of the deepest sorrow. I desire to add my humble tribute to the memory of our departed colleague. I was intimately acquainted with the late Senator Macdonald for many years, and learned to know his works and his high character. His appointment to this honourable House, without reference to political or party lines, was a tribute to that character. His appointment was alike honourable to him and to those who made it, and furnished a valuable precedent for the future. Hon. gentlemen have been witnesses of the able manner in which he performed his duties in the Senate. In business he was scrupulously honourable and fair in his dealings; by his ability and good management he succeeded in accumulating a handsome fortune, and he has been largely his own administrator during his lifetime in his bountiful bequests to many charities, and he never sent away the deserving applicants to his charity empty handed. When I heard of his illness and at about the same time the announcement of his princely charity to the hospital at Toronto, I wrote to congratulate him on his munificence and to say that I hoped he would soon recover his health, and that I should have the pleasure of seeing him here; but it has been ordered otherwise. His was home life with his family. He cultivated the home affections. We can all appreciate what a sad bereavement has fallen on those near and dear to him, but it may be some consolation to them to know that they have the sympathy of this House and of all who knew him.

Mr. Speaker—I am sure the House will permit me to trespass on their time for a few moments to add my humble tribute to what has been so well and ably said in reference to the excellence and worth of our late colleague, Mr. Macdonald. I have known him for so many long years that I could not allow this occasion to pass without expressing to this House my strong sense of the noble character of a man who lived not for himself alone or for his own pleasure and enjoyment, but who lived and laboured throughout a long life for the welfare of others, and who by his Christian example and influence, as well as by his munificent generosity, has done so much for his country and left a memory behind him which will long be held in reverence and respect. I shall say nothing of his political career, because that is well known to every one here, but I am sure I shall have the assent of every one who hears me when I say that from the time that Mr. Macdonald took his seat among us until the last time he appeared in this House, in everything he said and in every vote that he gave he was actuated by the highest and most patriotic motives.

From SIR OLIVER MOWAT, *Premier of Ontario.*

My first acquaintance with Senator Macdonald, personally, was about the time of his election, in 1861, as one of the members for the city of Toronto, and from that time until his death there was the warmest friendship between us. He was a genial, kind-hearted and liberal-minded Christian man, conscientious in politics as in everything else, a man of good sense, and possessed of great executive ability, as his long success in business demonstrated. The life of such a man as he was is the best of sermons to the community in which he was known. He both lived the life and died the death of the righteous.

O. MOWAT.

From REV. J. V. SMITH.

Rev. J. V. Smith, his pastor, who attended him during his illness and officiated at his funeral, says : "John Macdonald was a Christian in the best and truest sense of the word, and that all-important fact gave colour and character to the whole of his life. The great motto of his life was, 'Acknowledge Him in all thy ways, and He shall direct thy paths.' Insincerity, double-dealing and self-seeking he looked upon with all the scorn of a noble soul. He was a staunch defender of old-fashioned, time-honoured Methodism. He laid strong emphasis on the great doctrines taught in the Bible, such as sin, repentance, faith, regeneration and salvation for all through Jesus Christ. But he was more than a Methodist. In a high sense he belonged to all God's people. He was a lover of good men of all names and sects. He was the friend and helper of the poor, the fatherless and the widow. Many a cord of wood, many a ton of coal, and many a well-filled basket has found its way to the home of want as a result of his private charity. His public benefactions to philanthropic, educational and Christian institutions are known from one end of the Dominion to the other. But these benefactions were a means of grace unto himself. The last sentence he wrote was a marginal note on his Bible, the day before his death, stating where he had left off reading, and his last public utterance was the offering of a prayer at the Christmas service in Yonge Street Church.

From REV. J. G. MANLY.

My acquaintance with Mr. Macdonald extended through forty-two years, from his quest of health in Jamaica until his final illness. I knew him in England in the full tide of his business; in

Canada, as his guest on my way to the West for three months ;
and ever since, in the full flush of his prosperity and usefulness ;
and always as an able and honourable Christian man, without a
single step either backward or aside. No one that knew him
could question his veracity and integrity or doubt his good
judgment. In business, his course was an unbroken success ;
to the Church of his choice and whole spiritual life he was
always faithful and true, as he was also to his friends ; and to
every good cause and case that came before him he was thought-
fully and genially responsive, not to get quit of an applicant,
but to counsel and co-operate in a manner far above and beyond
the dimness and diminution of sectarianism.

He was a conspicuous example of *wealth without worldliness.*
No social attractions, no worldly indulgences, no fashionable
frivolity, no political rank or regard ever clogged or clouded his
Christian consistency, purity and duty. Nothing like ostentation or assumption belonged to him. He was a princely
merchant, a faithful steward of God, a truly good man in all
the varied relations of life : "He was a man ; take him for all
in all, we shall not look upon his like again." Never, in all my
life, has the loss of a friend so deeply affected me, making me
more conscious than ever of my love for him and of the greatness of our common loss. His provision for the sick is a Toronto
monument ; his commercial character and success should serve
as an example and incentive ; his practice in the churches should
quicken activity and rebuke bigotry ; and to his family, his
whole life is a precious legacy, a treasure and an inheritance.

I shall never forget my first official meeting with him in the
North Toronto Church, and the unostentatious, kind and liberal
spirit in which he helped to deal with questions of financial
obligation and difficulty. This spirit, in himself and all the
members of the Board, made the meeting for business a verit-
able feast of love.

"He is not, for God has taken him."

J. G. MANLY.

From REV. NATHANIEL BURWASH, LL.D., *Chancellor of
Victoria University.*

MY DEAR DR. JOHNSTON,—

You have asked me for a brief account of the connection
of the late Senator Macdonald with our recent University movements.

Mr. Macdonald was by an early classical education prepared

to take a very intelligent interest in all that concerned higher education. The literary taste thus acquired Mr. Macdonald cultivated to the close of life, and it was not an uncommon thing for those who were privileged with a more intimate acquaintance to find him of an evening preparing a rendering of some Latin poet in English verse for the enjoyment of his family and intimate friends.

His convictions, however, were opposed to the policy of making Victoria a rival of the Provincial University, and also to the policy of State grants for any denominational purpose. It was thus not until 1865 that he was induced to take a seat in the College Board. In 1867-8 the grants hitherto made to Victoria, Queen's, Trinity and Regiopolis were finally withdrawn, and Mr. Macdonald took a very active part with Dr. Ryerson, Dr. Punshon and Dr. Nelles in organizing an endowment movement to maintain our College work, contributing himself $2,000 for that purpose. At that time he favoured a project for removal to Toronto and affiliation with the University of Toronto; but finding that the sentiment of the Church was opposed, the matter was not pressed. He continued, however, to be an active member of the Board and a large contributor to later movements for enlarging the resources of the College down to the time of his death. At the same time he took a deep interest in the University of Toronto, and in 1877, was appointed a member of the Senate. In the autumn of 1883, Vice-Chancellor Mulock through Mr. Macdonald addressed a letter to the late President Nelles, making propositions for alliance of Victoria with the University of Toronto. Mr. Macdonald accompanied Mr. Mulock's letter with a lengthy letter of his own, expressing his sympathy with the project. In the negotiations of the various University authorities with the Ontario Government, which extended over the next twelve months, Mr. Macdonald assisted largely by his counsel and influential support. The next year was occupied in discussion of the scheme within our own Church and College circles, culminating in the decision of our General Conference in 1886, at which Mr. Macdonald made the generous offering of $25,000 for the work. The offerings of Mr. Macdonald, $25,000, Mr. Geo. A. Cox, $30,000, and Mr. Gooderham, $30,000, followed shortly after by Mr. Gooderham's noble bequest, gave the impetus to the financial movement without which federation never could have been accomplished in any other form than the establishment of a Divinity School in Toronto. This brief statement of facts may be of interest to some of your readers, and is due to the memory of a man eminent for his ability to guide wisely great public movements, as well as for the generosity with which he contributed to their support. His noble gift in memory of his daughter for the establishment of a hospital in connection with the Medical Department of the University, was another proof of the interest which he felt in University work and of his high appreciation of the noble mission of medical science for the alleviation of human suffering.

Wishing you every success in your praiseworthy effort to perpetuate the memory and the influence of the life of a great and good man,

I am yours sincerely,

N. BURWASH.

MR. THOMAS THOMPSON'S ESTIMATE OF THE SECRET OF SENATOR MACDONALD'S SUCCESS.

The question might be asked, have there not been instances on record of men having all the characteristics of Mr. Macdonald and yet not having succeeded in what is commonly called success ?

Now-a-days we hear the " secret of success " spoken of. What is that secret ? Will energy, probity and tact always insure it ? Or is there beyond all this some occult or hidden power that determines it ? Is it something that can be acquired, or is it something native to the possessor of it ? Is the science of money-making in mercantile life an exact one, or is it a combination of excellent qualities that make the prosperous business man, with fortuitous circumstances, as well as the thinking out and the balancing of probabilities and then combining the activity of the merchant with that faith in himself which not only deserves, but makes his ventures successful, like a Christian man answering his own prayers in the working out of what he is looking for.

Mr. Macdonald had his strong ambitions or delights, and which were to the other an alterative or rest, and, per consequence, each conduced to the strength of the other : for the mind and the body are so constituted that weariness invariably follows too close application to any given pursuit. So, if we may use a metaphor, the horse which has been resting comes freshly from his stall only too glad to be used by his rider, till it in turn retires grateful for its season of rest.

One of these means was, to put into shape and sometimes into rythm, his thoughts upon what passed before him in life's ever-changing panorama.

Being fond of literary pursuits, he took delight in the off-spring of his brain, and he had the ambition to do his work well; and the better clothed his thoughts were, the more he loved them and took pleasure in them.

The other delight was in his business, not directly in the continual aim to realize a good profit and to have a good balance sheet, but in the merchandise itself; and as spiritual things are spiritually discerned, even so there are many things in our material surroundings that need the lover's eyes to appreciate all their worth.

To Mr. Macdonald every department of his business had its history and romance. The gathering together of very much that was beautiful and curious in its manufacture enthused and gratified him, and made his daily business life not a mere routine of duty, but a never failing source of pleasure; and it is perfectly true that success sweetens labour, though many have to get along through life without this sweetening, and manage to survive barely, and perhaps serving their day and generation to the best of their ability. Even they succeed infinitely beyond the mere hoarders of money who, narrowed down to scrapers together of personalty and realty, and who as they slowly wend their way to their narrow graves, fancying that every one they meet is wanting their poor self-gotten pelf, self-made men in other senses (for self makes men very small), in some few instances some of whom may lay the flattering unction to their poor, starved, withered natures that they have arranged in their last will and testament some little sop in the shape of some small charity, and handing out the same from out their coffins with their bony fingers, thus putting themselves out of reach of the blessing that follows a generous act, the eyes becoming so blinded that they go away unblessed and with their dried natures unwatered.

Mr. Macdonald received his first training among shrewd Scotch drapers at a time when youths were taught to take an interest in the goods they were handling.

Perhaps the difference in fifty years ago and the present might be stated in this way. The object in view then was to learn the business in order to make a living. Now-a-days it is to get just enough knowledge of business to land them into a fortune, with the intention of discarding the business when circumstances will allow, forgetting that even in the prosaic work of buying and handling and marketing those goods that feed and clothe the body and adorn the home, as well as in the higher realm of furnishing the mind and heart, there is a spirit that must be wooed, won and loved for its own sake. No perfunctory or patronizing homage, but a spirit of devotion and faithfulness to its demands.

The loyal heart of Mr. Macdonald kept closely identified with the Church of his choice, his foster-mother the foster-mother of thousands who have lived and died in her communion, and who, when their own mother Church failed to reach out aliment to their hungry hearts, in the spirit of her Divine Master welcomed them to her sacraments and enfolded them in the invisible Church of the Son of God.

He made it part of his life work to extend her boundaries even to the islands of Japan, for with the shrewdness and culture of his redeemed nature he saw that the islands ever governed the continents. So with every sense quickened into activity he believed and acted up to the thought that the time was fast coming when from the rivers to the ends of the earth the teachings of Christ, the Son of God, would have universal sway.

THOMAS THOMPSON.

From REV. JOHN POTTS, D.D.

In the June of 1865 I was appointed to what is now known in Toronto as the Central Methodist Church, then better known as Yorkville Church. It was at that time that I first met John Macdonald. I found him an official member of the church and deeply interested in the prosperity of the cause of God in that congregation. As I look back to those days, nothing has made a greater impression upon my mind in relation to our departed friend than the spirit he manifested, especially towards those in the Quarterly Official Board who were not of the same social status. It seemed to give him pleasure to defer to their judgment in any matter that came up for discussion, and therefore his influence with them was correspondingly great.

John Macdonald was in many respects the foremost layman of Canadian Methodism. He possessed in himself several elements which, combined, made him easily the most influential layman in our denomination. He was to Toronto Methodism what Senator Ferrier was to Montreal Methodism. Senator Macdonald was a good preacher, a good debater, and a man of princely liberality, whose gifts found their way to benevolent objects beyond the bounds of his own Church. He was in the highest sense a connexional Methodist. His broad and statesmanlike views of the missionary and educational work of the Church made him invaluable on the Missionary Board and on the Board of Regents of Victoria University. While he was an intense Methodist from investigation and conviction, he evinced

a beautiful spirit of fraternity in relation to the other sections
of the Christian Church.   Perhaps more than any man in
Toronto he commanded the affectionate esteem of all classes of
the community as a philanthropist and an earnest and consistent Christian.

Mr. Macdonald was a constant and ardent student of the
Word of God, and cultivated a range of literature far beyond
that of most commercial men.   From a good deal of observation,
I came to regard him as a striking illustration of the principle
contained in that passage of Scripture, "Them that honour me,
I will honour."   Like the late William Gooderham, he recognized in a high degree the responsibility and privilege of Christian stewardship, and acted in all the relations of life as one
who expected to give an account of his stewardship.

JOHN POTTS.

From H. A. MASSEY, ESQ.

My first acquaintance with the subject of this sketch was when
he laid the corner stone of the Methodist Church in Newcastle,
Ont., on May 24th, 1867 ; but soon after this business relations
brought us together frequently, which gave me opportunities of
knowing Mr. Macdonald better, and which resulted in my forming a very high estimation of his abilities and personal worth.

He was always ready to respond to every call in any good
cause, and was devoted to the best interests of his country.
His untiring zeal in serving the Church in any and every
capacity that lay in his power, was worthy of imitation, and I
have no doubt that it stimulated others to similar good deeds.
By his death the Methodist Church lost one of its ablest and
worthiest members and most generous benefactors.   Would
that we had many more such men amongst us.

H. A. MASSEY.

From REV. W. H. WITHROW, D.D., *in* The Methodist
Magazine.

Seldom has the whole Canadian community been so deeply
moved by any death as by that of the Hon. John Macdonald.
To thousands who knew him only by reputation his loss was
felt to be a public calamity.   But those who knew him best
feel that the world is incomparably the poorer for his departure.
The readers of *The Methodist Magazine*, whose pages he so often
enriched with his thoughtful and inspiring papers, have reason

for regret that no more shall they be favoured with the
graphic productions of his pen.

The lessons of that life are writ so large that he who runs may
read. "Seest thou a man diligent in his business? He shall
stand before kings ; he shall not stand before mean men." By
his fidelity and energy Mr. Macdonald built up a colossal business, and yet found time to engage in schemes of widest usefulness, and was called to fill a prominent place and exert a potent
influence in the councils of his Church and of his country. But
while diligent in business, he was above all fervent in spirit,
serving the Lord. A prominent characteristic of his life was an
all-pervading sense of responsibility to God, of Christian stewardship. He seemed to hear ever the words, " Occupy till I
come." And how well he filled that injunction only the great
day shall reveal, for many of his benefactions were known only
to God and to the recipient. He was one of those who

> "Did good by stealth, and blushed to find it fame."

When he permitted his benefactions to be known, it was with
the object of stimulating others to Christian beneficence, to
more largely help the cause of God.

Religion was not to him a thing apart from his daily life, but
its very vital air. Religious subjects were not dragged into the
conversation, they sprang up spontaneously, like the daisies in
the meadows, as the most natural thing in the world.

In political life he maintained the same sturdy independence
which characterized his other relations. While from coviction
a Liberal statesman, he was no partizan, and commanded, as
few men have done, the confidence and respect of both sides of
the House.

Such men are God's best gifts to His Church. They are the
most striking " evidences of Christianity," demonstrations of
the power of godliness which the caviller and the infidel cannot
gainsay, " living epistles known and read of all men."

From REV. GEORGE DOUGLAS, D.D., LL.D., *Principal Wesleyan
Theological College, Montreal.*

It was in the summer of 1857 when I first met our friend, now
translated, Hon. John Macdonald. Somewhat slender in his
physique, medium in height, erect in carriage, handsome in
features, lined with strength, ample in brow, with questioning
but kindly eye, frank, cordial, genial in his manner, with a
shade of reserve militaire, graced with a Scottish cultus, this
was the man in the maturity of his youth who subsequently became the merchant prince, the parlimentarian, the potential

factor in all circles, social, commercial, philanthropic and religious. Recollection supplies no parallel to our friend in his steady and rapid ascent to status, to wealth, and to influence amongst his compeers.

His incisive intellect, his power of outlook and mastery of detail, his natural sagacity and coolness of judgment, the thoroughness which marked everything he undertook, ensured a success which was phenomenal, solid and enduring.

In our personal intercourse with the departed, we often admired his ability to lay aside all his pressing commercial cares and live for a time in the realms of thought and amid the attractions of literature. Naturally endowed with a measure of poetic genius, combined with philosophic tastes and tendencies, he had enriched his library with some of the finest poetic, biographic, historic, and evidential writers of the age.

All this gave to his conversation a peculiar wealth and charm. For the time the merchant was lost in the literateur. To the very close of life he delighted in those apologetic writers whose works authenticate from the human standpoint the verities of spiritual Christianity.

Though thus liberally gifted by nature, it was his absolute loyalty to Christ and His Church which gave nobility and strength to the character of our friend.

When he was blossoming into early manhood, grace supernal led him to turn his feet into the testimonies divine, the resultant of which was a clear, defined, experimental Christian life, a life which found its development in the Methodist Church of Canada until the close of his earthly career.

For the Church of his intelligent choice he cherished a profound admiration, and while strongly conservative both in relation to her doctrine and discipline, he was remarkable for the catholicity of his spirit. It may truly be asserted that he was one who loved our Lord Jesus Christ in sincerity.

Every official responsibility which the Methodist Church could confer on a layman was intrusted to our friend. His labours in the Sabbath Schools, the pulpits and the councils of the Church are an abiding record of his fidelity to Christ and his solicitude to make his life influential for the benefit of others.

Well do we remember our last conversation with him when physical decadence had begun, and the sombre shades of eventide were coming on apace. He then affirmed his growing delight in Biblical truth and an unfaltering faith in the ultimate realization of its eternal beatitudes.

Held in honour by all who knew him, well beloved by those who knew him best, enthroned in the undying love of those who shared his paternal regard, he filled a great sphere in the

Church as well as in the State. "Having fought the good fight, he finished his course and kept the faith."

Summers shall come and go with their blossomings and their fruitage which his eye shall never see, but his luminous example to the coming manhood of this Dominion shall in its influence be perpetuated by the admirable record of a noble life, furnished as a souvenir by one who along the years held him in honour, and is now his sorrowing friend.

"The righteous shall be held in everlasting remembrance."

GEORGE DOUGLAS.

How precious is the memory of a just and good man! Senator Macdonald was a remarkable man. If he could not be called great, he was not destitute of those qualities out of which great men are made. As a merchant he was enterprising and successful; as a statesman he was upright and intelligent: as a citizen he was patriotic and public spirited; as a benefactor he was generous and sympathetic; as a Christian he was devout, consistent and consecrated. His religion was not a mere creed or profession; it was a life, an experience. His name was a tower of strength to every good cause. He has left behind him a character above reproach, and his example will live for good through many generations.

> "Were a star quenched on high,
>   For ages would its light,
>   Still travelling downward from the sky,
>   Shine on our mortal sight;
>
> "So when a good man dies,
>   -For years beyond our ken
>   The light he leaves behind him lies
>   Upon the paths of men."

FINIS.

21

www.ingramcontent.com/pod-product-compliance
Lightning Source LLC
Chambersburg PA
CBHW031150120726
47905CB00006B/1893